M000224143

SHADOWMIND

DOCTOR WHO – THE NEW ADVENTURES

Also available:

THE NEW DOCTOR WHO ADVENTURES

SHADOWMIND

Christopher Bulis

First published in Great Britain in 1993 by
Doctor Who Books
an imprint of Virgin Publishing Ltd
332 Ladbroke Grove
London W10 5AH

Copyright © Christopher Bulis 1993

'Doctor Who' series copyright © British Broadcasting
Corporation 1992

ISBN 0 426 20394 1

Cover illustration by Christopher Bulis

Typeset by Type Out, Mitcham CR4 2AG

Printed and bound in Great Britain by
Cox & Wyman Ltd, Reading, Berks

This book is sold subject to the condition that it shall not, by
way of trade or otherwise, be lent, resold, hired out or otherwise
circulated without the publisher's prior written consent in any
form of binding or cover other than that in which it is published
and without a similar condition including this condition being
imposed on the subsequent purchaser.

Chapter 1

The bushtail chirruped impatiently as Donal Robson followed
him up the path between the great trunks of the spirecones. 'All
right Rusty, I'm coming,' replied Robson. 'Remember this is
work to me, even if it's no more than a scamper in the woods
for you.'

Squatting back on its haunches, the bushtail raised its forepaws
from the ground to hold them curled neatly against its chest,
and regarded Robson through blackberry bright eyes, now level
with the man's waist. 'Chirrip-chip-chip-choo,' it ventured, its
great golden-red billow of a tail forming a question mark as
though in emphasis.

'That's right,' confirmed Robson, 'another survey point.'

The bushtail sat patiently, watching Robson drive the sampler
staff into the ground, as though indulging a friend engaged in
some amusing, though incomprehensible task. He gave his usual
'chik' of satisfaction after the electronics package built into the
staff beeped when the sample was taken.

Robson wiped his brow in the warm, insect-speckled air and
brushed back his hair, sun-bleached by months of outdoor work.
His tanned skin accentuated the paler creases around his eyes,
the mark of those who gaze long at far horizons.

He compared his watch with the angle of the sun and the feel
of his stomach. 'Lunchtime,' he concluded. Resting his backpack and sampler staff against a ringpine trunk, he settled into
the hollow between two of its splayed roots and unpacked the
food: oak nuts and an apple for Rusty (greeted by approving
chirrups) and a generous stack of satisfyingly overfilled, thick-
crust rolls for himself. For a time there was no sound bar,
respectively, the cracking of nuts and the munching of bread.
Well content, Robson admired the view.

Framed between the spirecones and ringpine trees, the great

1

forest of Arden's northern continent rolled away before his gaze for a hundred kilometres until it faded into the afternoon haze. He had heard it said that Rusty's smaller arboreal cousins could travel three thousand kilometres across the continent before they had to touch ground.

In the middle distance, Lake Lysander glittered in the sun, fed by the Titania River, the line of its valley just visible as it snaked away to its source, high in the ranges to the north and east of him. Halfway between lake and foothills, the valley spread briefly, forming what was probably the largest expanse of level open ground for two hundred kilometres. It had been the obvious site for the landing field of Touchstone Base, presently the largest settlement on the whole planet.

'So far,' Robson amended his thoughts, 'and we hope it stays that way for a long time, don't we, Rusty?' The bushtail briefly delayed cracking a nut to give him a look which Robson chose to interpret as wholehearted agreement with these sentiments.

From where he sat, the tall trees hid from view the settlement he had left that morning, but Robson could visualize quite clearly the weather domes of Oberon Survey Camp, nestling in the lower slopes of the foothills of the Phebe Range, whose snow-topped peaks rose at his back for a good five thousand metres above the height he had reached today. He massaged his calves ruefully, and wondered, not for the first time, when they would get around to naming individual peaks. How many books had that ancient pre-atomic era Earthman written? And which classicist in the colonial department was responsible for . . .

He scrambled to his feet, stun pistol drawn, scanning the encircling wall of trees for the thing that had caused him to feel, with some unnamed sense, that he was being watched. Rusty paused in the preening of his white bib-front fur to chirp in puzzlement. Nothing troubling him, Robson thought. If there was an ursine on the prowl he would have shown it by now, he reasoned, so what is it that's making the back of *my* neck itch?

He circled the tree warily, aware of a pair of tree slinks in the branches above industriously boring a new nest hole, without any apparent sign of alarm. Insects droned and danced in bars of sunlight slicing through the trees. In the distance, a silver-wing gave its high, piping call. All was normal and peaceful, so what could be wrong? Maybe this was a touch of the 'watcher syndrome' others had reported — too much unpopulated raw nature for those addicted to crowded civilisation, so people create companions in their own minds and scare themselves with phantom taps on the shoulder.

Robson snorted in disgust at these thoughts and firmly holstered his gun. He'd been on Arden over a year and hadn't used it once. Even the predators here were shy of people. Arden was about the safest place he knew, and he *liked* it empty. He'd rather believe in Edonian spies than that there was anything wrong with Arden. Rusty had the right idea, he decided, observing him curled up, almost covered by his tail, unconcernedly enjoying a postprandial nap.

He lay back against the tree once again, making himself comfortable on the cushion of dry pine needles between the roots. Don't worry, that was the idea. He closed his eyes and enjoyed the warm sunlight and a full stomach. The scent of the pine was heavy and restful and a comfortable drowsiness settled over him, letting his thoughts wander easily, gradually becoming something apart, as though he were a mere spectator as they drifted gently through his mind.

Nothing on Arden need worry him, he thought. No Edonians were going to claim this wonderful world, no sir, no way. Wasn't that why the government had sent those soldiers here? Of course it was. Smart move. Nobody would risk anything now. Let the politicians talk, talk — thing they did best. Didn't bother him. Didn't bother him that people kept finding planets hundreds and hundreds of light years apart that had plants and animals and . . . and things so similar to . . . each other of course. Parallel evo . . . thing nonsense. Let the exobio people worry . . . didn't worry him. Didn't worry Rusty that he looked just like a giant squirrel taken to living on the ground, and he had some long Sci-latin name to prove it . . . Para sciurus vulgaris . . . something . . . He couldn't remember . . . didn't worry him . . .

He woke suddenly, choking, spluttering, certain for some reason he was drowning in warm and terrifyingly comforting darkness, with fluid filling his lungs. But all around him the wooded hillside was as reassuring as before, with Rusty at his side, blinking at him in surprise.

How long had he been asleep? The sun was low in the sky and reddening. The wood was filling with the shadows of evening and the air was cool. Oh well, he thought, not the first time I've fallen asleep in the woods.

Robson stood up, stretching and twisting awkwardly, feeling for a moment that his clothes restricted his body unnaturally. But the sensation passed, and he smiled down at his furry pet. 'Let's call it a day, Rusty. Back home the quick way, yes?'

The animal chittered and flicked its tail in anticipation as Robson unfolded the force-jet tubes from the backpack and strapped it on, then jumped into his special carry-frame without bidding. Extending the control arms, Robson checked the battery charge. Plenty left. My reward for using the jets sparingly on the way up, he thought, twisting the handstick. They lifted off soundlessly except for the hiss of expelled air propelled by the invisible fields, and scattering a cloud of dust and pine needles they sped off downhill.

As they slalomed between the trees, surprising the little gliding swoops, who thought they had the air to themselves, Robson's peculiar waking dream came back to him. What had inspired such a strange and, he admitted to himself, frightening image, he could not understand. He had never experienced any real near-drowning or serious choking that he could recall, and yet it had seemed so true and immediate. Perhaps he was . . .

Then he couldn't remember just what he was worrying about. The reason seemed to be dissolving and slipping through the grasp of his conscious mind even as he . . .

Then he couldn't remember being worried at all.

He was flying back to Oberon with Rusty. Everything was fine and just as it should be. Those unaccountable worries were tiny things now, smothered in warm comforting darkness, wrapped in velvet blackness and beyond recall.

It didn't worry him.

Chapter 2

Bernice Summerfield halted in mid-stride.

A deep feeling of timeless loss and regret had suddenly washed over her, and a window on her past had seemed to open – unbidden and unwanted.

For a moment, an image of a man had filled her mind. She bit her lip, hands tightly clenched. Isaac Summerfield as she last remembered him: strong, resolute, a loving father and devoted husband. She was a girl, tearfully waving her starship commander father goodbye. She never saw him again . . .

And then the sensation was past and her memories were back where they belonged: cherished, never forgotten, but under control. Realization dawned that the stimulus she had felt had come from without, not within.

Bernice looked about her, very aware, at that moment, how alien the place she now thought of as home really was. Of course, in her travels she had lived in many odd places, but this, she conceded, was certainly the oddest. She had still to fully grasp its possibilities – or its limitations.

She took a deep breath. Well, if something strange was going on, there was one person who had to be told. She strode purposefully off along the corridor.

The Doctor was in the TARDIS's control room as she entered, his small form hunched over one segment of the hexagonal main console, that sprouted like a hi-tech mushroom in the centre of the floor.

Apparently oblivious of her presence, he continued to read from the screen she recognized as usually displaying the autolog recording. On his face was an expression of timeless wistfulness so intense that she halted, unwilling to disturb his thoughts. Perhaps what she had to say could wait. After all, it was just a brief odd feeling.

She turned and started to tiptoe away, but the movement must have caught his eye because he said, in a vague, impatient manner without looking up, 'What is it, Barbara?'

Who? Bernice thought, turning back to him with a puzzled frown. As she did so, the sensation of loss poured through her once more, but far stronger than before. This time it was a picture of her mother that she recalled. For a moment it was happy and smiling — then the memory of the explosion tore through Bernice's mind and her mother was gone forever amid the flame and smoke . . .

And then everything seemed normal once again and her past was shut away in its proper place. But as she looked at the Doctor, it seemed to her, for a moment, that he *changed*. An elderly man with white hair and dressed in a period-style frock coat seemed to stand at the console. But he was looking at her with the Doctor's eyes: old, wise eyes, filled with more experience than reason would suggest was possible.

Then it was the small figure she knew as the Doctor standing at the console, his gaze falling back to the autolog display again. He said nothing more and Bernice was not sure he had even truly seen her.

She looked at the room about her, searching for something out of place. But all seemed as it should be. The monitor showed the featureless grey of the interdimensional void and the white walls of the room still curved irregularly, enclosing the space in an irregular geometry that, she suspected, served some complex but hidden function. The curves were formed of many panels, patterned with vertical ranks of recessed circular mouldings. Inset between some panels were Doric-style fluted columns. Inside the room was the same odd assortment of furniture as usual: a Sheraton chair, a glowingly polished Chippendale. A tall hatstand carried the Doctor's limp fedora hat with the paisley patterned hatband, and his red-handled umbrella. In one curve of the wall, in a large Chinese pot, stood a strangely formed plant, draping feather-like fronds that seemed to sway with a life of their own. A massive, brass-bound sea chest lay beside it. On a carved stand was a bust of Napoleon, while on its twin sat an ormolu clock. There was nothing out of place, to Bernice's eyes. There seemed to be no danger, but . . .

She looked again at the Doctor and noted the strong emotions playing across his features. In a puzzled silence she left the room. She needed to talk to someone who had travelled with the Doctor longer than herself. In fact, she only had one choice.

The phone on Lyn Shorren's desk trilled insistently. Without looking up, she said, 'Accept call.' The screen obediently lit up to display the craggy features of George O'Valle.

Lyn flicked her eyes to the screen for a moment 'Hello, George. How's everything at Oberon?'

'Fine, Lyn. All on schedule. Why don't you visit us more often and see for yourself?'

'Because the Colonial Department works its science co-ordinators too hard, that's why, George.' O'Valle chuckled.

The science coordinator's office at Touchstone Base was set in the upper level of the main dome. Through the window several other buildings were visible, clustered at the head of the landing field that ran along the shallow valley of the Titania River. A little way down the valley, the experimental crop fields formed a neat patchwork, where carefully introduced plants were being tested for growth under Arden's climatic and soil conditions. It was a view Lyn Sorren had become increasingly familiar with as the Arden colonization survey had gained momentum.

She finished her work on the desk pad and turned to the phone screen. 'Okay, George, how can I help you?'

'I wanted to ask about the, er, sample we sent you a week ago.'

'But I called you the other day about that. We were having problems with the analysis.'

'Yes, but since then some of my people have had some ideas about,' he hesitated, 'new tests. So if I could send someone over to collect the samples –'

'Oberonite.'

'What?'

Sorren grinned. 'Well, we had to call it something better than "that weird black glassy stuff" – it doesn't sound professional. Besides, it's the first unusual find you've come up with. Don't you approve?' She leaned forward confidentially. 'Are you

7

making a pitch for "O'Vallite"?'

O'Valle smiled, uncertainly. 'No thanks. I was just wondering if we could have the . . . oberonite back to run some tests because . . . ' He trailed off, as though puzzled by the direction his words were taking him.

'What's the matter, George? We've better facilities here than at Oberon.' Suspicion entered her voice. 'This isn't some kind of joke, is it? Those pieces of oberonite, especially the large segment with the embedded faceted nodules, they *were* found like you said, weren't they? Are you trying to tell me somebody's slipped some tinkered-up synthetics past you?'

'No,' O'Valle said positively, 'of course not. They were found as I told you. I just wanted them back, he became vaguer, 'for more tests . . . It's important.'

Sorren frowned. It wasn't like him to be so hesitant. 'Have you forgotten what I told you the other day, George? I was going to wait until I had more results before getting back to you about it. Remember, the lab couldn't make an accurate chemical analysis because of some peculiar trace impurity. Then they tried them under the electron microscope and couldn't get a clear image. Finally, they tried X-ray diffraction on one of those two crystal nodules to see if they really had a lattice structure, and both it *and* the other crystal reduced to dust in a few seconds, though the second crystal was nowhere near the one being irradiated — some sort of resonance effect they think. I said at the time it was mighty strange stuff and you'd have to wait for the lab to do some creative thinking on it. Found any more deposits, by the way?'

'No, Lyn. But we have these ideas for new tests, you see —'

'Well, you're too late. We've only got one piece left.'

O'Valle's face became more strained. 'You've used it up?' he exclaimed, thickly.

'What's got into you, George? No, we simply realized we hadn't the necessary equipment, so we shipped it back home for neutrino scanning yesterday. You'll just have to be patient — George? Can you hear me?'

'Sorry, Lyn, I . . . was thinking. It doesn't matter. Everything's fine. Thanks for telling me. Goodbye. End call'

The screen blanked.

8

Chapter 3

Ace sat at the desk in her room, examining her reflection critically in the mirror set above it.

Medium-length dark-brown hair tied in a ponytail, that hadn't changed. Face okay — regular features at least. Cheekbones high, call them distinctive. The set of her jaw, however, was tending towards the uncompromising; it suggested much experience of the sharp edge of life. The effect was moderated by her eyes, which were clear and keen, but not ungentle. Her mouth was wide and expressive — too expressive sometimes, it used to get her into trouble. Still, that was in the past.

All things considered, it wasn't a bad face. An unbiased observer might even have called it attractive. But it was beginning to remind her a little of her mother.

There was a time when she would really have resented that. Now, she thought, with a little effort she could come to terms with the idea. What was troubling her was the concept of 'womanhood'. Stupid how annoying a single word could be, but being labelled as a 'woman' had defined and limited her mother, Ace felt, whereas being a 'girl' meant you still had, well, possibilities — and anybody who said it sneeringly had better watch out . . .

She came to herself with a start. For a moment she had a vivid image in her mind of herself aged ten punching a boy who had said something to annoy her. Ace frowned. Several strong memories of the past had come to her in the last hour. They had caused her to check something which had been in the back of her mind for the last few days.

She sighed, and looked her mirror image squarely in the eye. 'Happy birthday, Ace,' she said. Then she smiled. Most people needed nothing more than an ordinary calendar to tell them when their birthday was. But then, most people had not lived in a time machine for a few years.

One of the problems of extended time travel, Ace decided, was reconciling the time duration you experienced with the changing world times around you. How old were you when you could travel back to a time before you were born? Answer: you were as old as the time you had *experienced*, of course, whatever order it came in. Over the years she had kept track of that total with watches of increasing complexity. Now it was all programmed into her wrist computer. Every so often, she checked to see what date it would be if she had lived these last few years on Earth, instead of, well, elsewhere.

And today, it turned out, was her birthday. And the realization came to her suddenly that her birthdays had not, as a rule, been happy days. Was it time to make this one different? Why not? The Doctor was bound to know somewhere nice they could go for a celebration, Ace thought. And this time she was determined to enjoy herself.

Pleased with her resolution, she was about to rise when there was a knock at her door and Bernice Summerfield entered.

Ace frowned at the expression on her face. 'Something the matter?' she asked.

Bernice came straight to the point. 'Have you felt anything . . . strange in the last few minutes?'

'What do you mean?'

Bernice sighed. 'I mean an odd emotion, a feeling that's not exactly your own, but makes you remember something from your past —' Bernice's quick eyes read the sudden change of expression on her face. 'Yes, I see that you have.'

'All right, Sherlock,' retorted Ace. 'Yes, I have been thinking of the past. I've just worked out that today's my birthday. What of it?'

'Congratulations, I'll bake you a cake later. Meanwhile, if you've been getting the same sort of emotional stimuli that I have, then there really is some odd force loose in here.'

'Something dangerous?'

'Perhaps not. But it's damned peculiar, and uncomfortable.'

'Have you talked to the Professor?'

'I tried to, but I don't think he wants to be disturbed just now. That's why I'm here. You see, when I saw him in the control

10

room, for a moment it seemed as though he changed —'

Ace sprang to her feet, alarmed. 'You mean he's regenerating? Mudbrain! Why didn't you say?' She rushed for the door but Bernice grabbed her arm.

'No, he wasn't *actually* different. It was an image, an illusion in my mind, I think. But for a moment it seemed so real. An old man with the Doctor's eyes. Then he was back to normal again, except that he seemed so preoccupied and, well, sad, that I thought it best to leave him until I had talked to you first. Does any of this make sense?'

For a long moment they faced each other, very different in appearance. Ace: small, compact, strong, looking fierce at the moment and as tense as a coiled spring. Bernice: taller, older, equally strong, equally concerned but more controlled, her expressive, sardonic face now thoughtful, her quirky mouth pursed and serious.

'No,' replied Ace after a moment. 'But there are some fragging awful things that have gone wrong in here before.'

'So I remember,' Bernice responded dryly, 'but what I mean is . . .'

Even as she spoke, another ripple of regret mingled with weariness seemed to discharge through them, almost like a build-up of static electricity being earthed. This time Ace recognized it for what it was. Old memories threatened to surface once again in her mind. For a moment, an image of Jan swam before her, then it was gone. She saw that Bernice had felt something similar.

Bernice ran here fingers stiffly through her short, practical hairstyle and managed a wry smile. 'The past,' she observed, 'is really a drag sometimes, isn't it?'

'Yeah,' Ace replied. For a moment there was a sense of fellow feeling between them. Two strong people, vulnerable only from within. Both wished the ghosts of what had been to remain well buried.

The Doctor was still standing at the console when they peered cautiously through the doorway of the control room. The atmosphere was heavy, tired, Bernice thought; filled, not so much with age, but a sense of *duration*; tightly packed with

11

experiences that could not find release, far too many for any human mind to contain. They felt the weight of memory press upon them as they stepped up to the console. The Doctor continued to stare at the autolog screen before him, apparently oblivious to their presence. His expression slowly changed as he read, from sad to wistful, then briefly smiling (they felt the mood in the room lift for a moment), then thoughtful. And it seemed to them as they watched him that more than his expression changed. Momentarily, other men stood before them, of different appearance, but all the same man, images of previous forms the Doctor had taken, somehow impressed upon their own minds.

It was disturbing and fascinating at the same time, but it had to stop. Ace coughed gently. 'Professor?' No response. She must forget her affectation for a moment and use the name he preferred. 'Doctor,' she said more forcefully, 'there's something wrong, please snap out of it.'

The Doctor muttered: 'Don't bother me now, Susan . . . Must finish this . . . '

'No, Doctor, I'm Ace — you must remember. Susan was somebody who travelled with you a long time ago. Please look at me.'

'And I'm Bernice, — Benny,' added Bernice, with gentle insistence. 'Do you know me?'

For a moment he blinked at them both in a puzzled way. The atmosphere in the room lightened as awareness flowed over his features. Then it was the Doctor they knew standing there, looking at them properly now, apologizing. 'Sorry, Ace, Benny — I was miles away. What is it, something wrong?'

The two exchanged relieved glances. 'You could say that,' Bernice exclaimed, with mild sarcasm, 'and I think it was *you*, Doctor.'

'We've been, somehow, sort of feeling your thoughts, Doctor,' Ace explained. 'Heavy stuff, most of it. Not nice. And with some powerful side effects, too.'

The Doctor frowned and examined the controls before him, his fingers dancing over the keyboard below the autolog screen. He 'tut-tutted' under his breath and moved around to the next segment of the console, his hands now flashing across the controls. Suddenly, he gave a little cry of satisfaction, made a couple of careful adjustments and stepped back, rubbing his hands together briskly. 'There now, that's better.' Two faces stared back at him expectantly. 'Oh, it was one of the telepathic induction circuits. Shouldn't have been linked up like that at all. Must have been amplifying and re-broadcasting my thoughts throughout the ship. Self reinforcing, positive feedback . . . Sorry if it bothered you.'

'So,' ventured Ace, cautiously, 'nothing nasty has got into the works — again — has it? Remember what happened last time.'

'My dear Ace, I can assure you that nothing "nasty", as you say, has come anywhere near "the works". It was just a slight misalignment of control settings.'

'Fine, panic over,' commented Bernice. 'But Doctor, if those were your thoughts we sensed, well, they were mostly pretty sad. Are you okay yourself?'

The Doctor smiled wistfully. 'I was simply looking back to my past. Bad mistake when you have accumulated as much as I have. Stay there for too long and look too deep and, well, it's best not to. It's a symptom, I suppose.'

'You're not ill?' Ace and Bernice exclaimed together.

'Pre-millennial angst, you might call it.' He grinned suddenly, boyishly. 'Just a state of mind, best cured by cheerful thoughts and external distractions.'

'Don't do that, Doctor!' Ace said with feeling.

'You really had me worried for a moment,' added Bernice.

'Again!' said the Doctor, pointing a finger dramatically at Ace. 'You have just called me "Doctor" again. After all this time calling me "Professor" to annoy me. Curiosity compels me to ask, why now?'

'I was just trying to get your attention,' Ace began, but Bernice interrupted her explanation, a mischievous gleam in her eye.

'It's her birthday, Doctor,' she said, poker-faced, 'and I think she's trying to get on your good side so that she can ask you a favour.'

'No I don't!' Ace exclaimed. 'Well, yes, I do . . . What I mean is . . . I thought maybe we could go somewhere . . .

I don't mean home, but — somewhere else.'

'My dear Ace, happy birthday!' The Doctor was transformed, striding about, zestfully rubbing his hands. 'Of course. Celebration. Somewhere interesting. Do us all good.' He turned to the console and started checking the planetary directory. 'Let me see: temporate climate; time period with stable civilization in ascendancy; varied sights; culinary expertise high — we mustn't forget the food; cosmopolitan society; music — depends on personal taste, I suppose.' He paused and suddenly turned to Ace, pointing dramatically. 'We go, on condition that *you*,' he wagged his finger, 'continue to address me as "Doctor" for the duration of our stay.'

'I'm not sure it's worth it,' Ace said. 'I've fought military campaigns more restful then your idea of a holiday.

'She has a point,' Bernice agreed. 'I could live without another outing courtesy of Club Zombie.'

The Doctor looked pained. 'Haiti was an unfortunate mistake; this time it will be different, I promise.'

Ace frowned, then smiled. 'All right, as long as I'm allowed to call you "Doc" occasionally.'

'If you must,' he sighed, and returned to his evaluations, musing over the requirements of their destination. Bernice raised an amused eyebrow and walked from the room This would be worth dressing up for.

Ace smiled, letting him chatter on to himself, as he lightheartedly selected their destination from a million worlds and a trillion different eras. Thomas Cook eat your heart out, she thought. Maybe birthdays can be fun after all.

Chapter 4

The stealth-contoured midnight-black fighter pulled out of its attack run and headed out for the stars at maximum acceleration. The crater-pitted surface of the dead moon fell away behind it, the horizon contracting and bowing into a ragged arc.

Three pinpoints of light swelled into brilliance on the ash plain below and slowly faded. 'Target strike confirmed,' said the computer running the wargame. 'End of attack phase.'

Nice shooting guys, said Lieutenant Kim Talevera.

She had not spoken the words, she had thought them. Her fighter comm system had translated them into a tight-beamed maser pulse and transmitted it to her wingmen. In the same way, she had not touched a control during the whole flight. In fact, she could hardly move.

People were always asking her what it was like.

'I tell you,' she would say, 'there's *nothing* like it. You *are* the bird when you fly one of these. Just you in command. Solo. And all your senses are boosted through the onboard systems. You think in fast-time. You see right through from infrared to ultraviolet and you "hear" the radio bands, and you're riding ten g's acceleration in the cocoon, but it's as though you're naked to the stars and your body is better and stronger . . . Yeah, it's a power high — ask any pilot.'

She was aware of her wingmen coming up on either side.

All in the green, Kim? enquired Dag Felden.

On the zero. Okay Nick?

Couldn't be better, Chief, Nicholas Cort replied.

Then let's head for home, said Kim.

The fleet's youngest captain surveyed the reflection in her cabin mirror critically. I wish I looked ten years older, she thought. Okay, I'd settle for five.

Fran Kausama had fought her looks all the way through the academy. Being tall, blonde and athletic, combined with having a clear olive complexion and striking features, would not normally be considered a handicap. But with her chosen career, her desire, as starship command, she had found otherwise. Like others before her, she had found it necessary to be that much better to prove she was just as good as the rest. In the end, her record spoke for her. When the position for the command of the *Broadsword* came up, she had ensured there was no other choice.

For a moment she felt the old self-doubt rise within her, knotting inside her stomach. Was she really worthy of command? To occupy the most responsible seat, where all bucks stopped? Could she make a decision which might quite literally mean the difference between life and death?

And then it had passed, as the psycho-test people said it always would. You wouldn't be fit for command if you didn't have *some* self-doubt, they had assured her. When the time comes, you *will* be able to make that decision. 'But will it be the *right* one?' she had asked. They had smiled, and shrugged.

She checked the time, squared her shoulders, and left her cabin for the briefing room.

The sound of the alarm buzzer jerked Kristen Barr rudely back to the present.

She had been dreaming, again, of some more advanced position with Systems Monitors Inc. Safety officer on a skystation; environmental monitor on a terraforming project? The reality of the present was the security division and the night watch at a university — albeit the largest on Tairngire.

The words 'UNIT MALFUNCTION' were flashing on a screen. The panel display indicated robomonitor eight had malfunctioned in a third-floor corridor of the Mineralogy Department.

For all his relaxed manner and comfortable proportions, her chief, Captain Portlyn, moved surprisingly quickly. He was at Kristen's side now, scanning the displays intently. Content but not complacent, she thought.

The screen that should have shown unit eight's visual transmission was blank. According to the diagnostic read-out, its sensor core had overloaded, causing it to shut down. Signals from the buildings' own alarm circuit were normal, and no other units showed anything unusual.

Captain Portlyn relaxed again. 'Nothing more dramatic than a system failure, Kristen.' There was a twinkle in his eye as he added, 'Sorry it's not more exciting for you.' He sympathized with her ambitions for greater things, but Kristen knew he did not share them for himself. He had found his niche and a way, if only by association, to join the cloistered world of academia. Watching him take one of his paternal daytime strolls through the campus, exchanging polite words with the tutors and dispensing encouragement to the students, it was obvious to her that he was there for life.

She grinned back at him. 'I'll try to fill at least half a page in the log with it. Shall I go and check it out?'

'Please do. Take the manual override key with you and power it down, just in case it decides to start up again. We don't want it running amuck because it can't see its way round properly.' As she went out of the door, he was already contacting the maintenance company. 'Robosec Repairs? This is the University Security Office. One of your PRM units has just overloaded . . . That's right, probably couldn't stand the excitement . . . '

Outside, the night air of the University of New Byzantium was refreshingly cool. Kristen stepped onto her power scooter and sped off silently along a glowkerb-lit pathway. Scattered lights showed where a few of the university's residents still laboured on into the early hours, but most of the buildings bulked darkly against the sky-glow of the city.

She passed a wall of glass before she reached the Mineralogy Building. It was the exhibition hall of the University Museum of Industrial Archaeology. Halfway along she tried to spot one of her favourite exhibits in the reflected kerb-light. Yes, she could see the regular bobbing motion of the ancient pumping engine oddly named a 'nodding donkey'. Old Earth had been covered with them, apparently. They extracted crude oil which was distilled to obtain lighter volatile fractions to power things called 'internal combustion engines', which drove vehicles which polluted the air and destroyed the climate. She thought the exhibit told you more about the nature of people than machines.

The oil extracted from the small field under the city was passed through another of the museum's working exhibits: a small-scale reproduction of an oil refinery. The fuels produced were used to power its precious collection of primitive vehicles. Kristen had seen them on one of the special exhibitions days. How did people live with such noise and smell back then? She preferred force motors and power cells.

The Mineralogy building rose impressively before her: boldly coursed stonework softened by thickly spreading ivy; its windows reflecting the kerblights but dark within. Kristen parked her scooter and mounted the broad flight of steps to the main entrance, triggering the doorlights. As she keyed her way into the reception area, more unseen sensors obliged by lighting her way, illuminating a spacious hall and stairwell and glittering off prestigious columns of richly veined marble. Elevator doors beckoned, but she virtuously chose the stairs — it was only the third floor, after all.

The upper levels were less ostentatious than the entrance hall, containing laboratories, workrooms and computer-terminal alcoves. One room was packed with cabinets and shelves full of specimens: a solid reference library of minerals.

She entered the corridor containing the malfunctioning unit and stopped, mildly surprised.

The automatic lighting, which had so efficiently lit her way up to now, was not working. The corridor was only dimly illuminated by the lights from the room behind her. Turning on her torch, she tried the manual wall switch. Nothing happened.

Kristen unclipped the handphone from her belt. 'Captain? I think we're going to need more maintenance here — the corridor lights aren't working either. Maybe it was the same thing that affected the monitor unit? I can see it halfway down . . . Just going along to it now. Looks all right on the outside.' She examined the sensor dome on top of the squat, angular body. 'I can't see any obvious damage. I'm going to turn off — ' There was a crackle of static from the 'phone, a whisp of smoke curled from the earpiece and the casing was suddenly hot in her hand.

18

The torch flared brilliantly then went out, leaving the corridor in darkness, save for the dim, distant light of the room she had entered through.

Beside her, silently, a door started to open.

She flung the useless torch and 'phone at the widening opening and sprinted down the corridor towards the light. She nearly made it.

There was a whining, buzzing sound. Cloying coldness wrapped itself about her body. Numbed legs, that seemed no longer to be hers, refused to support her. She hardly felt the impact as she hit the floor.

It was remarkably quiet as she lay there, paralysed and helpless. Soft footsteps down the corridor became muted, as whoever it was that had stunned her returned to the room they had come from. Then there was only the distant sound of unidentifiable objects being moved about.

You wanted excitement, well here it is, Kristen thought, with savage self-mockery.

She knew she had been hit by a stun weapon, but the very centre of the beam must have missed, otherwise she would have been unconscious. Even so, most of her body was cold and senseless, like an arm too long slept on.

She was lying sprawled on her front close to the side wall of the corridor, her face turned inwards, right cheek pressed hard into the bonded floor covering. It had been too thin apparently; she could taste blood in her mouth and deduced a split lip. She had a side-on view across the corridor, illuminated by a scattered fan of light from the room at the end. Her out-stretched left arm was visible − and, she realized with elation, tingling with returning sensation. Desperately, she tried to will her body to move, finding her left leg also coming back to life. It too must have caught the very edge of the stun-field effect to recover so fast. But she could move nothing else.

How long had she lain there? Surely not more than two minutes. Did Captain Portlyn realize what had happened? How soon would help arrive and would the intruders (a pair of them she guessed from what she could hear) still be here? What had they been after anyway? How fast can you crawl on one arm and one leg?

Then there were footsteps in the corridor, coming quickly towards her, and Kristen realized they would pass her as they made their escape. Good sense made her ignore the impulse to attempt something heroic and pointless. There was nothing she could do, and no one would blame her for lying quiet.

From the floor below came a sudden commotion: thudding doors, pounding feet, someone calling her name. The intruders quickened their pace; she saw a booted foot actually step over her outstretched arm. Suddenly, common sense seemed to lose its appeal. Why not? she thought, and, forcing herself up on her one good arm, she kicked out hard with her one good leg.

She had a momentary impression of a dark-clothed man falling awkwardly, losing his grip on a box he had been carrying, which burst open as it hit the floor with a stony clatter. Kristen managed to kick out once more, and hard, before she heard the whine of a stun gun for the second time that night . . .

After she had recovered the next day in hospital, and had answered innumerable official questions put to her by a surprisingly long list of interested parties, Kristen Barr managed to find out what the thieves had actually taken. What pieces of rock had been worth stun guns and pulse fusors?

The answer, along with one other peculiarity of the night's events, left her just as puzzled and oddly resentful.

Her senior officers were seated around the briefing-room table as Kausama entered. She nodded to them and took her own seat. For the record, she spoke formally.

'Fifth day of combat trials of the CSS *Broadsword*, taking place in Concordance wargames system Delta Epsillon. Ship's status reports. Commander Warwick?'

Her first officer spoke with a smile. 'General status is good, Captain. All systems operating within projected parameters, crew efficiency in top percentage band.'

'Chief Engineer?'

'Only minor work required, Captain. A slight recalibration of one of the drive stacks, already made and logged. Otherwise every wee thing is just fine.'

Kausama smiled slightly. 'Weapons systems, Commander

Foss?'

'Some frequency adjustment needs to be made on one of the main blaster batteries, Captain. I've got a team on it — they should be finished tomorrow.'

'Do you need any assistance from general engineering?'

'No, Captain, we can manage. I'm missing having Manten of course. It was bad luck to lose him so close to departure like that, but Pandril seems to be a good replacement. Uh, off the record, Captain, may I ask if there's any further news about Manten?'

'Still in base hospital but recovering slowly, according to the last report — it was a bad accident — and your enquiry will stay *on* the record, Chet; the Fleet cares about its personnel.' Foss smiled quickly.

Kausama continued taking reports around the table. Finally she sat back, allowing a slight smile of pride to show, while still speaking formally.

'Notification to Admiral Vego, Fleetcomm, Tairngire. Final combat trials of CSS *Broadsword* proceeding well. Expect *Broadsword* to be ready for active duty within two days.'

Chapter 5

'We are about to dock at New Byzantium shuttle port. Please prepare to disembark. Travel tubes from this terminal link directly with New Byzantium Central. Captain Sympson and her crew would like to thank you for travelling with Tamura Spacelines, and hope you had a pleasant flight.'

Gerry Ostman gratefully found a single corner table in the port's dome-top restaurant and ordered a late breakfast. He watched distractedly as another shuttle touched down as his had earlier, transforming itself from aerospace craft to seaplane and dropping gently onto the blue waters of the Strait of Byzantium. The craft trailed a 'V' wake of foam behind it as it taxied over the water to lock into the embrace of the docking arms and passenger tubes radiating from the floating geodetic dome of the shuttle terminal.

He was trying to get used to people by the thousand once again.

Waiting for the food, he tried to analyse what he suddenly found so disturbing, even slightly threatening, about the crowds in the main concourse. What had generated a feeling strong enough to make him change his plan to go straight to his hotel and instead seek a kind of refuge in the restaurant? After all, he wasn't that hungry.

What was it about people in large numbers that he had, apparently, only just noticed for the first time? Was he on the edge of some significant insight here, or was it simply that he'd been out in the wilds too long? Through the internal windows he looked down on the people moving through the concourse.

After a few minutes, he realized it was not the number of people that troubled him, it was the way they *moved*. They walked about, rode the escalators or waited for arrivals in a manner that certainly had purpose but seemed to him to be —

what? Uncoordinated, that was it. There was a general pattern imposed on the flow of people by the layout of the dome, but now he was aware of the eddies and irregularities in that motion as individuals disturbed the order: pausing to look around, crossing through other files of people, suddenly calling and waving, running to greet a new arrival. Strange that he hadn't noticed that before. It was something he had *seen* but never truly *appreciated* until this moment. Not that it was his province. Crowds were entities best studied by people who liked that sort of thing, like sociologists or psychohistorians. Gerry was a botanist. Was his plant prejudice showing, he wondered?

The food arrived and, as he ate, the odd trail his thoughts had taken seemed to fade away. He tried to reconstruct the sense of it, but it suddenly seemed so inappropriate to his normal reasoning that there was nothing to hold onto. The observation slipped through his mental fingers and was gone.

He sat there, perfectly at east with his surroundings, idly admiring the view through the transparent dome canopy. Shuttles and pure seaplanes arrived and departed, distant bulks of cargo-ships moving through the strait, with the purple hills of East Byzantium beyond them.

What should he do now? His luggage had been sent onto his hotel by cargo-tube, so he was free to play the tourist for the rest of the day if he wished. There were some acquaintances he had promised to call in on if he ever visited the capital, but they could wait until tomorrow. After all, he'd only been to the great city once, when he was a child, so why not look around a little first?

He took out his memopad and keyed it into the City Information Channel: places of interest. Text and maps started to cross the screen.

Shortly afterwards, his itinerary decided, Gerry Ostman left the restaurant in the direction of the travel-tube platform. He was not aware of the two men following him; the same men who had been seated at a table not far from his, and whose faces had, briefly, become fixed and expressionless each time they glanced in his direction.

He boarded a tube capsule. His shadowers took the one behind.

* * *

In a park, not far along the coastline from the shuttleport, there was another, but unscheduled, arrival.

Amongst the curving gravel paths, neatly trimmed hedges and scattered variform sculptures, a strange sound had become audible. A distant keening whirr that rose and fell rhythmically, gaining strength but without any visible source. The sound grew louder still, the pulsations more rapid, almost like a series of deep groans now, as though the very fabric of reality were being distorted by vast energies — which it was.

On an empty patch of grass, a rectangular box-like object materialized, fading into existence where, a moment before, there had only been thin air. The pulsating noise reached a crescendo with a surprisingly solid thump of reality, then all was quiet.

It was a form out of its proper place in time and space.

A student of twentieth-century Earth history might have recognized it as a police call-box, a communication facility predating the use of personal radios, once used in the geopolitical region known at that time as the United Kingdom.

A narrow door in the box's side opened and the Doctor stepped out, examining his surroundings with owlish concentration. After a few moments he gave a bright, self-satisfied grin and absently patted the battered side of the police box, as though it deserved congratulations. The TARDIS had materialized into its usual deceptive, improbable external form, that gave no hint of the space-time craft contained within its transdimensionally engineered interior.

Ace appeared in the doorway and looked about her more critically. The Doctor had promised to take her somewhere interesting, and this didn't look like it. Acutally, it reminded her of the grounds of a country house she had been taken to when she was seven. That had been full of boring statues she was supposed to admire and signs saying: KEEP OFF THE GRASS.

'Okay Doc, it's a sculpture park,' she said, disappointed. 'What happens here?'

'Very little happens here,' replied the Doctor, examining the identification plaque at the foot of one of the exhibits. 'Although you may find some of the works not without merit and the atmosphere pleasantly restful. It will serve, however, as an ideal temporary repository for an otherwise potentially inconveniently anachronistic, but nevertheless essential adjunct, to our little holiday; permitting us the convenience of accommodation adjacent to a central location without the need to find a hostelry for transient visitors.'

'You mean,' said Ace, after a moment's translation, 'we can leave the TARDIS here, close to where the action is, so we don't need to find a hotel?'

'Precisely.'

'Why didn't you say so?'

'I just did; you understood me, didn't you?' He beamed with pleasure at his little word game.

Ace opened her mouth to argue, then half smiled. She put on her mirror shades and sauntered off along a gravel path.

The Doctor watched her go and a thoughtful expression crossed his face. He could tell she had some personal reason for disliking their landing site, but she was controlling it. Not so long ago it would have been a different story. It was something he was having a little trouble coming to terms with.

In the three years of her time that she had been away from him, she had matured considerably, but for all his experience of the apparent changes in people brought about by time-jump contractions, he couldn't help thinking of Ace as the confused teenager he had first met on Iceworld. Of course, he mused, humans had to mature rapidly or their emotions tore them apart. They were such a short-lived and hectic people — was that why he found them so fascinating?

Bernice appeared from within the TARDIS. She had changed from her preferred, rather utilitarian, shipwear, and was now wearing a bright, varicoloured one-piece costume, a large straw hat and a pair of sunglasses. 'Where's the Birthday Girl?' she enquired.

'She's just gone on a quick tour of the exhibits,' replied the Doctor. 'I hope she likes them.'

Somewhat to her surprise, Ace had started to quite enjoy her surroundings. The Doctor had been right: it was restful, even interesting.

The park basked peacefully in what seemed to be mid-morning sunshine. The air was already warm and filled with insect drone and flower scents. The path wound through a chequerwork of hedged glades, each with a display of sculpture or statuary. Some of the materials she recognized: granite, marble, bronze and wood. But what was that one made of? It looked like a huge exploding blob of mercury a metre or more across, sitting on a jet-black cubic plinth.

Walking over to it, she tried to stroke the mirror-like finish, but as she reached out, the surface dimpled in front of her hand, as though retreating from her touch. Surprised, she pulled her hand back, but the ghostly impression of her fingertips remained. Ace laughed. Do-it-yourself sculpture and no mess, she thought — wicked! She reached out again, the palm of her hand flat, fingers spread, and the strange material responded as before. Then she leaned forward face first, eyes closed. When she pulled back and looked, there was a negative mask of her face, cast in quicksilver.

The second exhibit in the glade was a tall hexagonal glass column. Its surface seemed both transparent and semi-reflective in a way that Ace could not understand. Some trick of internal refraction threw out the sunlight from each face in rainbows across the grass. As she moved around it, she was surprised to see her own image passing around the faces of the column, first reflected, then inverted, changing direction, or standing still apparently trapped within. The rainbow beams cast on the grass rotated in time to this, presumably holographic illusion. Ace wondered if machinery was needed to produce the effect, or whether it relied on solid-state optics within the material of the column. She thought it must be hollow, but couldn't tell for sure.

The last piece of sculpture had been the least appealing to Ace, not only in comparison to the other more eye-catching works, but also because it reminded her, at first glance, of the statues in that pretentious country-house garden. Now she felt drawn to examine it as though it had gained in value because of that very difference. Perhaps that was the idea.

It was a group of a dozen or so nude figures that she'd first thought represented some sort of pointless mythical Greek allegory — that country-house garden, she recalled, had been full of them. Ace smiled to herself, remembering how she had brought up the question of fig leaves and hadn't let it go; the outing had been downhill all the way after that. These statues, she was pleased to see, went honestly without that sort of prudish adornment. They were a mixed group of figures: male and female, children, youths and adults. All were looking into the sky in the same direction: the children laughing and pointing; the older figures reaching out and upward, but with more thoughtful expressions, turning to each other as though in doubt, seeking reassurance. The level of detail and expression was remarkable and they would have seemed uncomfortably real, except that they were formed out of what seemed to be veined marble, deliberately avoiding representing ordinary skin tones. Paradoxically, the hard stone seemed unusually warm to Ace's touch and she supposed that was intentional. She looked at the plaque beside the figures; 'Choice,' it said simply.

She was still deciding whether to take the work at face value or not, when a couple entered the glade through an arch in the hedge. Ace observed them from the corner of her eye, realizing, with mild annoyance, that she hadn't asked the Doctor anything about the local inhabitants.

They seemed quite human; a man and woman in their early thirties, she guessed. The woman wore a skin-tight bodysuit that shaded from deep purple at her feet to crimson at her shoulders, with a high-ruffed collar and cuffs. The man wore a costume, in pale blue, of a loose-topped jumper, sashed at the waist, which formed a sort of straight kilt falling to just above the knees.

The pair nodded politely to Ace and started to walk round the exhibits. She listened to the comments they exchanged for a few moments. They were admiring the crystal column and the woman said that she liked the simplicity of the form. Her companion said he preferred the artist's more adventurous earlier works. Surely he didn't think his work of the previous year was anything but preliminary to this, she queried. Well actually he did, he replied; in fact, now that she mentioned it . . . Ace smiled to herself and followed the path out of the glade.

Local fashion was not choosy, she decided, and they had accepted her own midnight-black military-style combat suit without comment. Language, of course, would not be a problem. To her it seemed to be common English, in the same way as had the writing on the exhibits' plaques. She knew if she concentrated on what she read or heard spoken, she would become aware that it was Trans-anglish or Galacticspeak or some entirely new language, but at the moment it was convenient to think of it as her mother tongue. Once again, the TARDIS had telepathically induced the local language through her subconscious mind. In Ace's opinion, it put twenty-eight-day taped language courses and pocket translators severely in the shade.

Eventually she reached the edge of the park, where the path turned to skirt a low boundary wall, and she got her first view out across the Strait of Byzantium and along the coastline to the great rising tiers of the city itself, the towers and domes gleaming under the bright sun. She looked down over the wall to the water's edge where shallow waves broke languidly over the rocks. The water looked clean and clear; not a crushed drinks can, plastic bottle or oil slick in sight. She drew in a deep breath of fresh, slightly salt-tanged air. Yes, she thought, this might really turn out to be a good idea.

When Ace returned to the TARDIS, she found Bernice examining one of the exhibits in the glade, whilst the Doctor was lying back on a convenient bench with his hat over his eyes, apparently dozing: a casually comfortable figure in his crumpled cream-linen suit and two-tone brogues. As she approached however, he murmured: 'Have you been enjoying yourself?'

'Yes, I really did. You know, I thought it was going to be seriously tedious, but there's some weird stuff around here and – oh, sorry I was so long, I didn't mean to be.'

'That's all right Ace, it is your birthday. And I have not been idle.' He gestured to the base of the TARDIS, where Ace now saw a plaque bearing the words: 'TARDIS, by A Doctor.'

She laughed. 'That's great, Doc. Now it'll fit in fine. Oh yeah, I forgot to ask – what is this place and what's the year?'

The Doctor smiles. 'This is New Byzantium, capital city of the planet Tairngire, and by your calendar the year is twenty-six seventy-three. For which purposes I have also prepared these.' He handed both Ace and Bernice, who had just wandered over, a pair of small plastic cards. 'Identification and credit cards. Perfectly valid, I assure you. They don't use cash money here and, after all, it wouldn't be a holiday unless we could buy at least a stick of rock and a "Kiss-me-Quick" hat, would it?' He beamed.

'Okay,' said Ace, 'let's go.'

The Doctor rose, hooking his umbrella over his arm, but Bernice interjected, 'She's not wearing that,' pointing to Ace's combat suit. 'This *is* meant to be a holiday.'

'Quite true, Ace,' added the Doctor. 'Your costume does not really convey the true holiday spirit.'

Ace took a deep breath. 'All right, I'll change,' she conceded suddenly, stepping towards the TARDIS. Why did nobody understand how comfortable she felt in the combat suit? She'd still wear black though, she decided, but it would be her black jeans and tee shirt with the silver trimmings, and her old badge-encrusted bomber jacket – with an inside pocket for . . . Well, they didn't need to know what for, then they wouldn't worry. Both the Doctor and Benny were too trusting sometimes, she thought. She believed in being prepared.

Ace paused on the TARDIS threshold and smiled at them. 'You know, I really think I'm going to like this place, there's not a 'Keep off the Grass' sign anywhere!'

Chapter 6

The dark bulk of the *Broadsword* swelled and blotted out the stars, dwarfing the last flight to return. The three fighters came to a stop outside the brightly lit mouth of their hangar bay. Force-field manipulator beams locked on and drew them through the pressure curtain and into the ship. As they settled gently on the deck, the space doors slid closed behind them.

The side hatch of Kim Talevera's fighter opened and the pilot's cocoon split and unfolded. Kim felt the computer-link terminal disconnect from the base of her skull. Suddenly she was back in the world of five limited senses and a frail human body again. She sat for a moment, as usual, regretting the loss. Then she climbed stiffly out and onto the deck and pulled off her helmet, ruffling her crown of tight dark curls. She blinked in the light, waiting for her eyes to adjust to ordinary seeing again.

Her wingmen came over, helmets under their arms.

'That's it then,' said Dag. 'Last exercise completed and we passed very neatly even if I do say so myself.'

'You,' said Kim, contriving to sound censorious, 'very nearly spread yourself over the landscape on that second pass.'

Felden looked aggrieved. 'The mission profile said "low" and I was,' he protested, grinning.

'There's low and there's suicidal. If I check the underside of your bird, I bet I'll find scrapes in the paint from that last ridge.'

'Debly's coming,' said Cort quietly. They turned to the approaching figure of their flight commander.

Kim saluted. 'Flight reporting, sir.' She handed over the memory card she had pulled from her cockpit. 'My copy of the flight log and record of the exercise.' Felden and Cort handed over their cards. Debly nodded.

'Your flight's the last in, Kim. We can hold the mission debriefing tomorrow morning, since the trials are effectively over as of now.'

'How does it look?' Kim asked anxiously.

'Officially, Lieutenant, we wait for the word from Fleetcomm after they've analysed the data. Unofficially . . . ' He smiled at the three expectant faces. 'I would be most surprised if the *Broadsword* wasn't on the active list within the next few days.' He regarded the mutual backslapping between the flight members with an amused eye, and started to walk away. Then he turned suddenly.

'Oh — Felden?'

'Sir?'

'You won't try anything as stupid as that again, will you? You may be expendable, but fighters are expensive.' And he walked away, leaving Talevera and Cort to laugh at the expression on Felden's face.

'Okay,' said Kim after a minute, 'it's me for the showers. See you in recreation later?'

'Sure,' replied Felden. The more reserved Cort appeared hesitant.

'Well, actually . . . ' he began.

'Alternative plans? You quiet ones are all the same — move in when nobody's expecting it,' Kim exclaimed.

'Ahhh, light dawns. Is a certain new weapons tec coming off-duty shortly?' Felden enquired with a grin.

'What if she is?' replied Cort defensively.

'Nothing. It's an ill wind, that's all.'

'Huh?'

'After all, poor old Manten's accident didn't do him any good, but it brought the delightful Toni Pandril into your life, didn't it? There's always a plus side if you can find it.'

Night lay softly over New Byzantium, drawing a silent blanket of mist up from the water front to veil the lower terraces, until the tallest spires and towers seemed to float unsupported beneath the stars. The mist transmuted the controlled city lights into a pale, hazy glow, recombining the vari-tinted sources into a uniform opalescence.

In a district on the city's outskirts, one patch of multicoloured light remained, burning too vividly for the mist to conceal. The famous Lantern Market was in full swing.

'It says here,' Ace said, raising her voice over the noise of the crowd flowing past her, 'that the Lantern Market of New Byzantium — hey, what happened to Old Byzantium?'

'Byzantium is the original name of Constantinople,' Bernice informed her. 'Named after the Emperor Constantine. That was the capital of the Eastern Roman Empire until the fifteenth century, when it was captured by the Turks and later renamed —'

'Istanbul,' Ace cut back in again. 'Thanks for the lecture, Professor, I remember now. But why pick that name anyway?'

'I should imagine it was a question of geographical similarity,' ventured the Doctor. 'Both cities are set on what is practically an isthmus of land, cut through by a strait linking two seas. Or perhaps somebody simply chose the name because it sounded pleasantly lyrical.'

Ace continued reading from the Cityguide infopad: 'The Lantern Market commemorates the trading stalls set up by the colonists shortly after their first landing on Tairngire over three hundred years ago.'

The Doctor smiles. 'I have observed this before in human cultures, and it may be another answer to why the city is named as it is: the need to establish a sense of place in the present by commemorating even the most trivial events of the past. The mystique of age and tradition give spurious justification for an inaccurate re-creation of what, probably started out as the best the first settlers could do in the circumstances.' He gestured at the strings of large, Chinese-style, coloured lanterns that looped from the trees and bedecked each trader's stall. 'Originally, those must have been temporary working lights running off the landing craft power cells. They put a few scraps of coloured plastic or paper over them to brighten things up a bit, because they *needed* the diversion. Starting life on a new world, even one as benign as this, is hard, often dangerous, sometimes fatal.' His eyes took on a distant look. 'Believe me, I know.'

'You mean they would have preferred to find a supermarket

chain megastore waiting for them when they landed?' queried Bernice, sarcastically.

'We could always go back and ask them, if you like.'

'Oi, Doc! Benny! Don't spoil it!' exclaimed Ace. 'It's been a great day, I'm having fun, the people are having fun. Let's just keep on enjoying ourselves, okay?'

'I'm sorry, Ace, by all means keep on enjoying your birthday. This *is* a jolly place and the people *are* having fun. But that would be so whether this was an accurate re-creation of the first market or not. Enjoy the present because the past may be unreliable, do you see?'

Ace brightened. 'Point made, Doc. Now let's see if we can find a bargain.'

They joined the flow of people once again, allowing the tide of shoppers and tourists and chattering, excited children to carry them along the paths between the stalls. Bernice smiled. She especially liked to see children having fun.

Under the multicoloured lanterns the market was filled with iridescent highlights glinting off polished trinkets and carpeted with flickering, many-hued shadows. The smell of roasting peanuts, hot chocolate and honeycomb from the snackbarrows filled the air. Strolling between the stalls were a pair of buskers playing an accordion and penny whistle, whilst over the heads of the crowd, they could see a stiltwalker with a clown face, bowing and doffing his absurd hat as they let him through.

They passed stalls selling mirrors and masks, perfume and candles, pottery and badges, flowers and jewellery, parasols and balloons and . . . Ace stopped trying to keep count. She made some purchases just for fun, while the Doctor chattered foolishly and wittily with the traders. Bernice bought balloons for some children who had been innocently fascinated by the varicoloured brilliance of her costume. Inwardly Ace hugged herself — it had been a *good* day, full of undemanding pleasures.

New Byzantium itself had proved as fresh and elegant as her first distant view of it had promised. In fact, it was what people of her time would have wished a futuristic city to be like: towers, spires and domes that managed the difficult architectural feat of being both majestic and impressive without being over-powering. It thronged with people, but the efficient powered walkways and sinuous, transparent travel-tubes with their silver bullet capsules eliminated the expected crush of private traffic.

Amazingly, as she now thought of it, she had chosen to visit an undersea centre twenty kilometres out to sea and reached by submarine travel-tubes. Not so long ago she would have considered visiting an aquarium incredibly 'naff' – as she would forcefully have pointed out. But now, well, why not? And she had enjoyed it. Life was fascinating if you allowed yourself to enjoy the pleasure of looking, she decided.

Returning to shore in the afternoon, they had spent a few hours in the Unreality Park; which, Ace decided, left laser lightshows and hundred-track sound systems standing. It was entirely frivolous and probably very juvenile and extremely silly – and she loved it. Perhaps you had to grow up a little before you appreciated simple pleasures. Bernice, who had obviously been observing her closely, had said: 'Yes, simple pleasures are wasted on the young: they're not old enough to appreciate them.'

'Cynic,' Ace had retorted with a smile.

'I like to keep in practice,' Bernice had replied.

And now the homely bustle and strictly low-tech coloured lanterns of the market, melding with cool, misty evening air, were a welcome contrast and a perfect way to wind down.

Ace felt pleasantly tired but happy. It had been a good day. Very possibly the best birthday she could remember. She wondered if she could pretend to have made a mistake and that in fact tomorrow was her actual birthday – and could they do it all again?

It had been a growing nightmare of a day for Gerry Ostman.

He was now certain that he was going mad, and equally certain that he could do nothing whatsoever to help himself. He knew this because he had tried to ask for help, and then . . . And then . . . His memory closed in upon itself again, his line of thought washed away, and there was only the present moment in his consciousness.

Gerry looked about him in mild surprise. He was on the edge of a large, tree-lined square, filled with people and open-air market stalls lit by many coloured lanterns. He found himself undecided; should he join the crowd or keep away from it?

Suddenly this seemed a very important decision to make and he didn't know why. What was it about a crowd that simultaneously attracted and repelled him? For a moment he felt like running and there came a tentative recollection that he *had* been running from . . . He couldn't remember. His clothes, he realized, were damp with sweat — that was correct if he had been running — but he wasn't breathing hard and his legs didn't ache, and that was wrong, he thought uncertainly. Suddenly, feeling emotionally shaken, he sank gratefully onto a seat under a tree. Automatically his eyes flicked between the crowd and the entrance to the square nearest to him, alert for . . . what? With an effort of will, he buried his head in his hands and forced himself to try to remember.

His day had gone wrong from the start. He distinctly recalled intending to visit the xenobotanic gardens and somehow he had found himself in the Central Library, knowing he had been searching the references, but unable to remember why he had been doing so, or what he had been looking for. He had left in a dazed state of mind, wondering if he had experienced some sort of blackout and thinking seriously about finding a doctor when . . . there was another blank, and he found himself leaving a public building — the office of somebody important, he was sure — knowing that he had been asking questions about them but without the slightest idea why he had been doing so! Really frightened, he had looked around for help and seen a patrolman (the uniform had never seemed so reassuring) and had started to walk towards him, intending to ask for help . . . And then it was half an hour later and he found himself sitting at a table in a quiet walkway restaurant.

Desperately, he had tried to ask the people at the next table for help, but the words would not come . . . Then another blank and it was an *hour later*. He was leaving another office building with the impression that he had been making enquiries about some important people, but he *still* couldn't remember why.

At some point in the nightmare, he became aware that he was being followed, then his moments of lucid thought between the blackouts had become briefer and more disjointed. He could remember starting to run, though he did not know from whom or what, and the terrifying thought came to him that he might be a criminal suffering from memory loss. Why couldn't he go to the police if he was an honest citizen? Perhaps it was the police following him . . . And then his mind blanked out again. When he recovered this time, he had seen the lights of the market — and here he was.

He forced himself to sit quietly. Every time he had tried to ask for help his mind had blanked out. Perhaps if he just waited until the right person walked past close enough, he could ask them — calmly, rationally — for medical aid, without pushing himself over the brink again.

Some children ran past him, laughing, batting a large red balloonball between them. He tried to draw reassurance from their innocent pleasure, waiting for somebody more suitable. He felt absurdly deserted at the edge of the crowded square. Why didn't someone come? His thin veneer of calm was slipping away. He scanned the nearest line of stalls, hoping to catch someone's eye, but all their attention seemed to be on buying and selling — no, there was one young woman, dressed in black, looking at him. For a moment he relaxed his control and let the fear inside show on his face.

The man with the bowed back, slumped on the bench beneath the lantern-hung tree, had caught Ace's eye because his whole attitude was so different from every other person she'd seen that day. Yet it was at the same time very familiar. In twentieth-century London, he would have gone unnoticed among all the other hopeless, friendless loungers. But here in twenty-seventh-century New Byzantium, so well-ordered, secure and prosperous, he was terribly out of place. His eyes met hers and she saw an expression of agonized entreaty cross his face. The unspoken appeal for help was impossible to refuse and she stepped towards him.

As she walked forward, she was vaguely aware of two men jogging purposefully along the line of the trees towards the man on the bench. She saw him glance round at them and his face went blank. He leapt up and sprinted off towards one of the many small alleyways that opened onto the square, the two men in hot pursuit. Their faces, she realized, were just as blankly expressionless as their quarry's had so suddenly, unreasonably, become.

'Doctor! Benny!' she called behind her. 'Something's happening – this way!' And she dashed off after the three men without waiting to see if they had even heard her.

There was no sign of hunters or hunted as Ace raced into the alley, leaving the buzz of the market behind her, but ahead she could hear the clatter of running feet and she followed them. Something was very wrong, both with the frightened man and his stone-faced pursuers. What it was, she didn't know, but she was going to find out.

She was running through a maze of small, twisting streets. Arched passages and flights of steps branched off invitingly, hinting at hidden arcades, quiet mews and tiny curio shops waiting to be explored. Behind several windows, homely lights glowed through the misty air, but for the moment Ace ran unseen through deserted ways, silent except for the pounding feet ahead of her, seemingly just around the next corner, but out of sight when she reached it.

The Ace found herself in a tiny square with three streets radiating from it. There was no sign of the men she was chasing. Panting, she jogged to a halt under the hazy radiance of a standard-mounted light globe in the middle of the square, straining her ears over the thump of her heartbeat. There was no sound of running feet to guide her, neither did the glow-kerbing that lit each of the diverging streets give her any sign as to which way she should go.

Footsteps rang in the right-hand street, coming towards her. She tensed, but it was only a man and a woman who appeared, arm in arm and obviously without a thought for anyone but themselves.

Suddenly there was a reflected flicker of blue light from the middle street and the echo of a cry, sharply cut off. Ace sprinted forward, through a broad archway and along a narrow curving street which turned around the back of what seemed to be walled house gardens, for the tops of trees and shrubs spilled over them.

Then there were three figures before her: two upright, frozen in the act of lunging forward by her unexpected appearance, the other in the process of slumping down the wall at his back, one hand vainly twisted in the trailing strands of its shaggy ivy crown. For a moment the tableau held, then one of the standing men jerked up his arm. Ace leapt sideways as a lance of blue fire singed the air and stonework cracked and bubbled behind her.

She made a tumbling shoulder-roll and came upright in the welcome shelter of a recessed arched gate. She tried it; locked! She *knew* she should have worn her combat suite − and her blaster. How long until they realize I'm unarmed, she wondered − five seconds? She grinned. *Almost* unarmed, she amended, unzipping an inner pocket of her jacket. Always be prepared, she told herself. She drew out a handful of white spheres of assorted sizes, resembling uninteresting boiled sweets. Choosing a small one, she popped it into her mouth for a moment, then withdrew it. Now it was a deep red. She tossed it down the street and hugged the shelter of the archway.

The explosion was most satisfactory, reverberating and echoing along the narrow streets and pushing a billowing hole through the misty air. The patter of descending chips of stone was like a round of applause to Ace's ears.

She snatched a quick look down the street. One of the men was on his hands and knees; the other was staggering upright, still holding something in his hand. She pulled her head back into the protection of the archway as another beam flared past. She activated a slightly larger piece of her explosive 'confectionery' and threw it after the first.

This time, after the dust had settled, she heard a pair of dragging, unsteady footsteps disappearing down the street and into the night. She fingered a third sweetbomb for a moment, but restrained herself. When she emerged cautiously from her shelter, there was no sign of the hunters. Only the body of their victim remained.

Ace ran towards him, past the two small craters her deceptive sweetmeats had created. The Doctor disapproved of her fascination with ordnance in general and explosives in particular, but even he (she was sure) would agree that *this* time there had been no choice. The opposition had been packing some pretty severe hardware of their own (she would point out) and didn't mind using it. And she *had* resisted the quite reasonable impulse to fragment the murdering pair of . . . Somehow, she knew, the Doctor would still not approve.

The body of the man Ace had first seen on the bench at the market lay where it had fallen, his head and shoulders doubled up against the ivy-topped wall, his right arm still reaching above him, fingers entwined in the trailing strands. She saw an intelligent, thoughtful face, surmounted by a head of blond hair, cut in a practical, conservative style because the owner had more important things to think about than fashion. The face was frozen in a rictus of surprised death, the eyes open and focused on infinity. There was a scorched and smoking fist-sized hole in his chest.

Ace stared down at him and for the first time felt the familiar sense of sickness and anger swell within her. This was it — the reality after the action, the big pay off when the exciting bit was over. She felt for a pulse in the big carotid artery of the neck without hope — nothing. 'Sorry I couldn't get here sooner, mate,' she murmured, regretfully.

Then the dead eyes turned to look at her and a dead hand grasped her arm in a vice-like grip. The body jerked up; the mouth twisted to form words. 'Drowning . . . ' he gasped, then his features relaxed into a terrible calm and he sank back.

Ace struggled to free herself from that unnatural hold, then froze, choking in horror, as a small, bloody, blackened thing pulled itself half out of the hole in the man's chest and then lay still. She tore free and, pale and trembling, she scrabbled on hands and knees across the roadway until she rested against the far wall, hugging her shins, staring with fearful eyes at the body. She hadn't moved when the Doctor and Bernice found her a few minutes later.

Gerry Ostman felt his mind leave the ruined body and the sensations of death faded away, until there was only the warm, fluid darkness to cocoon him. The nightmare was ended and now there was peace and rest.

Chapter 7

Inspector Quillon stepped out of the groundcar into the narrow back street of the Old Town. The kerblights were still pulsing, warning the small crowd of the arrival of further official vehicles as he came up to the police line being maintained by two air-patrol officers. One of them let him pass.

'Air Patroller Ord,' she introduced herself. 'The victim's over there, sir.'

Quillon saw the figure slumped against the wall a few metres along the street. A man and a woman were apparently examining the body, while a younger woman stood a little apart. 'And who are they?' he enquired mildly. 'It is not the custom of this force to allow civilians to paw over our corpses in public, is it, Officer Ord?'

'They were involved in the incident, Inspector. I think you had better speak to them . . . ' There was an odd look on her face that made Quillon withhold further reprimand. He walked over to the man wearing the strangely cut suit and the brightly dressed woman. The younger woman was looking annoyed with herself, he noticed.

'Excuse me, sir, ms,' he said firmly. 'I must ask you to keep clear of the body. If you're not accredited by the city for this sort of work, you must leave it for our own specialists.'

The brightly dressed woman commented wryly: 'I think your specialists are going to need some help with this one.'

The small man turned two intense grey eyes, fiercely bright, to meet his gaze. 'Specialists? I *am* a specialist.' He returned to examining the body.

'A specialist in what, sir?'

'Almost everything — I generalize in specialities, you might say. Besides, I doubt if you have anyone qualified to deal with this. Take a close look at the chest.' Curious, drawn on by his words, Quillon squatted down and peered at the chest wound and the bloody lump disgorged from it. Suddenly he jerked up; white, thin-lipped, swallowing hard.

'Yes,' beamed the little man, with an enthusiasm Quillon considered misplaced in the circumstances. 'You see what we're dealing with now. There may have been a murder, but this is not the body of the victim, because it's *not a body*. This is an extremely lifelike exoform; designed, I should imagine, to provide mobility and a disguise for the small creature that lived in the chest cavity. It's a pity the creature was so badly mutilated, but you can see the remains of tiny, but very well-developed and dexterous looking hands. I wonder how intelligent they can be as individuals, hmmm?' He looked at Quillon as though inviting him into a consultation, but for the moment Quillon could think of no suitable response.

Interview rooms of police stations, Bernice thought, even such comfortable and civilized ones as provided by the city of New Byzantium, are not ideal places to spend long periods of time. The atmosphere contrives to make even the most honest citizen feel uncomfortable. She looked at her companions, suspecting that they shared her opinion on this point.

The Doctor sat forward in a chair, resting his chin on his red-handled umbrella, and gazing into the middle distance with a look of glum resignation on his face. Ace was methodically pacing the room and peering occasionally out of the window at the city lights beyond. Her expression varied between an occasional 'I told you so' look, cast in their direction, and a scowl of deep annoyance.

The first expression was easy to interpret. Ace was reminding them that they should not have talked her out of wearing her combat suit. Bernice returned the look with a wry smile. The latter expression's meaning, however, Bernice could only guess at, but she suspected it masked Ace's little slice of personal shame. Seeing the creature emerge from the 'body' in the alley had shocked her, and she resented it. She knew Ace had seen plenty of carnage and suffering, probably more than she would admit to. But by some quirk of chance, this incident had slipped in under her guard. Dead people should stay dead, she probably thought, and things shouldn't crawl out of them.

Bernice sighed inwardly and slumped back in her chair once more. Idly, she flicked her hat in the air and caught it again.

Ace stopped her pacing. 'It's nearly midnight – how long are they going to keep us here?' she demanded impatiently. 'The inspector took our statements hours ago!'

'Forty-eight minutes and twenty seconds ago, to be more precise,' replied the Doctor, without, apparently, consulting a watch. Bernice experimentally threw her hat higher so that it touched the ceiling, lost stability and crashed onto the table like an errant flying saucer.

Ace glared at her as she retrieved it. 'Yeah, well okay, but it's still too long. I mean they checked everything: IDs, credit cards – *and* they took my minibombs!'

'I've been meaning to speak to you about those,' the Doctor said sternly. 'Some time ago, you promised me you would be making no more nitro-nine.'

'And you told me this was a peaceful planet.' countered Ace. 'No need for a combat suit, you said. Good thing I did have those bombs, wasn't it?' She became more contrite. 'Anyway, what I actually said was, I'd finished with making up nitro-nine; this is *neo*-nitro – much better stuff. This formula is perfectly stable until it's activated by saliva and it's easy to graduate the strength of the charges and so –'

'Spare me your enthusiasm, Ace. I admit your ingenuity, but what happens if somebody mistakes them for sweets and does not merely suck, but actually *swallows* one?'

'Now, that's a good question,' endorsed Bernice.

'Well actually, Professor, they're broken down harmlessly by gastric juices,' replied Ace, with some pride. 'Gives you a bit of heartburn, though.' She paused and lowered her voice a little, returning to a subject that had been troubling her. 'Doc, those credit cards and identifications, they were kosher, weren't they? I mean, I didn't even know you had them until you handed them to us this morning.'

'Now that also is a good question, Doctor,' said Bernice with feeling. 'I was wondering about them myself.'

'They are perfectly genuine,' the Doctor reassured them. 'Their source may be a little unusual, but quite impeccable as far as this time period is concerned. You see, complex societies demand the production of the right number and the right reference so often, that any, shall we say, *widely* travelled person such as myself, sometimes finds it easier to establish a source of genuine bona fides, rather than having to evade the issue.' He mused for a moment. 'It's a pity though. More primitive cultures are so much more ready to judge the *person*, rather than a set of numbers, and take you on trust.' He paused. 'Of course, they may cut your head off because your hair is the wrong colour . . .'

Inspector Quillon re-entered the room.

Bernice found him interesting: a young man for his rank, tall, slim and academic looking, with a pleasant open manner, slightly nervous gestures and sharp eyes that, Bernice guessed, would not miss a thing.

'Sorry to keep you waiting, Professor Summerfield, Ms Ace and, er, Doctor.' He glanced again at the name on the Doctor's identity card and decided not to attempt to pronounce it.

'Have you got them yet?' demanded Ace.

'A very thorough search of the area is being made, I can assure you. And all the ports and travelways are being watched. Of course, it would help us if you could give us a more detailed description of the two men.'

'It was the best I could do while being shot at,' retorted Ace, sarcastically.

'Yes, quite,' conceded Quillon. He hesitated, as though unwilling to broach a delicate subject. 'While we're waiting, there is one small detail I'd like to clear up. According to your statements, you all arrived in Byzantium this morning from off-world, but we can't find your names on any passenger list of any of today's shuttle landings, nor any recent starliner arrival at any skystation.' He smiled. 'Now perhaps you can explain just how you got here,' he requested in an ingenuous, but un-compromising tone.

Ace glanced at the Doctor. Hadn't he just implied everything would be fine?

'I have a private shuttle lander,' began the Doctor, in his best matter-of-fact manner. 'We landed in a small flying field outside the city. Probably nobody noticed us; it's a very small craft.'

'But deceptively spacious,' added Bernice, automatically.

'I'm sure it is,' said Quillon. 'Now if you could give me the name of the field and the registration of your vessel, we can sort the matter out.'

'I thought there was free access to Tairngire for all galactic citizens with the proper identification documents? They *are* in order, I assume?' The Doctor reached out for the cards, but Quillon held onto them.

'Yes, Doctor, they are in order, but they do not excuse compliance with certain formalities usually observed by visitors to this planet. And considering that, half a day after landing here, you are associated with an, ah, incident, with possible off-world connections, and you cannot give a satisfactory account of how you got here . . . That entitles us to be a little suspicious, does it not, Doctor? What do you expect us to think?'

'What I expect you to think of,' the Doctor said, forcefully, 'are the full implications of the artificial body, the creature within it and the two mysterious assassins, because they are far more serious than you yet comprehend!'

'What other implications are there? If you have any further information, you must tell me. Convince me of your good faith Doctor, and perhaps we can overlook your infringement of regulations.'

'Very well — but I don't think you're going to like it.' His smile was ironic, almost pitying. Quillon's face set. 'Firstly, I believe you will find, when you finish checking his identification, that the "body" is an exact copy of a real person. Not simply a realistic replica of *a* man, but a specific person, probably a citizen of Tairngire. So, where's the original, and where did the substitution take place?' Quillon started at this, but the Doctor continued remorselessly. 'Secondly, it is probable that the two "men" you are hunting are also replicas. Again, where are the original people? Thirdly, I think you will find the creature that was living inside the exoform to be an unknown species, so where are you going to start looking for them?' Quillon was looking distinctly unhappy now, but the Doctor was saving the worst for last. 'Finally, instead of worrying about our slight infringement of the rules, think how many other *really* illegal aliens there may be on this planet right now — and how are you going to find them?'

There was a long silence after this, broken by the beeping of the desk terminal screen. Quillon scanned the information displayed, then turned apologetically to the Doctor. 'The body — if we can call it that — has been confirmed as exactly resembling one Gerry Ostman, age thirty-four, citizen of Tairngire. Occupation, botanist, just back from off-world studies this morning. Also, preliminary search has so far failed to match the remains of the creature living in the "body" with any known species in the galaxy. It seems you are right, so far, Doctor.' The Doctor beamed in a satisfied manner.

'He told you so!' chimed Ace.

'Our cards, please,' requested Bernice politely, holding out her hand. Quillon solemnly returned her cards and the Doctor's, but hestitated over Ace's.

'I would like to remind you,' he said, looking sternly at her, 'that we take a very dim view of the unauthorized possession of explosive devices — and even more so to their use. You are lucky that, under the circumstances, we're not bringing charges.'

'Self defence!' exclaimed Ace. 'Besides, you'd never have known about those fake people with the little rats hiding in them if I hadn't been there, 'cos odds on, those two thugs wouldn't have left the body around for you to find, would they, Doc?'

'Most unlikely,' confirmed the Doctor.

'Nevertheless, there will be no more home-made explosives,' said Quillon firmly.

'Can I have the rest of the bag back?' asked Ace, innocently.

'Only when you leave this planet.'

'Okay,' replied Ace, with a sudden meek acceptance that caused both the Doctor and Bernice to look at her suspiciously. But further discussion was interrupted by the communicator on the desk.

Quillon took the call on the handset, listened for a moment, said, 'All right,' gruffly, and replaced the receiver.

'That was from the City Marshal's office. It seems the military are worried about the possible space defence implications. They're overreacting a bit,' he muttered, half to himself. 'Anyway, Marshal Talevera would like to see you in person and they've sent transportation over.' He scowled. 'It seems they

45

don't even trust the civil police to get that right.'

Bernice sympathized. Quillon seemed quite a decent type; an honest man doing his job to the best of his ability. She could see he felt this intervention from above implied lack of understanding of the value of his investigation.

'Well, we'd better go down to meet them,' said Quillon, with barely disguised annoyance. 'They'll be here shortly.'

As Quillon guided them through the building, the Doctor followed, his thoughts uncertain. While he needed to talk to the most senior people about what he suspected might be happening, there was more information he wanted from Quillon, whose trust − to a degree − he felt he had already won. Besides, there was a slight doubt in his mind . . . 'Tell me, Inspector,' he said, as though just making conversation, 'where do you go to get away from the pressures of the job? A place in the country, holidays abroad, or perhaps somewhere more exotic?'

Puzzled by this sudden interest in his domestic affairs, Quillon replied rather sharply, 'Well, if you must know, we have a small villa on one of the Cerulean Sea islands. We always go there for holidays.'

'And your work keeps you tied to the city, I suppose?' continued the Doctor. 'You don't need to travel far in the course of your investigations, as a rule?'

'No, not for some years. Why do you ask?'

'For the best of reasons,' murmured the Doctor, 'the very best.' He lapsed into a thoughtful silence.

They reached the exit where the transport would collect them and the Doctor turned to Quillon. 'Well, goodbye for the moment, Inspector. I'm sure we'll be seeing you again very shortly. There's a lot more to do, you know.'

'I am fully aware of that, Doctor,' replied Quillon, a little stiffly.

'Good, good,' enthused the Doctor. 'Hold that thought and, *be prepared*,' he added, with sudden emphasis.

That's my line, thought Ace.

'What for?' queried the Inspector.

'Almost anything!'

The vehicle that drove out of the night and stopped under the entrance-way awning was a broad, low-slung eight-wheeled troop carrier, painted in military olive drab. For all its bulk, it was surprisingly quiet, powered by high-efficiency force engines like all the other vehicles they had so far seen on Tairngire.

A smart young officer stepped out and gave a courtesy salute to the civilians. 'Inspector Quillon? Lieutenant Tesseni reporting with escort. Doctor, Professor Summerfield and Ms Ace? This way please.' Ace brightened, impressed by the powerful vehicle and by being treated as somebody important. She climbed eagerly through the side hatch door with the drop step.

Bernice followed, less than enthusiastic about things military, especially the military mentality. She fervently hoped they would not encounter any brass-hatted stuffed shirts or she would start speaking her mind . . . She started telling herself not to lose her temper in advance.

Inside the long, low interior, the lieutenant indicated they should sit on one of the double row of bench seats that ran down both sides of the vehicle, while he sat down opposite them. There were two other soldiers inside, seated near the rear double doors and looking alert.

Bernice eyed them all with tolerant disfavour, while Ace wanted to find out more about what was state of the art for military equipment on Tairngire. However, it was the Doctor who monopolized the conversation. As the motors hummed with power and the transporter rolled slowly out of the police head-quarters car park, he said, 'This is a large vehicle just to collect the three of us, Lieutenant. Does the Marshal expect any danger?'

Tesseni replied simply, 'The Marshal's orders were very specific about it, Doctor. He's a very careful man; I'm sure he knows best.'

'Of course, of course. By the way, shouldn't we have turned left if we're going to the Defence Building? I'm sure I recall seeing it marked in the other direction on the map of the city I saw this morning.'

'No, the Marshal's at his own residence — we're going there. It has full communication facilities; the Marshal can work just as well from there . . . ' He trailed off. It was hard to read his dark face in the dim interior, intermittently lit as it was by the passing streetlights shining through the driver's windows, but the Doctor thought he was frowning, almost uncertain.

The Doctor replied understandingly, 'I see, very sensible in the circumstances.' This time he clearly saw the flash of teeth as Tesseni smiled, as though reassured by his acceptance. Then, surprisingly, the transporter slowed and stopped.

'Hello,' said Bernice, 'broken down? Or are we picking up another fare?'

Tesseni replied stiffly, 'We have to wait here.'

'What for?' Ace asked, puzzled. Before there was a reply, the double back doors of the vehicle were thrown open and two more soldiers climed in, carrying between them the unmistakable form of a body contained in a heavy black plastic bag. The other pair of soldiers helped them lay their grisly burden down, the doors swung shut and the transporter moved off again.

'I see we're taking the remains of the ersatz Mr Ostman with us as well — no doubt the Marshal wants them specially examined,' remarked the Doctor, mildly.

'But I thought the police labs were doing that?' exclaimed Ace, cold suspicion seeding within her even as she spoke.

'Now now, Ace,' reproved the Doctor, 'The Lieutenant is just following his orders, like a good soldier should. Isn't that right, Lieutenant?' Tesseni was nodding in reflex. The Doctor sat forward, full of friendly interest. 'And where did the orders for your last posting take you, Lieutenant?'

'My unit was part of the garrison on . . . ' Tesseni stiffened visibly, his voice losing inflection.' We had a home posting, Doctor.'

'Oh, that must have been nice for you.' The Doctor sat back, as though he had noticed nothing unusual. Ace sat very still, coldly tensing herself as realization sank in. Bernice's eyes flashed around the vehicle, assessing their chance, then settled on the Doctor, waiting for his cue.

The Doctor appeared to have more mundane things on his mind, for he was patting his stomach and smacking his lips audibly. 'Do you know, it's been hours since I've eaten.' He turned to Ace. 'I'm sure you have *another* bag of those sweets of yours, haven't you?' Ace nodded, not trusting her voice at that moment, and reached inside her jacket. The Doctor turned back to Tesseni. 'You really must try one of Ace's sweets — they're her own recipe. Of course, they are a little strong for some people, so I'll only have a small one . . . ' Ace produced the bag, offered it to the Doctor and Bernice, then popped a small white ball into her own mouth. ' . . . just to test the mixture.' He sucked thoughtfully for a moment, then made a face and delicately removed the sweet, now a deep red in colour. 'A little too strong, I think.'

'Not good bon bons?' queried Ace, spitting out her own sweet. Bernice appeared to be examining hers thoughtfully.

'No, better *Boom, Booms*!' And he flung the activated bomlet forward over the drivers position and into the control panel. It exploded only a fraction of a second before Ace's bomb blew open the rear doors.

The heavy vehicle slewed widly across the roadway with a squeal of tires, smashed through the central lane barrier and onto the opposite carriageway. A robot-controlled maintenance truck heading in the other direction could not stop in time, cannoned into its armoured hull and was swept aside as the transporter crossed the lane, ploughed through the kerblighting strips and into the tree-lined bank that flanked the roadside. The vehicle shuddered to a halt, its nose buried in the soft earth amid splintered saplings.

The side hatch sprang open, spilling out four figures onto the churned turf. Bernice rolled clear, but Ace and the Doctor struggled to free themselves from the ersatz Tesseni's grasp. The duplicate of Tesseni fought with more than a man's strength, and the desperate kicks and punches that Ace and the Doctor rained upon it seemed to cause it no pain or injury. They could not escape from its implacable grasp. Frantically, Bernice clawed up a handful of soft earth and rammed it into the thing's face and eyes. For a moment it seemed to be distracted and they tore free. Staggering to their feet, ears still ringing from the double explosion within the transporter, they ran unsteadily along and over the embankment and into the cover of the trees. As they ran, Bernice activated the bomlet she was still holding and flung it behind them, to discourage pursuit.

Suddenly, they found their escape blocked by a high wall,

previously hidden by the foliage. They started to run beside it, looking for a gap.

A lance of blue fire illuminated the darkness and a tree beside them burst into a shower of burning splinters and crashed to the ground. All three fell flat, twisting round to look back between the trees to the transporter, where three of the duplicate soldiers, survivors of Ace's exploding confectionery, had joined Tesseni. Two of them kept up a hail of energy bolts, pinning their targets down, whilst the third, carrying a heavier barrelled weapon, angled it over their heads and fired. A grenade exploded behind them, blowing a tree out of the ground by its roots.

'They're out of throwing range,' yelled Ace, clutching at her bag of neo-nitro 'sweets'.

'But not out of range of *this*!' the Doctor shouted back, pulling a catapult from his pocket. Ace whooped ecstatically.

Her first shot knocked over the soldier with the grenade launcher; the second scattered the two firing the energy rifles, who took cover with Tesseni behind the bulk of the transporter. Succeeding shots started to blow chunks out of it − Ace had run out of the smaller-sized charges.

Then the kerblighting along both sides of the broad roadway started to flash in warning and there were sirens in the distance. Bernice saw one of the soldiers fire into the air as a police air patroller, twisting his glidewing sharply to avoid the shot, swooped overhead.

Police cars appeared and slewed to screeching halts in a wide halo around the crashed transporter. Figures poured out and started to return fire. The air filled with the buzz of high-intensity stunners and the crackle of energy bolts. A thin haze of smoke, harsh with the smell of scorched metal, rolled over them as they crouched amid the trees. Ace saw a policeman fall, hit by an energy bolt. She wished she had her own blaster, because as far as she could tell the police stunners did not seem to affect the soldiers. The police must have realized the same thing and broken out heavier weapons, for she started to see them returning fire with energy bolts. One of the soldiers sheltering in the wreckage of the transporter jerked backwards −

Then, without warning, the surviving soldiers stopped firing. They dropped their weapons and simply collapsed to the ground, like puppets whose strings have been cut.

There was a long moment of surprised silence. Cautiously, a few police officers started to edge forward. The Doctor sprang to his feet and started to run down the embankment, arms windmilling, bellowing out. '*No!* Keep away from them! It's not safe.'

Streamers of vapour fluttered from the still figures and they burst into brilliant, caustic flames that hissed and flared as they were consumed. As the watchers backed away, secondary charges blew the burning fragments apart. In a few moments, nothing even remotely human-like remained. The Doctor stood, fists clenched, helpless and angry. 'I wanted them *alive*,' he muttered. 'I might have been able to reason with them.' As the fires died, he turned to find Inspector Quillon by his side, stun pistol still in his hand.

'Two minutes after you left headquarters,' Quillon explained blandly, 'an aide from the Marshal's office turned up and was very surprised to find you gone. Then the lab came through to say the body of Ostman was missing. Well, you did say be prepared for anything.'

'I had a hunch,' the Doctor said. 'It seemed a possibility that the communication from the Marshal's office might not be genuine. But I couldn't be certain.' He walked back along the verge to where Bernice was sitting on the grass bank, looking disgruntled.

She looked up as he approached and waved a hand vaguely around her. 'This has done nothing to improve my opinion of things military,' she commented.

Ace was sprawled on her back on the grass bank. Her clothes were torn and dirty, her face scratched and bruised, and her hair singed. Her eyes were closed and she was apparently oblivious to the commotion of police cars and newly arriving fire engines that by now had woken half the city. The Doctor stepped forward anxiously. 'Ace, are you hurt?'

She turned her head towards him. One of her eyes was beginning to swell. 'Doctor,' she said simply, 'next time I ask you to take me somewhere for a birthday treat, just kick me down a flight of stairs instead — it'll be less painful!'

Chapter 8

City Prefect Annis Delray rubbed her eyes tiredly, trying to shut out the uneasy murmur of conversation around her. She pushed back the swing arm of the chair carrying the infopad display and stretched. The screen continued to scroll through the latest reports, but they would have to wait for a few moments. Less than an hour ago she had been sound asleep, and emergency or not, her body was taking its own time to accept this unexpected activity in the early hours. Her only consolation was that practically everyone else in the room was in the same condition.

There was a tap on her shoulder and she found Peter van Buran beside her, holding another beaker of highly carbonated lemon and lime and a small, blistered-packed capsule.

'Thanks for the drink, Peter, but no stim-tabs.'

'You're going to need it, chief. If you think this is going to be a long night, just wait for tomorrow. Besides, everybody's having one — didn't you see the Marshal take his a few minutes ago? It's not cheating, you know.'

Annis sighed. 'Needs must, I suppose. Thanks for the common sense nudge, Peter.' She swallowed the medicine. 'Watch the latest reports for me while this stuff does its thing.'

Half of the curving wall of the massively buttressed Command Room in which she sat was taken up with a glass-panelled gallery, opening onto the secondary information-processing areas manned by the command support personnel. The rest of the wall space was filled with an arc of display screens, illustrating on a giant scale the progress of events as the situation developed. At present the only display was a map of the city with several locations picked out in red. The floor of the room was dominated by a circle of twenty or so large conference seats, each with its own infopad arm. Radiating out in wedges behind them were the seats for assistants and advisors.

The Command Room was housed in a sub-level of the Defence Building, ready to be activated in direst emergency, whether natural disaster or military threat. It formed the centre of a communications web that embraced not only the capital city of New Byzantium, nor just the world of Tairngire, but its entire star system and, via hyperlink, the command centres of the seven other systems in the Concordance.

Annis Delray remembered the time she had used the facility, years before, as a junior assistant in the Prefect's office during the Ranger skystation disaster. Now, for the first time since that day, she was back in the command room for something other than an exercise. But now she sat in one of the inner-circle seats as Prefect of New Byzantium, de facto leader of Tairngire.

She glanced at the solid, grey-haired, fatherly man seated across the cirlce of seats from her. Marshal Talevera was calmly taking briefings from his subordinates and checking information on his chair screen. The discreet row of medal ribbons across his chest was testimony to a great and hard-won experience. He was in this room during the Sidril War, she thought. My fortune to have missed that — and my thanks he's here now.

The last of the key personnel were filing hurriedly in and taking their places. Among these, the Prefect noticed, was Inspector Quillon of the city police, ushering in three strangers. One was a small man, dressed in some unfamiliar off-world style, who gazed about him with sharp interest. The next was a young woman in a black badge-encrusted jacket that looked much the worse for wear, who walked with a tired, dragging step. Beside her was a taller woman in a brightly coloured one-piece costume, also soiled, who was fanning herself with a large hat in a very deliberate manner.

They took their places in observers' chairs to one side of the main circle. From her briefing notes, Annis knew who they must be and what they had gone through, and sympathized, especially with the younger woman's condition. She was just going to ask Peter van Buran to check the woman had received any necessary medical aid, when she saw the woman's male companion, who was apparently some sort of doctor according to her notes, lean across and gently touch her temples with his fingertips. Even at this distance the effect was noticeable. The vitality seemed to flow back into her; she sat straighter and her eyes brightened and she managed a smile of thanks to the strange little man.

Well, thought Annis, you are something special. Where were you earlier, Doctor, before I had to take that blasted pill?

With her watch showing it was still a few minutes short of an hour since the emergency had been declared, Annis Delray touched a control on her chair, sounding a chime that stilled the buzz of conversation. Assistants in the outer circle continued monitoring the data channels, while their superiors in the inner seats turned to face her.

'This emergency council session is now called to order. Thank you all for your swift attendance. For the benefit of those last in, and as an aid to coordinating our efforts, I'm going to give you a brief summary of the significant events — so far as we've been able to piece them together. At oh-nine-forty yesterday morning, Tamura Lines flight two-oh-six berthed at Byzantium shuttle port carrying a passenger by the name of Gerry Ostman . . . '

From the welcome comfort of her seat at the side of the chamber, Ace listened to the briefing with half an ear, while trying to work out how a room she had never seen before could inspire a strong sense of *déjà vu*. It took her a few minutes thought before she realized it was not this *exact* room she was familiar with, but this *style* of room, with its attendent atmosphere of power and controlled tension. She must have seen its like dozens of times on television, usually with the American President talking earnestly into a red telephone, surrounded by anxious faces, while on a huge display screen behind him ominous radar traces grew across a map of the world . . . She smiled grimly at the thought and returned her attention to the summary of the strange last day of the pseudo Gerry Ostman. Apparently, he had been visiting government offices enquiring about department heads' personal travel histories.

When she heard her part of the story described as, 'A brave pursuit without regard for personal safety, made by a visitor to our planet,' Ace felt the curious approval of many eyes and, to her surprise, felt herself blushing in response. Bernice, sitting beside her, silently clapped her hands together in mock applause.

She received a very wry smile from Quillon, as her use of the bomblets was transmuted into, 'Single-handedly driving off the attackers with an unorthodox self-defence system.'

But as the attempted kidnapping of the three of them, together with the theft of the Ostman 'body' by the duplicate soldiers and the consequent battle was described, they could feel the level of concern and discomfort rising. The leaders of a peaceful, well-regulated society were trying to come to terms with the idea that there were imposters amongst their own trusted and respected military personnel. The concept was not easy to accept. Prefect Delray finished her briefing. A troubled silence fell in the chamber as the council members exchanged uneasy glances. One of the older councillors spoke up:

'While I accept we have been given an accurate summary of yesterday's events, Prefect, I must admit my credulity is taxed to its limits by the proposition that "duplicates" of up to nine people have been made − by some unknown alien race − that are so realistic that they can walk about our city masquerading as humans! And further, that we are being asked to consider the implication that there may be even more of these undetectable duplicates about. I'm sorry, but I cannot believe anybody could be fooled by such things for a moment, much less someone who knew the real person.' There was a murmur of approval at this assertion, but it was cut short by a quiet, authoritative voice.

'I'm afraid they can, Councillor Cheyney.'

All eyes turned to Marshal Talevera. His was the sort of voice that did not need to be raised to command attention, thought Ace. He sat squarely in his chair, fingertips touching to form a neat pyramid. His face was grave but his manner still conveyed calm, unshakeable, self-control. 'I have just received new information that, unhappily, shows just how perfect these, ah, duplicates are. When I was informed of the vehicle despatched to police headquarters, supposedly on my authority, a search was made to find who actually did initiate the order. It has now been confirmed that it was from Major Olaf Brandel, who serves on my staff. He is, or perhaps I should say he *was*, a thoroughly reliable officer of long service whom I know well, and indeed spoke to several times yesterday. Unless some sort of substitution was made in the brief period after I saw him last — and such a substitution would have to have occurred in the upper levels of this very building — that order was given by the same Major Brandel. Or something that looked like Major Brandel.'

There was another long silence in the chamber, even more strained than before as the implications sank in. 'What's being done with the Major?' queried the woman councillor sitting next to Cheyney.

'He cannot be found, Councillor Wharton. Naturally, a search for him is under way,' replied Talevera. 'We are also investigating the possibility that the two, as yet unidentified, killers of the Ostman duplicate are also servicemen, as it seems that all the other duplications we know about, so far, have been of military personnel.'

'Commissioner Lahat has taken personal command of the search for the two killers,' added Annis Delray, 'in conjunction with the military police. He'll be reporting to us later. Inspector Quillon is here if we need more first-hand information about last night's events.'

At the side of the chamber, Bernice glanced over at Quillon, who was paying more attention to his chair screen, which was relaying police reports, than to the deliberations of the council. She smiled. I'll bet he would rather be out on the street, she thought, than hanging around waiting to give evidence to some committee. Beside her, she noted that the Doctor was also studying his infopad, flicking between different source channels. But she had no doubt that his peculiar mind was quite capable of listening to the debate simultaneously. She wondered how long his patience would last, and when he would step in to *really* get things moving.

The discussion moved onto technical matters, with Chief Pathologist Strek answering a question about the physical nature of the duplicates and the creatures inside them. Bernice studied him with interest and a growing smile. He was a tall, lanky man with unruly hair. His enthusiasm for his subject was very apparent and he almost tripped over some of this words in his eagerness to share his new knowledge.

'To a degree,' he was saying, 'the creature dwelling in the chest cavity is less interesting than the synthetic body it was directing and, presumably, built. You see, although the creature is of an unknown species, its composition is of the widespread carbon-based, warm-blooded, oxygen-breathing classification – our own, in other words – which is common to many known worlds and, probably, even more unknown ones. If you were on an off-world trip and came across this creature in the wilds, as it were, you'd hardly give it a second glance. The specimen we have was rather messed up, but here's the xenobiological department's reconstruction of it.'

The screens displayed the computer-generated image of a small creature, covered in mottled brown fur, somewhere between a miniature monkey and an upright bipedal rat. It had a vestigial tail, neat five-fingered hands and a large head for its size which, according to the scale shown, was about seventeen centimetres. Ace shuddered as she recalled the bloody thing she had seen crawling out of Ostman's chest.

'Note that the head,' Strek continued, lapsing into a lecture-room manner, 'is proportionately quite large, with the surface of the cerebrum highly convoluted – a common indicator of intelligence. However, the actual cranial volume does not seem to be sufficient to support the level of intellect we would assume, bearing in mind where it was found. It's a possibility that the neuron configuration is unusally dense, or more interlinked, which we're still investigating. That aside, there is nothing very remarkable about the creature. We are, of course, checking details of its amino-acid structure and any unusual trace elements in the body, to see if we can match them to a known biosphere, but that will take a little more time.'

The image on the screens changed to a three-dimensional schematic representation of a male human body, with various organs picked out in different colours.

'Now here we have the duplicate of the Ostman body,' Strek continued, with growing enthusiasm. 'This *is* something original. When we started the examination we thought we might need to bring in the roboticists to help take it to pieces, thinking it would be essentially mechanical in nature. Well, there wasn't a wire or servo in sight. It's an organic hybrid, part human clone with some addtional substances resembling organic plastics, plant sap, resin and various vegetable-like fibres.'

'It sounds as though you're suggesting this body was grown in a pot rather than built, Professor Strek,' Delray commented.

'In a manner of speaking, I think it probably was,' he replied simply. 'So far, we've found nothing in the body that could not be formed from an organic base, except for some traces of ceramic powder in the midbrain which are a bit odd. We haven't yet identified it —'

Councillor Cheyney interrupted. 'This is all most interesting to the biochemists, no doubt, but it does not help us in our first requirement, which must be to find a method of detecting these things!'

'A good point, Councillor,' agreed Marshal Talevera. 'Can you suggest some method, Professor? Bearing in mind that these duplicates seem to carry in-built self-destruction devices, and that we may have to test large numbers of people, some method of remote — and unobtrusive — sensing would be preferable.'

Strek ran a hand through his hair irritably. 'Well, so far, and please remember the body was only brought to us a few hours ago, I can't suggest any reliable method. We are dealing with a remarkably accurate external replica, right down to Ostman's own fingerprints, according to the records. They might even pass a casual medical examination. You would need a high-definition contact soundscan to show the indwelling creature — there is a diffusing layer round the cavity it occupied, which was surprisingly small in fact. A blood test might show unusual traces, but again you would have to be looking for them. The body we examined could bleed, so a minor injury would appear quite natural, but otherwise all the usual functions of a human body were duplicated: digestion, excretion, sweating and so on. It has, or rather it *had*, as far as we can estimate, a realistic body temperature, so a thermal image might show up the chest cavity, but I'm not sure . . . Given more time we may come up with something.'

'We all appreciate the efforts of you and your team, Professor,' the Prefect said, understandingly. 'Is there any other information you can give us?'

'Only that the Ostman duplicate did not carry any in-built self-destruction charges or incendiaries as the others did — I'm not sure if that is significant.'

'I see, thank you.' Annis Delray turned to the rest of the council. 'Are there any comments?'

'What can we say?' exclaimed Cheyney. 'Beyond generally increased security, how can we make specific recommendations when the imposters we are looking for can only be detected by direct examination — upon which they will, presumably, explode? Neither have we any idea what these — beings — are after. What is their purpose on Tairngire? Perhaps . . . ' He hesitated. 'Perhaps they have established a clandestine base here — in some wilderness area maybe. I think we should investigate that possibility. In fact, I believe we should institute a planet-wide search for something of that sort; proceeding with due caution, of course.'

'I agree, in principle, with Councillor Cheyney,' said the Marshal, 'However, we cannot act effectively without knowing how many people have been duplicated. On this evidence, it could be anybody, even me,' he finished mildly.

Cheyney looked shocked. 'Marshal — I wasn't suggesting . . . '

'Or you,' the Marshal continued. Cheyney stopped abruptly.

'But you'd hardly suggest the idea if you were a duplicate,' somebody put in quickly.

'How better to divert suspicion?' Talevera replied simply. He scanned the circle of anxious faces. 'And how can we proceed until we know we can trust *everybody* in this room?' There was an awkward silence.

'I think I can help you there,' said a penetrating voice.

All eyes turned to the Doctor, who had risen, and was holding one finger solemnly in the air as though modestly calling attention to the inevitable. He returned the stares with an encouraging smile and, ignoring Quillon's hissed, 'Sit down, man!' walked calmly into the inner circle of seats. Here we go, thought Bernice and Ace simultaneously, and followed him. The Doctor settled himself in one of the vacant conference chairs and they slipped into two of the staff seats behind him.

Suddenly, the assembly became aware that the small, oddly dressed man in their midst radiated a confidence and self-assurance that was impossible to ignore. 'I offer my services to this council as a special advisor, based upon wide, if not unique, experience of the type of threat probably facing your city — perhaps even your world.'

'Prefect, please have this man removed!' exclaimed Cheyney.

'One moment, Councillor.' Annis Delray turned to the Doctor. 'Putting aside, for a moment, the fact that you are not a member of this council, simply a witness who has yet to be asked to give evidence, how do you believe you can help us, Doctor? We do not lack advisors or ability, nor do we have time for interruptions, however well meaning.'

'Believe me, Prefect, when I say no one values time more than I! But the worth of time is nothing unless you mean to spend it wisely, so I say to you *listen to me now*, and you will find it time well spent.' With all their attention on him, the Doctor turned to Marshal Talevera. 'I see you have known the bitter teaching of war, sir, and acquitted yourself bravely. But has any of that knowledge prepared you for the circumstances now facing you? If it is a war that is planned, then it may already have started. But there has been no declaration and the enemy, unknown and unsuspected, may have been infiltrating your highest ranks, perhaps for years, building its strength by these subtle substitutions.' He looked around the circle of intense faces and back to the Marshal again. 'Well, sir. Your past gives you the courage to face what is to come, does it not also guide you to seek advice from one who has knowledge of situations such as this from *personal* experience, just as hard won as your own?'

'I don't see how this man can justify such a claim,' interjected another councillor, and the garrulous Cheyney nodded vigorously in agreement.

'Do you wish to hear the litany, Councillor?' returned the Doctor. 'Daleks, Cybermen, Yeti, Ice Warriors, Autons . . . I could continue, for it is a sadly long list, but I have faced them all — and they often employed schemes of infiltration very similar to what seems to be happening here. But I can offer more than advice. If it is possible, I wish to talk directly with the beings responsible for these duplications, to see if conflict can be avoided. That I also have experience of. Negotiation is preferable to outright war, and I will make the attempt if it is at all possible. I can fairly say that my mediation during the conflict between Earth and Draconia, for instance, proved worthwhile —'

'That was a hundred and thirty years ago!' interjected the Marshal. 'You cannot possibly be —'

'But I can, Marshal, because I am not human. And I present myself as an unbiased third party, only interested in a peaceful resolution. Earth and Draconia have never fought again, have they? You might find mention of my efforts in the records, though my appearance was somewhat different then.'

For a long moment the Marshal's bright, unfaded blue eyes locked with the Doctor's own deep-set eyes of unfathomable grey. Then he turned to an aide and whispered something which set her to work at her own console. Facing the Doctor again, he said firmly, 'I am listening, Doctor. What help can you give us?'

'Firstly, I have some equipment in my ship that will help to detect these duplicates at a distance. That is an essential first step in establishing communication.'

'We can bring anything you need from your ship, Doctor,' said Annis Delray. 'Just tell us where it is and I will arrange it.'

'Thank you, but no. One of my associates will fetch the items, with the help of some of Inspector Quillon's people, if that can be authorized.' The Prefect glanced at Talevera, then nodded to Quillon. The Doctor fumbled in his pockets and then produced an old notepad and pencil. He wrote speedily, talking at the same time. 'Security, as you realized, is a problem. It really would be best if the fewest people possible know about this, since, as you have already speculated, it is possible there is a duplicate present.' He finished the note and handed it to Bernice, who took it to Quillon. He read it, gave an understanding nod, and started typing out a message on the secure channel of the infopad. The Doctor then glanced enquiringly at Ace, who nodded. He started scribbling a second note.

'Even if there is a duplicate among us, Doctor, it could not communicate any intelligence while in this room. All communication channels are monitored and this sub-level is insulated against all unauthorized transmissions, in or out.'

'I hope so, Marshal, I really do. However, I am minimizing the risk as far as possible.' He finished the second note and handed it to Ace. She was feeling refreshed now and, though the Doctor was starting to make interesting things happen here, she preferred to be doing something practical. In any case, she wanted to get back to the TARDIS to change into her combat suit — and pick up her blaster.

She read the note quickly, smiled, said, 'Okay Doc, I will,' and walked to the door where Quillon was waiting for her. The Doctor watched them go, then turned to the assembly once more.

'While we wait for the equipment, we can turn to the next problem: where do the beings activating these duplicates come from?' He rubbed his hands together briskly, almost gleefully, as though he were brushing away other thoughts, eager to tackle a new challenge. His eyes sparkled and he grinned at those about him. The Prefect watched him and sighed inwardly. I can believe you're not human, she thought. Where do you get your energy from?

'Now this should be fairly straightforward, as I think we have some useful clues to work from.' He studied the keys on the chair arm for a moment, then pressed the one that opened a channel to the computer operators in the gallery. 'Could you please make records search for the following: timespan — three years back from today; search area — Off-world travel records; subjects — Gerry Ostman, botanist, Major Olaf Brandel, defence staff, Lieutenant David Tesseni and troopers . . . ' He named the duplicate soldiers identified as having been with Tesseni. 'Display results, crosscheck and indicate any coincidences.'

'Can it really be as simple as this?' queried the Marshal.

'I think so,' the Doctor replied.

Within moments, the information started to appear on the screens. It was soon apparent that one name was common to all the lists.

'Tell me more about a planet called Arden,' said the Doctor.

Chapter 9

The Doctor's note to Quillon read:

'Using a secure channel, arrange for an *unmarked* ground car to collect Ace from a side entrance. Have it driven, if possible, by those two air patrol officers, Ord and Kirin, we met earlier this evening. They already know something of the affair and have met Ace. Tell them to check the car before starting, to be armed (not just with stun pistols), and to take Ace wherever she directs. See Ace to the car *yourself*, and have a *police* escort waiting for her return at a *different* entrance. You may not be able to trust the military.''

Ace walked beside him as they made their way up to the ground level of the building. She felt a distinct spring in her step. Just as she had expected, the Doctor had manoeuvred himself right into the thick of things. Her note read:

'Quillon will arrange transport. Don't say where you are going until you have left the building. Start in a different direction first and check you are not being followed or bugged. From the TARDIS storeroom bring a delta-beam projector, a focusing stabilizer, synchronizer module, control/display unit, power cell and the small tool kit. Return by a different route. *Be careful*.'

They did not have to wait long at the service entrance to the Defence Building before an unmarked ground car appeared. It was driven by officers Ord and Kirin, dressed in plain clothes.

Ace smiled as Quillon gave them their instructions, and her elevation to the status of one carrying out Emergency Council business, by order of the Prefect herself, was made clear. Very shortly they sped off into the night.

'Where do you need to go, Ms Ace?' enquired Ord, in a distinctly deferential tone.

'Just head north for a bit — and take a few side roads to make sure we're not being followed.'

'Yes, Ms. The Inspector said we were to take care.' She held up a small device with a pulsing green light on it. 'This will detect any scanning, and we already checked for tracers.'

After a few minutes, Kirin, who was driving, said, 'I'm pretty sure there's no one following us.'

'Fine. Now turn south and make for the coast road. We're going to a place called the Vanaheim Memorial Park — know it?'

'Certainly, Ms. Er, can we know what we're going there for?'

Their deference was beginning to annoy Ace. 'Just call me Ace, okay?' She grinned, 'And what we're going for is to fetch some equipment from our, ah, spaceship. We landed it there.'

'In Vanaheim Park?' exclaimed Ord.

'Yeah. See, it's not what you'd call a standard model . . . '

'But these duplicates cannot come from Arden,' said Marshal Talevera. 'There is *no* indigenous intelligent life there.'

'What *is* there, then?' the Doctor queried.

Tamsyn York of the colonial office answered. 'It's a new colony world, Doctor. We started developing it nearly three years ago. It is a stage one colony — no children — of about five thousand in all. There are plenty of native life forms, but the Marshal's quite right when he says these duplicates can't come from there, because we survey any prospective colony world first, as per interstellar law: "No permanent settlement can be attempted if it will cause significant harm to the planet's ecology, or if the planet already has intelligent or proto-intelligent life forms".'

'Perhaps they were simply hiding from you,' murmured Bernice with a hint of sarcasm.

The Doctor smiled dryly. 'That is not improbable, you know. Small creatures might be very good at that, especially if they *are* intelligent. Have there been any problems with the colony?'

64

'Not really, apart from the dispute with the Edonians. They claimed colonization rights at the same time as we did.'

'We sent a token garrison there to discourage anything underhand,' explained the Marshal, 'while the interstellar court settles the matter.'

'That's why Major Brandel and Lieutenant Tesseni had visited the planet, of course,' the Doctor mused. 'And Ostman went there for botanical studies . . . ' He trailed off, scowling in deep concentration for a moment, then turned to York again. 'Gather as much information on Arden as you can: physical data on the planet, fossil record, flora and fauna, progress of the colonization project, the Edonian's claims and anything odd that's been reported. Benny, perhaps you'd like to monitor that as well. Maybe we can find some more "coincidences".' York nodded and set her staff to work on the search.

Annis Delray realized that the Doctor was rapidly taking charge of the proceedings. Partly to regain the initiative, she asked: 'Doctor, you imply you are familiar with the concept of the duplication of people. Can you explain how these creatures that control the duplicates can make them *behave* so convincingly, so exactly like the individual they have replaced? That seems to be a more complex task than reproducing an accurate physical replica.'

The Doctor smiled slightly, as though pleased by a perceptive question. 'You're quite correct, Prefect. The duplicates we have so far encountered, though significant feats of bio-engineering, would be useless if they could not mimic the fine details of an individual's behaviour − all those mannerisms and peculiarities unique to that one person, by which they convince you, often on a subconscious level, that they are who they are. One method of endowing a duplicate with these characteristics is to copy the complete memory pattern of the individual into the duplicate's brain. You see, these creatures are not controlling the duplicates as you would a ground car on manual steering, because, for practical purposes, the duplicate's mind *is* the original person's mind, directing the body in the same way as usual. The only time it would behave out of character, is when the alien actively superimposes its thoughts or commands over that of the copied mind. I suppose you could say these duplicates make perfect spies; since they don't know they *are* duplicates, they behave perfectly naturally.'

'Great heavens, Doctor,' exclaimed the Marshal, openly shocked, 'you make it seem as though these duplicates are actually self-aware!'

Bernice did not look up from her screen, but her penetrating undertone cut in again. 'You'd better believe it. These aren't clockwork soldiers you're dealing with here.'

The Doctor blinked at the assembly, as though surprised. 'Sorry, was that not obvious? Any copy that is as perfect as these have to be to function, must give rise to a similar state of consciousness. Leaving aside any theological concepts of ''soul'', a duplicate would think it was the real person, assuming the incident of the duplication process itself was wiped from the mind. As I said, perfect spies.'

After a long moment, Annis asked in a strained voice, 'What about the original people, once they've been copied?'

'We must just hope these little creatures still have a use for them,' he said simply.

During the thoughtful pause that followed, Inspector Quillon re-entered the chamber, gave a quick thumbs up to the Doctor and resumed his seat. Then the Prefect found Peter van Buran by her side, whispering something that made her call up a certain file on her chair screen. Shortly, she attracted the Doctor's attention again.

'I've been reminded, Doctor, that there was an incident at the university the other day that concerned Arden, at least tangentially. There may be nothing in it of course, but if you call up channel five on your screen, you can read the investigation report.'

After a few moments of speed reading, the Doctor looked up, his expression very thoughtful. 'So, the only samples taken were those from Arden awaiting analysis. I would very much like to see the specimens dropped by the thieves, when the security guard interfered with their escape. Also,' he turned to face Chief Pathologist Strek, 'I would like to examine a sample of the ceramic powder you found in the brain of the Ostman duplicate.'

'I'll have them sent here immediately, Doctor,' Annis assured him. 'You think they are important?'

'If they are what I think they might be, Prefect Delray, then the situation may be more complex than I had feared.'

With that ominous possibility in mind, Annis decided to call a brief recess.

Only the park entrance was lit when Ace, Ord and Kirin arrived: a little hazy dome of light in the misty night, illuminating the powered walkway stop outside the gates and a small parking area. As Ace climbed out into the cool, moist air, she realized with surprise that it had only been eighteen hours since she had arrived on Tairngire in this very park. A lot had happened since then, she told herself. What you might call a 'full day'.

The ornate double gates were closed but not locked. They pushed through, their feet crunching on the gravel. The officers switched on their torches, revealing several paths disappearing between the trees and tall hedges. 'This way,' Ace announced, as she found her bearings and strode off briskly down a pathway.

When they reached the hedged glade that featured the TARDIS as an unofficial exhibit, the two police officers reacted rather as Ace had expected.

'You're telling us that's a spacecraft!' exclaimed Kirin, playing his torch beam over the facsimile of an ancient police call box. 'It's hardly bigger than an escape pod.'

'And it's such an . . . odd shape,' added Ord.

'She's called a TARDIS,' Ace countered sternly. 'And don't call her odd — you'll hurt her feelings.' She patted the battered craft affectionately, then drew out a key from her shirt front where it hung from a long black neck ribbon. Opening the narrow door, she grinned at her companions, now illuminated by the strangely diffuse light from the control room within. 'You should know at this point that TARDIS is an acronym for: Time And Relative Dimensions In Space. It may help you understand because, as my friend told Inspector Quillon earlier, she's a deceptively spacious craft. Why don't you come in and see?'

Ace left them goggling at the control room, with a warning not to touch anything, while she passed through to the storeroom to collect the items on the Doctor's list. A few minutes later, carrying a small armful of equipment, she went into her own room and turned out her backpack to make a convenient carrier.

She changed, throwing her torn and dirty clothes into the clean-and-repair unit. Pausing before the full-length mirror of her wardrobe for a moment, she checked her injuries, but they seemed to be fairly minor. The first aid she had received had relieved most of the pain and swelling, and the mental pick-me-up the Doctor had given her was keeping her natural tiredness at bay. She donned her combat suit gratefully, delighted as always by how it fitted tightly about her, yet did not inhibit her movements. She drew her blaster, checked it was fully charged and slipped it back into its holster again. The weight of it felt good against her thigh.

Ace paused for a moment, debating, then pulled on the sleeve extensions with the elbow reinforcements which linked her gloves to the suit's own sleeves. She picked up the customized helmet from the worktop. There were still some adaptions she wanted to make, but most of its main circuits were functioning. She slipped it over her head, plugging in the optical fibre connector that ran inside the left sleeve of her suit, linking her wrist computer, collar radio and throat mike to the helmet. Now, she thought, I'm properly dressed.

With her backpack slung over her shoulder, she returned to the control room in time to hear Kirin saying flatly, 'After seeing this I swear I'll believe absolutely anything . . . '

'Oh, I always believe everything,' Ace said as she entered, 'except on alternate Tuesdays.'

As she moved over to the console and activated the scanner, she was aware of their eyes upon her. The shiny black close-fitting suit, with 'ACE' emblazoned in glitter across the back, she knew was not unflattering to her figure. Their eyes, however, seemed to dwell on her helmet, perhaps realizing that there was something familiar about it. As she adjusted the scanner sensitivity, until the scene outside seemed as bright as day, Ord asked hesitantly, 'Is that made from what I think it's made from?'

'It is,' confirmed Ace, rotating the scanner. 'The original owner didn't need it anymore.' She allowed herself a dash of pride. Few people owned headgear cut and shaped from the dome and sensory antenna of a Black Dalek Supreme.

She saw nothing out of place outside, and switched off the scanner and lifted the plunger knob that opened the main doors. Ord and Kirin filed out through the broad opening revealed by the heavy double doors and, in some dimensionally distorted manner, found themselves almost squeezing out of the narrow doorway of what still appeared to be, externally, a twentieth-century Earth police box. Ace followed, locking the door.

As the illumination from the TARDIS's interior was cut off, Kirin hastily snapped on his torch. A cone of light cut through the mist, angled upwards into the night sky — and illuminated a camouflage-suited figure wearing a military flightpack, rising with a soft rush of air over the tall hedge opposite them.

Chapter 10

.

Inset underneath the Command Room gallery was a row of small, curtained alcoves. They supplied the councillors with private rest areas and adjoining washrooms, should the facility be in use for an extended period. More importantly, they provided relaxation, if only briefly, from the pressure of the inner circle seats, where all the worries of a world, literally and metaphorically, were focused. However, the alcoves represented a very small and ephemeral suspension of responsibility — the inner circle was only a ten-second walk away.

Prefect Delray lay on an alcove couch now, enjoying what time there was left of the brief adjournment she had called. She had felt the council needed a little time to assimilate the torrent of information and ideas they had been subjected to, before being expected to make snap judgements on them.

One concept was causing her particular discomfort.

At this very moment, she thought, perhaps within fifty metres of her, something that looked human might actually be a synthetic duplicate, directed by an alien creature within it, and mimicking exactly the original. And what of the real person? Was the original body and mind still alive and whole, or had it been destroyed after duplication? Perhaps it was better to be dead than alive but helpless, knowing a monstrous replica of yourself existed, free to mix with unsuspecting colleagues, friends — and family.

Doctor, why have you given me a new nightmare?

Kirin's torch beam bought them the briefest of delays.

The unexpected flash of direct light from the powerful beam upset the flyer's aim for a fraction of a second. Kirin yelled, 'Down!' and lunged backwards, catching hold of Ace as she turned from locking the door, throwing her sideways. Ord fell

70

to the ground, shoulder-rolled and came up with gun drawn, loosing off a snap shot at their assailant. As the soldier fired, the brilliant thread of the laser pulse from Ord's pistol missed him by mere millimetres.

Ace heard a deep whining buzz that set her teeth on edge as the broad-beam stun effect struck down Ord and Kirin. All that saved her was that she had twisted to avoid falling on her backpack and had rolled into the partial shelter of the corner of the TARDIS. Even so, she felt a wave of numbness strike her outstretched right leg. She pulled it to her and crouched against the side of the TARDIS, her own blaster drawn, knowing that her suit gave little protection against stun effect.

Kirin's torch had gone out and the only light in the glade came from the faint skyglow of city lights, which made dark silhouettes of the surrounding trees and hedges. The only sounds were her own rapid breathing and the rush of air from the force jets of the soldier's flightpack.

Ace flipped down the helmet visor over her eyes and the glade appeared to spring into sharp relief, lit by an unnaturally brilliant sky. She was now seeing through the image intensifier of the Dalek eyeball unit mounted on the front of the helmet. 'Command: sound: augment,' she whispered. The throat mike picked up the almost inaudible instruction and her hearing seemed to become acute, amplified by the sound discs recessed into the helmet sides. There was an increased directional quality to the boosted sound, building an aural picture in her mind's eye of the position of the flyer relative to herself. She could hear him on the other side of the TARDIS . . . Moving low over the ground . . . Getting nearer . . . Will he come left or right? Nearer . . . Rising . . . He was coming over!

Ace fired upward as he crested the TARDIS's roof and his stun burst whined harshly but went wild as she saw a flare on his shoulder where her blaster beam winged him. She scrambled around the TARDIS again, cursing her numbed leg. The flyer was still airborne, from the sound of it, so her shot had done no serious damage. He started to circle the TARDIS and so did she, keeping close in. He suddenly reversed direction and she nearly fell over doing the same. I can't play bloody 'Ring-O-Roses' around the TARDIS all night, she thought.

Is there time to unlock the door while he's on the opposite side? she wondered. No. How long before he stops trying to take me alive and adjusts the frequency of his weapon to KILL? Anytime. Is he expecting reinforcements? Very possibly. Then I've got to get a clear shot at him, she decided, and right now.

Ace skipped backwards away from the shelter of the TARDIS as fast as her numbed limb would allow. 'Come and get me, slughead!' she shouted.

There was a rush of air and the flyer hurtled into view around the side of the TARDIS — and she fired.

There was a flash of light and a sharp crack as her beam hit his flightpack. She had a brief image of the battle-suited figure outlined in an aura of sparks, then came the shrill of an unbalanced jet and the flyer twisted and spun through the air, like some ungainly aerial ballet artist, as he desperately struggled to regain control over his machine.

Ace dived to the ground as the flyer almost crashed into her in his uncontrolled gyrations. Ducking and weaving, she scrambled for the shelter of the nearest hedge as her opponent whizzed dangerously about the glade. As she ran, she realized that it would be a bitter irony if the flyer succeeded in knocking her down by accident now after failing to shoot her by intent.

Then, for one moment, she thought he had regained control. He soared clear of the ground, crested the tall hedge that bordered the glade — and crashed heavily into the upper branches of a tree. The jets cut out in a final shower of sparks and there was a sudden silence. The flyer hung limply in the tree like a discarded scarecrow.

Prefect Delray sat up on the alcove couch and slipped on her shoes. Once again she wished she'd thought to put on a more comfortable pair when the alert call had woken her. Next time, she told herself — and I hope there never is a next time — I'll make it a rule that everyone wears whatever they feel most comfortable in. She found herself chuckling in dark humour at the notice she would post:

Crises are not fashion-conscious events,
there is no need to dress up for them.

Between the curving wall of the chamber and the last

row of seats was a broad walkway, a step above the level of the central floor area. Scattered along this were little knots of people, taking the chance to stretch their legs or converse in muted tones. A good place for informal words, she mused as she surveyed the chamber. Only one of the inner seats was occupied, where the unmistakable figure of the Doctor was leaning back in his chair, legs splayed out in front of him, hands folded, eyes closed. In the chair behind him Bernice was reading from her chair screen. Annis frowned. Her briefing notes said she was Professor Summerfield, but not what she was professor of. And who actually *was* this Doctor – whatever that incomprehensible name was? And why did it seem so easy to allow him almost to dominate the proceedings? She saw Bernice lean forward and say something to the Doctor, and he responded instantly. So, he was lost in thought then, but not sleep. The possibility came to her that he might not even need to sleep.

She became aware of the Marshal standing beside her.

'Wondering about our strange friend?' he asked, nodding towards the Doctor.

'Yes. I was just realizing how little we know about him. He said he's not human, but then, what *is* he? I saw you'd started some enquiries – any results yet?'

'Very soon, I hope. Of course, in the circumstances, the only important things are: is he as all-knowing as he seems and do we trust him? For my part . . . I think I do. He inspires confidence, in his odd way, doesn't he?'

Annis smiled. 'Thank you for saying that. I thought I was almost letting him take charge without any justification. But now you may have put the reason into words, because, deep down, I also have a strange confidence in him.'

'My dear Annis,' said the Marshal, 'don't go reading so much into an old soldier's opinion.'

'But you are a good judge of people.'

'I try to be, but I'm not infallible. Look, Quillon's over there. He made enquiries when they brought the Doctor and his companions in for their statements – he may know something more about him.' He waved Quillon over. As he reached them, the aide the Marshal had detailed to search the historical records appeared, looking both excited and deeply puzzled.

73

'Found any references to our mysterious Doctor, Lieutenant Khan?'

'Yes, sir!' she exclaimed, then, trying to be more reserved, continued, 'I mean, I have got some information on the Doctor, sir, though I can't quite believe it. Both in the military and government records of the twenty-five forty Earth–Draconia conflict, there were several references to a mysterious "Doctor" – with a young woman companion – who seems to have been instrumental in keeping the sides from all-out war and revealing the Dalek interference in the affair. There is no accurate description of the man, unfortunately, and nobody seems to know what happened to him afterwards.'

'That is extraordinary. Well, thank you, Lieutenant –'

'There's more, sir. When I couldn't find references to the Doctor after twenty-five forty, I ran the search program backwards before then, hoping to find some earlier mention of him . . .'

'And? Don't keep us in suspense, Lieutenant.'

'I found references to a "Doctor" of unknown origins, in the old records for mid-*twentieth*-century Earth! He was a special scientific advisor to an early international security force called UNIT, created to investigate the alien incursions of that time. I found a security-pass picture of him – but it doesn't look anything like that man over there . . .'

'Oh . . .'

'But then, according to the records, the Doctor who worked for UNIT was known, on at least two occasions, to *completely change his physical appearance*!'

There was a suitable pause to digest this piece of information, then the Marshal enquired mildly, 'Any other little bombshells you'd like to drop, Lieutenant ?'

Khan couldn't help grinning. 'Just one more, sir. When I was searching the twenty-five forty records, I sent a request via hyperlink to Draconia to see if they had anything on the Doctor. The reply came through a few minutes ago. I think you'd better read it youself, sir.' She handed Talevera a message slip.

He scanned it silently for a moment, then read aloud: 'From the Imperial Court of the Draconian Empire, He who is called The Doctor is, by venerable decree of the Fifteenth Emperor, a noble of Draconia. He has the eternal favour of the Draconian Empire while its line endures. Transmitted by the hand of Lathilar, Archivist to the Court. By order of Xaxil, Twenty-fourth Emperor of Draconia.'

There was, once again, an impressive silence after Marshal finished reading. Then Inspector Quillon said, 'I can't top that for a reference, but there was one interesting piece of information my earlier check on the Doctor turned up.'

'You might as well tell us,' said the Marshal mildly.

'Since their arrival here was a little suspicious, as you know, we ran a validation on their IDs and credit cards. Now, the cards were drawn on the First Galactic Bank — which is about as solidly reliable, alloy-cast secure as you can get — and the cards were good. Ms Ace's and Professor Summerfield's had a very comfortable limit of a hundred thousand. The Doctor's simply came up as "UNLIMITED CREDIT". In other words, if he wants to buy New Byzantium to ornament his poolside, Madam Prefect, then you may treat it as a serious offer!'

'I'm glad I decided he was someone special before I knew all this,' declared Annis Delray, matter-of-factly, 'because otherwise I would have been feeling very foolish right now.'

Chapter 11

Ace sat for a moment where she had taken cover, watching the flyer hanging in the tree in case he started moving. She flexed her toes inside her boot, tring to restore life to her numbed right leg. Ridiculous, she thought — the third time in less than a day that those counterfeit goons have tried to kill or kidnap me; and I only came here for a birthday treat!

A little awkwardly, she got to her feet, reslung her backpack, and started to limp towards the TARDIS. She had to check Ord and Kirin were okay, then contact the Emergency Council and . . . She froze. From the direction of the main entrance came the clang of gates being burst open, the growing hum of powerful engines and the rapidly approaching swish and crackle of a heavy vehicle ploughing uncaringly through hedgerows.

Friend or enemy, she could not tell. Either way, she knew she could not get back inside the TARDIS before they arrived — and she could not risk being wrong. She ran as fas as she could back to the hedge, wishing she had not turned out her backpack to make room for the detection equipment. There were heavier weapons amongst its normal contents that would have given her a chance against armour.

Holding the pack before her, she forced her way into the base of the hedge, trying to find a gap between its many stubby trunks. There was a crash behind her as the last hedge went down, and she tumbled through onto a pathway in the next exhibition area. To her boosted hearing came the sound of a heavy vehicle slewing to a halt. Then a hatch opened and there was the thump of many pairs of feet. Ace crouched down for a moment in the shelter of a monumental free-form stonework sculpture.

'Command: radio interface: local multiple transmissions: synchronize and relay,' Ace instructed her computer. She moved in a limping run to the next exhibit, which seemed to be a series of roughly trimmed tree trunks driven into the ground to form a leafless miniature forest. As she reached it she heard a voice over her helmet earphones. It faded and wavered as her computer started to lock into the soldiers' command net, then sharpened as it started to predict the frequency-hopping sequence they were using. ' . . . units six to nine, left forward flank to perimeter and encircle. Units ten to fourteen, mirror on right flank. Target is armed. Proceed with caution. Capture her alive if possible.'

Not friends, thought Ace. She ran on, angling away from the glade containing the TARDIS and the troop transporter, trying to get clear before the net closed about her. She had no illusions about winning a shooting match against an infantry section with the resources she had to hand. They were professional soldiers or facsimiles of them, anyway — and they would be equipped at least as well as she was. It might be possible to pick off one or two, but that would only signal her position to the rest via their comm-links or whatever other monitoring channels they might have. With more time she might be able to tap into them. With more power she might be able to overload their whole system . . . Wishful thinking, she chided herself.

She limped on, flitting from the shelter of one exhibit to the next, keeping off the noisy gravel paths, cautiously scanning ahead with her augmented sight and sound. Her best hope was to get clear before the flanks joined and started to close in. Her only piece of luck at the moment was that they had no airborne scanning. Perhaps she had knocked out their only flyer.

There came the sound of heavy boots incautiously scraping across gravel ahead and to her right. Ace altered her course, putting a hedge between the source of the sound and herself. The hedge turned out to be backed by an ornamental wall, which gave her a slight hope — a wall provided much better screening. She hoped there were a few more of them.

Grass rustled ahead of her. 'Command: thermal imaging,' she whispered. Her surroundings dissolved into a mass of faintly shimmering heat patterns. Through an intervening hedge she could see a ghostly form, perhaps twenty metres away, moving stealthily in her direction. She halted, biting her lip. The encirclement had been completed. Should she wait to ambush one soldier and try to break the line? Ace assessed her chances coldly. With two good legs, maybe, but as she was, no. She could not get clear in time once they had her position. Time! If only she had somewhere she could hide while her leg recovered. And surely the duplicates could not waste too long searching for her? They must realize she would soon be missed.

Ace started to retreat, looking for a hiding place proof against the electronic senses of those pursuing her. Her suit was good, but not undetectable — or indestructible. Where would she be safe?

She realized she was retracing the path she had taken the previous morning — how long ago that seemed. Suddenly she was in the exhibition area next but one to that containing the TARDIS and the soldiers' transporter. She could go no further. She had, she estimated, about two minutes to find somewhere to hide.

The Doctor, with a jeweller's lens screwed tightly into one eye, examined the fist-sized piece of glassy black rock intently. On the table beside it was a small phial containing something that might have been the same rock, reduced to sand. Scattered across the table were several sheets of tests results, which Bernice was reading out to him whenever he requested it.

Standing around him, exhibiting varying degrees of impatience, were the Marshal, the Prefect, Inspector Quillon, Professor Strek and Councillors York and Cheyney.

When the samples the Doctor had requested had arrived, it had been decided that the most convenient place for him to examine them would be the small medical room, adjacent to the main chamber. This, fortunately, limited the size of his audience, since by now the entire council realized that the mysterious Doctor was something special.

Finally, the Doctor removed the lens from his eye and surveyed the ring of expectant faces. 'This is, as I feared, hypergem ore,' he stated flatly.

'We believe you, Doctor,' said Annis Delray. 'Now would you *please* tell us what is so special about it!'

The Doctor picked up the lump of rock, passing it restlessly from one hand to the other. 'Hypergems, which can be extracted from this ore, are rather rare crystals with the interesting property of being able to transmit — between matched pairs of gems — low-energy, wide-band signals, instantaneously through hyperspace, without any extra power input or transmission equipment.'

The Marshal visualized a starship's bulky hyperspace communication apparatus and the power it drew, and tried to imagine it replaced by a small piece of crystal. 'Speaking for the Navy, Doctor, we would be very interested in these hypergems.'

'So is someone else. So interested that they risked stealing them from the university. Assuming the thieves were more duplicates, which I think is likely —'

'Why are you so sure?' cut in Cheyney.

Bernice answered. 'Because, according to Kristen Barr, the security guard they partially stunned, she tripped one of the intruders during their escape and managed, very commendably, to vigorously kick him in the groin before she was stun-beamed again. She is certain the blow connected and the man was not wearing any protection but, surprise, surprise, he made *no sound* — which is unusual in those circumstances. Reasonable conclusion: the man was duplicate and the creature controlling it blocked the pain sensations so it could continue its escape.'

'I must say this sounds very thin reasoning,' responded Cheyney. He turned to the Doctor. 'And are you *sure* these rocks are what you think they are?' A look of open suspicion grew on his face. 'All we've had from you, has been a fantastic tale of the properties of these "hypergem" things and a lot of talk that seems to have led us to suspect Arden, but might just as easily be pure coincidence. And all this has taken *time*. Time which we could have spent starting a search for these aliens on Tairngire, instead of having our attention diverted elsewhere, and waiting for this "equipment" to come from your ship. I'm beginning to wonder about you, Doctor.'

'I am perfectly satisfied with the Doctor's credibility, Councillor Cheyney,' Annis Delray said firmly.

'Well with respect, Prefect, I am not. And I'm not the only councillor who thinks this man is having far too much influence on these deliberations which, may I remind you, are supposed

79

to initiate *emergency* measures, not to sit around listening to dubious and unproven speculation.'

'We cannot take action until we understand what we are dealing with,' the Marshal stated. 'A rapid response is not automatically the correct response. I am prepared to wait a little longer for sound advice before initiating further action.'

'Assuming the advice *is* sound —' began Cheyney, but the Doctor cut him short.

'To extract hypergems from their parent rock,' he declared seriously, tossing the chunk or ore in the air,' you must know how to handle them correctly.' He grinned at his puzzled audience for a moment, then stood up and flung the rock with tremendous force at the medical-room wall.

There was an unusually sharp crack, as though of an electric discharge, and the stone burst into a shower of fragments. Amongst the splintered remains, four black polygonal gems, the size of walnuts, bounced and rolled across the floor.

'They always form in pairs,' remarked the Doctor conversationally. Bernice gathered up the newly formed hypergems and placed them, pointedly, on the table in front of Cheyney.

For a moment the councillor seemed about to speak, then he turned abruptly and stalked from the room.

'Doctor, what other uses are there for hypergems?' asked the Marshal, breaking the awkward silence that followed.

Professor Strek interrupted 'A psionic interface! Of course! There were hypergem fragments in the duplicate's brain — they were part of some sort of mental relay.'

'Well anticipated, Professor,' the Doctor commended. 'That is, I think, the reason behind the university theft. Their need for hypergems is so great that they can't even do without the samples sent here. Or perhaps they were simply trying to keep them secret a little longer. Before I knew hypergems were involved, I assumed the duplicates were animated by *copies* of the original brain. Hypergems, however, allow a direct, continuous, real-time link between copy and original, with the creatures inside overriding when needed — a simpler solution.'

'At least it's possible that the original people are still alive!' said Quillon. 'There's a chance for them.'

'True,' agreed the Doctor. 'Their bodies are probably kept

in a state of isolation, so that the sense signals received from the duplicate bodies take their place. The illusion that nothing has happened to them can still be maintained. They are still perfect spies. In addition, you must realize now that any duplicate you uncover and destroy, or force to self-destruct, means a possible sentence of death for the original.'

'Oh, yes, I suppose −'

'Further,' the Doctor continued, 'there is still the question of the Ostman duplicate. That doesn't fit with the others we know about. It was duplicates, apparently, that killed him. So was he one lone rogue individual or, remembering the odd enquiries he was making, did he represent an opposing faction amongst these duplicate makers? Unfortunately, however, that is not your most pressing problem . . . '

'Yes?' Marshal Talevera said after a pause.

The Doctor held up a hypergem. 'It is almost impossible to shield hypergem signals. If there is a duplicate among you, everything overheard may already have been passed on.' His eyes darkened for a moment. 'When I sent Ace off, I did not reveal where she was going on general principles. If I had known then that hypergems were involved . . . No. Anything I do now may make it worse. We must just wait for her to bring back the equipment, so I can confirm my suspicions about who the duplicates are in the council, giving us a chance to isolate them without forcing self destruction, and then . . . '

'You mean to tell me you already have specific suspects in mind!' exclaimed the Marshal. 'Doctor, I must insist on knowing your reasons now. I appreciate the risks to the real people, but I firmly believe they themselves would understand our proceeding immediately to expose their duplicates. Humanitarian restraint must be balanced against the threat to the greater good.'

The Doctor scanned the faces before him and saw they agreed with the Marshal. With an odd grimace of resignation, he took a strip of print-out paper from his pocket, and handed it to Talevera.

'During the recess I did what you would have done yourselves very soon, once the full consequences of the Arden link had sunk in. I had your records compile a list of all the councillors and their staff present who have visited Arden, crosschecked against medical files for any examinations they have had *since* returning. It is a reasonable assumption that though they may be able to pass an examination, duplicates will avoid full medicals if possible. For instance, you were on Arden last year, Councillor York.' The woman gave a shocked start of apprehension. 'However, you had a routine medical three months ago.'

'Don't frighten me like that, Doctor!'

'In the end there were five names left. On the top of the list, Marshal, you will see the name of someone who has twice *cancelled* routine examinations since returning from Arden.'

Trooper Jodee Flyn warily approached the entrance to the next exhibition area. She switched her goggles to thermal imaging and scanned the thick hedgerows about its entrance. They were clear, but there appeared to be a cluster of heat sources on the other sides, almost like a small crowd of people.

Weapon at the ready, she crouched down and snatched a quick look around the foliage. She seemed to see a group of naked people with arms raised, still as, as statues — but warm? Of course, thermo-rock sculptures. She switched to image-intensifier mode for a moment. Yes, she could see the marble-like veins on their surfaces now.

Back into thermal imaging, she skirted the open area, and there was a flicker of heat radiating faintly from a tall, hexagonal column set in the grass. She froze and the heat source stilled. She moved and there was another flicker; a pale shadow of body heat seemingly from within the sculpture. Flyn switched to intensifier mode, and the column was revealed to be transparent. She had been seeing her own body heat reflected and refracted back at her.

Annoyed by the illusion, she moved on to the last exhibit. This time she was prepared for something deceptive, and recognized the great twisted silvery blob on its black plinth for what it was, before the reflections of her own body heat fooled her again. She was about to pass it by when the realization struck her that it was a perfect hiding place. Suddenly tensed, she circled the blob. Yes, if it were hollow and had been shaped from within to form an opening at the top, above her eye level . . .

'This is unit eight.' She mouthed her words for her throat mike to send on the open command channel. Odd, but she felt she was using the radio link more out of routine than necessity at that moment. 'Possible target. Weapon on stun — firing now.' She levelled her weapon. The blob rippled and dissolved into a cloud of silver droplets as the vibrations of the stun field tore through it.

Bernice and Quillon left the medical room by a side door. Their faces were set and each strode quickly and with purpose.

Shortly afterwards, Delray, Talevera, York and the Doctor filed into the main chamber and took their seats once more. Annis called the meeting back in session.

'Before proceeding further, I would like you all to listen to the Doctor, who, on my personal authority, I have appointed special advisor to the council while this emergency lasts. Doctor, please address the council.'

With great deliberation, the Doctor stood up and began to pace slowly round the disc of floor at the centre of the inner ring of seats, his hands thrust deep into his coat pockets. He looked intently at each councillor in turn as he passed in front of them.

'You are all aware of the peculiar events that have occurred today. The duplication of some military personel you have already heard about. The possibility of some of the people in this very room being duplicates has also been suggested. I can now tell you, that possiblity has become a certainty — we know there is a spy amongst us!' A whisper of concern ran through the chamber, as its occupants unconsciously shrank from their nearest neighbours. 'Before I reveal the identity of the duplicate, I urge the entity in control of the body to come forward voluntarily to prevent any further violence.' There was silence. Nobody moved. 'As you will,' said the Doctor sadly. 'I have done my best. The spy is — you Councillor Warton.'

He had stopped just in front of her. She gaped, astonished at the Doctor's dramatically condemning finger thrust towards her. 'We know all about your secret journey to Arden. That

83

was when they duplicated you!' Every eye in the room was on them now.

'No! You're mad,' Warton gasped, finding her voice. 'It's a lie, I've never been there. I'm not a duplicate — I can't be! I've never been to Arden, I tell you. I'd *know* if anything had happened to me!'

'That's just what a duplicate *would* say!' snarled the Doctor in return. 'Which is why I must do this —' With a speed few humans could equal, he drew his other hand from his pocket, now holding a stun gun, twisted round and fired it at point-blank range.

The harsh whine of the stun effect faded away.

The myriad globlues coalesced into a perfect silver sphere, but no unconscious body fell from concealment within. Flyn reversed her weapon and probed the pseudo-solid metal with the butt. There was nothing inside. 'Eight reporting. Negative target. Continuing sweep.'

She moved on, still treading carefully, for the target was armed and had already killed their scout flyer. But her orders were to take her alive if possible, and the orders came from the very top. From . . . Jodee Flyn paused, suddenly, ridiculously unsure what she was doing or why. Her motivation seemed very unreal at that moment. Was this a training exercise? Why was their target a young woman called Ace? Somehow her capture seemed very important . . .

Something was wrong . . .

It must be . . .

What had she been thinking?

Trooper Flyn continued her search, as per orders. In the back of her mind was the vague thought that some of the trees in the park reminded her of the garrison she had been posted to, on Arden.

The Doctor fired his stun pistol into the chest of the man sitting beside Warton: Councillor Cheyney.

At point-blank range the field effect penetrated the duplicate body and stunned the creature within. The Cheyney duplicate sagged in its chair, arms and legs twitching uncontrollably as impulses from the real Cheyney's mind fought to actuate the deadened synthetic spinal column. Its eyes rolled, unfocused, in a face frozen in a rictus of surprise.

There was a roar of sound in the hall. Shouts and exclamations merged with the thud of feet as people rose, trying to see over the heads of their fellows, unsure which way to move. Then, in quick succession, there was the sound of four more stun-weapon discharges. Suddenly there seemed to be uniformed police everywhere, pushing through the delegates who were scrambling away from four more stunned bodies, each guarded by an armed plain-clothes officer. The Prefect's amplified voice rose over the din, ordering the chamber cleared.

Professor Strek pushed through the crowd to the Doctor, who had been standing guard over Cheyney. Ripping the councillors shirt open, he ran the contact head of a portable ultrasound scanner over the man's chest. 'Duplicate!' he confirmed, and half ran to examine the next suspect, now ringed by police and an emergency crew, who held fire extinguishers at the ready.

Police and paramedics were now beside the Doctor, pushing a stretcher trolly. Without ceremony, they heaved the Cheyney duplicate onto it and, with the Doctor beside them, ran the trolley out of the chamber, bursting through the main doors, turning sharply and dashing madly down the corridor, like some bizarre parody of a hospital drama. Through more doors, a sharp turn and then ahead was a pair of doors manned by guards who threw them open at their approach. They skidded to a stop in the middle of a large refectory hall, hastily cleared of furniture.

Amidst the paramedics and safety personnel, standing ready, was Bernice, waiting beside a table laid out with medical instruments. She handed the Doctor a laser scalpel and watched tight-lipped as he deftly cut into the duplicate's chest, excising a plug of synthetic flesh and bone to reveal a small furry body curled within. Behind them the doors of the hall burst open to admit a second trolley, with Strek in attendance. Ignoring the commotion, the Doctor gently lifted the creature out of its unnatural resting place and deposited it in the container held in Bernice's steady hands. All this time, the arms and legs of the thing in Cheyney's form twitched and jerked with pseudo life, and the eyes darted about in an all too realistic mimicry

85

of agonized appeal. One of the policemen who had pushed the trolley turned from the macabre scene and was unashamedly sick on the floor.

There was a hissing. Heavy vapour issued from pinhole vents about the body. 'Incendiary!' shouted the Doctor. Extinguishers sprayed foam and frost over the trolley, but despite their efforts, with a pop and rush, coloured flames flared into life. 'Get clear!' he ordered, and shoved the trolley with its gruesome burden into the farthest corner of the hall. A screen of expanding room dividers was pulled across to shelter the rest of the room. With an echoing bang the duplicate erupted into blazing fragments. Strenuous efforts by the fire fighters contained the damage. The emergency crews had plenty of practice that night.

The glade remained still for some moments after the trooper had left. Then the right leg of one of the statues in the figure group trembled slightly. Not yet, Ace told her disobedient limb. She could feel the pins-and-needles of sensation returning, but she would not move too soon.

It had undoubtedly been a mad idea, she thought, and yet there was a certain logic to it. Her suit could not completely protect or conceal her in the circumstances. The soldiers were looking for a black combat suit because the flyer would have relayed a description. They expected her to fight or hide out of sight, so . . . The phrase, 'Hiding in plain sight,' had tumbled through her mind as she started to strip off her suit, praising quick-release fastenings. The title *The Purloined Letter* had followed it as she bundled suit and boots into the backpack. Pack and helmet she had thrust up into the depths of the adjacent hedge. She had smeared streaks of earth and mould from amongst its roots across her body to simulate the marble-like veins of the other statues, and had taken up her pose in the middle of the group. She had had almost thirty seconds to still her breathing before the soldier had entered the glade.

Keeping still had been one of the hardest things she ever did. She had been aware of a vague shape crossing the glade, but dared not even move her eyes. She had kept them fixed on the same indefinite point in the sky the other statues contemplated, her arm outstretched towards it. She had positioned herself next

86

to a figure whose head was half turned from the focus of their interest. Now it appeared he was seeking her opinion on the matter.

The soldier moved beyond her field of vision. Ace concentrated on immobility, ignoring the dew being deposited on her by the cool, misty air. Think of something else, she told herself. Pretend you are a statue. Statues . . . There was a game she had played when she was young called statues. Someone turned their back and the others tried to creep up on them. They turned round suddenly and the rest had to 'freeze'. If you were seen moving, you were out of the game. Just like now, she thought.

Why was the soldier taking so long, she thought with exasperation, knowing in truth it had been less than two minutes. For that matter, why were they after her in the first place, and why try to capture her alive? Just what were the duplicates really —

The stun-beam discharge seemed, to Ace's straining ears, to go off right beside her. She flinched and her muscles locked as she fought the natural urge to run, or jump or do *anything* but remain absolutely still. Another interminable minute passed and the faint sounds made by the soldier faded away. It was then that she realized that her right leg was tingling with returning life.

Slowly, very slowly, she broke her pose. Crouching down she rubbed her leg vigorously, squeezing the calf muscle and flexing her angle. Carefully extricating herself from the figure group, Ace cat-footed over the wet grass and retrieved her bulging backpack from the hedge. Should she dress now, or would she need the statue dodge a second time — and had she the sheer chutzpah to carry it off? Were there still soldiers on the perimeter, and what would happen when they drew in their net and found it empty?

The muffled thumps of a repeating grenade launcher brought her answer. As a projectile whistled overhead, she rammed on her helmet, image intensified mode coming on automatically as she pulled down the visor. Slinging her pack, she started to run, pistol in hand, in the direction of the park boundary and the strait beyond.

Something struck the ground to her right and burst with a rushing, hissing noise. Gas! Probably not lethal, but she was not going to risk finding out. She ran and ran.

And then a soldier stepped out into a brick archway in the hedge before her. He must have seen her just on the edge of his field of vision, for he twisted suddenly, rifle coming down to target — and hesitating for a fraction of a second in surprise at the naked figure wearing a Dalek-style helmet who was sprinting towards him. Ace fired three rapid shots. The second struck his chest, the third his visor. She leaped over the body without breaking stride and hurtled through the archway.

Gravel pricked her bare feet and the low wall dividing the perimeter pathway from the narrow shoreline of the strait was before her. She vaulted the wall. Pebbles and loose shale sprayed up as she hit the tiny beach and rolled into the water.

Half wading, half swimming, Ace surged through the shallows towards the dark rocks that formed a humped and ragged line, marching out into the strait. Amongst these she found a niche in chest-deep water, out of sight of the shore path. She slipped off the pack and wedged it clear of the water, then clung to the rocks, panting. Exhaustion was claiming her. There had been too many battles and jolts of adrenalin at the end of a long day. It was good that the water was half supporting her, she thought, because otherwise she would probably fall over.

Bernice looked around the smoke-blackened refectory.

In the end they had saved three of the alien creatures and one, now completely lifeless, duplicate body. Of the suspects on the list, only one, a councillor's assistant, turned out not to have been duplicated, and she was recovering well from the stun effect. The single duplicate body saved was due to Strek; seeing the others self-destruct, he had cut the hypergem from its brain before removing the alien creature. The gem itself had disintegrated a few moments later. One creature was found to be dead upon removal from its host, possibly from a too intense stunning.

Bernice realized the Doctor was standing beside her.

'Will you help the Professor take care of the creatures?' he requested. 'Watch out for them in case they start to revive.'

He frowned. 'Meanwhile, I suppose I'd better let the Council know how we've done — and suggest they get the decorators in.'

The pre-dawn pallor was flushing the sky and the distant lights of Byzantium city were losing their sharpness as Ace worked her way back along the line of rocks to the shore. With augmented sound on full intensity, she listened for any sign of the duplicate soldiers. There was nothing. She scrambled up the beach between the rocks and rested against the base of the shore wall, shivering in the cold morning air. There was nothing but the sluggish wash of waves over shingle.

She dressed as hurriedly as cold fingers would allow, forcing her suit on over her wet skin. Reconnecting her wrist computer she listened for any signals on the command bands she had tapped into earlier. They were silent.

Luckily, the heavy coursed stone-work made an easy climb and she was soon sitting on top of the wall, surveying the pathway and the park beyond. Everything was still and peaceful. Satisfied that the soldiers had gone, Ace set her computer searching the wavebands for the police frequencies. Now she was safe from detection, it was time to let the Doctor know that things had not gone exactly as planned.

'And that is the situation as it stands,' the Doctor reported to the reconvened, and still shocked, Council. 'By the way, apologies to you, Councillor Warton — I hope you understand the need for a distraction, in the circumstances.' Warton managed a weak smile in acknowledgement.

'When the creatures recover,' the Doctor continued, 'we shall attempt communication. But they probably relied on their mental link, via the hypergems to the original brain, for translation both ways, so language may be a problem. Also, I suspect, they are not very intelligent as individuals, so we may not learn much from them.'

'Surely they made the duplicates and that indicates extremely high intelligence,' someone pointed out.

'I think that was a product of *group* intelligence,' replied the Doctor, 'but we shall see.'

The Marshal spoke: 'Now we can rely on the security of this

chamber, I can reveal the measures we have taken so far. All units that have had garrison duty on Arden have been confined to barracks, using the excuse, contrived by the Military Chief Surgeon, of possible contamination by a supposedly debilitating, though not dangerous, alien virus. Similar orders covering space crews have also been issued. Arden itself has not been mentioned by name, and other groups of personnel and vessels, chosen at random, were added to the list to disguise the intent. This probably means confining a lot of innocent soldiers as well, but that cannot be avoided. Civilian contacts with Arden may prove harder to trace and deal with.'

'How do you know your orders have been carried out?' asked Annis Delray. 'can you trust the people who report back to you?'

'That had occurred to me, Prefect. I have arranged for officers with no recorded contact with Arden to be examined by the Chief Surgeon, then to proceed to all the bases and ships, on or off planet, with full authority, to see that the orders *are* obeyed. I realize there is some risk in such examinations, but in the circumstances it is justified.'

'Why not simply tell the truth?' someone suggested. 'Order a general alert.'

'Because that will lead to doubt, mistrust and panic. While the duplicates are not forced into revealing themselves, I'm hoping they will "stay in character" shall we say. Only certain key people will be told the truth.' The Marshal rubbed his eyes tiredly. 'Councillors, I know this is not an ideal option, but I have considered the other alternatives with my staff and this seems the least destabilizing. The duplicates, or rather, the creatures directing them, will know something has happened because they have lost their operatives in the Council. But I hope to conceal as far as possible our next moves against them.'

'I'm not sure we know for certain how much the duplicate controllers know has happened here,' Annis Delray suggested. 'Doctor, how much information could be sent via this hypergem link you spoke of? Enough just for the exchange of sensory data to animate the duplicate body, or is there sufficient "bandwidth" for creatures to, ah, "talk" to home base at the same time? Perhaps they can only send extra information when the duplicate body is sleeping, for instance.'

The Doctor smiled grimly. He knew what the Prefect was hoping for, but he could not indulge her wishful thinking. 'I'm afraid the hypergems do have sufficient capacity, Prefect. How well that is exploited by the small creatures, I cannot tell, but I would advise proceeding on the assumption that they already know everything that has happened here. I regret to say. Marshal, that your actions, though eminently sensible, may already be too late.'

'Excuse me,' Quillon interrupted the discussion. 'There's a call coming through for the Doctor. It's from Ms Ace, relayed through headquarters. I think there's been a problem. Channel three, Doctor.'

The Doctor pressed the appropriate button and Ace's voice came through clearly.

'Am I through now? Doctor, can you hear me?'

'Yes, Ace. Are you all right?'

'Totally knackered and I've picked up a few more bruises, otherwise okay. But there must be a security leak somewhere —'

'We know,' the Doctor interrupted dryly. 'We've already taken steps to plug it.'

'Well I wish you'd done it sooner. We must have been followed by an army scout in a flight pack — you'd better check local air-traffic control for rotten apples. Anyway, we got hit by him as we were leaving the TARDIS, then a bunch of his mates came along in an APC and we had some fun and games.'

'Where are you now?'

'Still in the park. It's okay, the soldiers have gone. I'm just on my way back to check on Ord and Kirin; they got stun-beamed earlier. Nearly there now — yeah, they're still there. I'll just — oh *shit*!' Here expletive rang out clearly through the chamber.

'Ace! What's wrong?'

'Doc, it's the TARDIS — it's *gone*!'

Chapter 12

Two minutes after Inspector Quillon left the Command Room for the Vanaheim Memorial Park, the Prefect's voice rose above the murmur of converstion. 'Your attention, please. I have just received news which I fear may be linked with the current situation. A few minutes ago the hyperwave link with Arden through its skystation went down. All efforts to trace a fault have failed and it seems as though the transmitter at the other end has been switched off. There are more details on infochannel nine.'

Bernice leaned over the Doctor's chair. 'You thought something like this would happen, didn't you?'

'I'm afraid so. The duplicates have had plenty of warning and by cutting the link with Arden they deprive only us of information. They still have their hypergem links.'

'They work over *light-year* ranges?'

'Oh yes. Properly aligned their range is practically limitless.'

Bernice chewed her lip for a moment. 'And the TARDIS? What do they want with it?'

'I don't know yet, but I'm glad Ace said she locked the door . . . ' He broke off, aware that the Marshal was looking at him.

'It appears that you were correct, Doctor. Well, there is no point in pretence any longer.' He raised his voice. 'Councillors, I am ordering an immediate general alert as from now.'

Lyn Sorren heard the noise just after eleven, Touchstone local time. There was shouting from outside the dome, an isolated scream, then the whining buzz of a stun shot. For a moment she was frozen in surprise, then she pushed back her chair and sprang to the window.

At first her mind could not take in the scene below her. There were bodies lying on the ground. From the shelter of two opposing buildings, garrison soldiers were firing at each other, not with stun beams now, but flashing, deadly energy bolts. Little knots of colonists were huddled in whatever shelter they could find. On the edge of the settlement she could see a group of people, hands over heads, being driven along by troopers with levelled rifles.

A thudding crash from within the dome itself impinged upon her shocked senses. This was *real*; this was actually happening. A voice in the corridor shouted, 'This is crazy —' then was silent. She lunged for her door, not knowing at that moment whether to lock it or run through it. It burst open in her face.

A battle-suited soldier stood before her, rifle pointing at her chest. From behind the blast visor a flat voice said simply: 'Outside.'

In the corridor, Governor Narvik was lying on the floor with blood on his head. The soldier urged her past before she could tell if he was alive or dead.

'Doctor, the TARDIS is missing — how can you be so calm?'

The Doctor swung his conference chair round to face her. 'Would it really help if I ran around tearing out my hair?'

'Of course not, but — you know, can't we *do* something?'

'I am afraid, Benny, that we — and the TARDIS — have become inextricably bound up with whatever purpose the duplicates have on Tairngire. In this room we are in the best position to discover what is going and and give what advice we can. We know Ace is safe and Quillon will be taking charge of matters at the park very shortly. So for now we must just sit and think.'

'I'm not a professional chair-warmer.'

'No — that takes practice. But somehow I don't believe we will have to wait long.'

The amplified voice of one of the gallery staff came from the speakers: 'Priority emergency call from Devonport Field direct relay.' One of the main screens lit to show the head and shoulders of a middle-aged woman in military uniform, hunched awkwardly in front of the viewer. There was blood trickling down a cut on her forehead. Behind her, sections of a smoke-hazed control room could be seen. A body was sprawled over one of the consoles and personnel were frantically clearing damage.

'Admiral Lombardo, Devonport Field . . . ' She coughed 'Request emergency assistance . . . Control centre and other facilities sabotaged. Transporter vessel *Atlas* and two fighters have made unauthorized lift-off . . . Unable to intercept . . . '

Talevera was issuing a string of instructions to his staff. The Prefect spoke: 'Admiral, help is on its way. Can you tell us what happened?'

Lombardo seemed to realize for the first time that she was bleeding and pressed a handkerchief to her head. 'Within the last hour, Prefect, a Major Brandel from the Marshal's office came on the line following the medical alert . . . appeared to have full authority. He ordered the preparation of the *Atlas* for immediate launch, said it was something to do with the medical problem, top priority. Loads came in from all over and went straight on board. But there was something strange about one of the last ones, sticking out of the back of an APC . . . '

'The TARDIS!' Bernice hissed. The Doctor nodded.

'Macnikol − our chief loadmaster − queried it. And they shot him . . . ' She coughed. 'Then all hell broke loose − explosions, gunfire . . . Brandel's aide is dead, but Brandel got away cool as ice . . . Saw him on a monitor actually *walk* on board the *Atlas* seconds before she lifted. It was inhuman . . . '

'Yes, Admiral,' said Delray, 'it was exactly that. Civil and military assistance will be with you shortly. We will handle the missing ships.' The Admiral's image faded.

'I am in contact with navy skystation *Olympus*,' announced the Marshal. The big screen now showed a stiffly upright man in a Commodore's uniform.

'Your orders have been received and have been implemented, Marshal,' he responded briskly. 'We are tracking the target craft now. They have left the atmosphere and are heading for deep space. A squadron is preparing to intercept.'

'How long until the targets can make hypespace?'

'At present acceleration . . . Less than forty minutes,

94

Marshal. But the interceptors will reach them before that.'

'Understood, Commodore. Issue instructions that your ships are to prevent them making the jump if possible, as long as there is no risk to themselves. If they resist, the targets are to be classed as hostile — is that clear?'

'Quite clear, Marshal.'

The Doctor interrupted. 'Marshal, are any of the interceptor ships on your quarantine list?'

Talevera started. 'You don't think . . . Commodore, did you hear that?'

'Why, yes, Marshal. The *Adamant* and the *Skua* are on the list, but in the emergency I thought . . . '

'The general alert superseded those orders.'

'What alert, Marshal?' The man looked mystified. 'I have received no communication of a —' The image blurred and trembled and a reverberating boom could be heard. The Commodore staggered and clutched at his desk. Alarms sounded and there came the thump of emergency pressure doors. The Commodore disappeared from view.

'External views now!' The Marshal's voice cut through the noise. Secondary Command Room screens lit to show views from the *Olympus's* central tower down onto its radiating docking arms, each with its surrounding cluster of ships at berth. The cameras trembled and the space about the station was filled with a mist of flying fragments that twinkled as they caught the sun. Some of the docked craft hung askew to their passenger tubes or were tumbling slowly away from the station. Only two ships were moving purposefully, manoeuvring clear of the devastation about them.

'The *Adamant* and the *Skua* I presume,' said the Doctor.

The main screen cleared to show the Commodore again, looking considerably shaken. 'Stop those ships!' the Marshal shouted, raising his voice for the first time.

'Weapon Control: any turrets still functioning, targets *Skua* and *Adamant* in enemy hands — priority red.'

The fleeting ships disappeared behind the glowing shells of their force-fields as the invisible energy beams and strings of incandescent plasma bolts struck. They sped away, with the station's weapons still locked on, bombarding their flaring force-fields. Bernice found herself willing the ships' destruction, caught up in the momentary desire to pay back the duplicates for what they had done. There was a blaze of light and one of the shells was gone, replaced by a disintegrating mass of wreckage tumbling into nothingness.

'Reporting the *Skua* destroyed,' the Commodore said in a strained voice. 'The *Adamant* is now out of effective range.'

Quiet, reserved people make careful plans and do not like them to fall through without good reason. When Toni Pandril was twenty minutes late, Nicholas Cort went looking for her.

As he emerged into the corridor surrounding the central access core on the seventh level, he saw Pandril drop past him down a conveyor, carrying a parcel under her arm. 'Hi Toni . . . ' But she seemed not to hear. He stepped quickly into the next conveyor unit and dropped down the tube after her.

She got off at level fifteen, the engineering control deck at the very bottom of the shaft. Cort stepped out of the tube as she was striding determinedly towards the engineering control room door.

'Toni! Hey, what's so important? Toni?' She paused for a moment, then turned. Her face was impassive. 'Toni . . . ' He reached for her — and she kicked him in the stomach. He doubled up and she kicked him in the face, lifting him off his feet and sending him crashing against the wall.

For a few seconds he must have been semi-conscious. When he recovered and clawed his way dizzily to his feet, alarms were sounding, merging with the ringing in his own ears. He stumbled into the engineering control room. One technician was sprawled on the floor; another was slumped over a control panel in about the same state as Cort. He became aware of a repeating computer voice.

'Warning — engineering compartment lock in use — neutral atmosphere beyond — breathing equipment must be used. Warning . . . '

On a monitor screen he saw Pandril step calmly out onto a walkway slung between the massive reaction-mass tanks and climb down a railed flight of stairs.

'She'll last only as long as she can hold her breath,' the

engineer grunted. The cameras followed Pandril as she strode purposefully along the lower walkway. Cort stared incredulously, shaking his head, as he watched Pandril approach the power core. She pulled the object she had been carrying free from its wrapper as she went. It was a mine.

'Where's the speaker control?' Cort shouted at the engineer. The man touched a switch. 'Toni —' his voice echoed around the machine spaces. '*Toni*! Think what you're doing.' Taking no notice of his plea, she started to arm the mine. He was aware of people crowding into the room behind him and Commander Stirling's distinctive voice demanding to know what had happened.

'How long can she last?' muttered the engineer. Cort was aware of men pulling on breathing gear and making for the lock, while Stirling worked at another control panel.

A second screen came to life, showing a remote handling unit gliding forward along a track over the walkway. In the control room, Stirling was hunched intently over the panel, guiding it with deft touches. They saw Pandril glance up quickly, finish arming the mine, then lean out over the walkway rail to place it on the power core. A manipulator arm extended down and caught her arm, jerking her off her feet. The mine fell from her grasp and clattered into the depths of the machine spaces.

They froze, bracing themselves uselessly . . . Nothing happened.

For some seconds, Pandril beat at the mechanical arm holding her; they could hear the relayed sound of incredibly violent blows. Cort swallowed as he saw the flesh on her arm tear as she tried to pull free. Then she went limp. 'Bring her out, please.' There was a hissing noise from the speakers. Oxidant-fed flames blazed about Pandril's body. Stirling jerked the blazing form away from the power core, running the handling unit back down the walkway as fast as it would go.

The body exploded, twisting the handler off its tracks, causing it to grind to a halt. There was silence.

Cort stared slack-jawed at the screen, shaking his head in horror. He was aware of orders being given and people moving about the control room. Then he heard Stirling's voice clearly, 'Whatever it was, Captain, it wasn't human.'

97

'Hyperlink emergency priority call: Captain Kausama commanding CSS *Broadsword* to Fleet Admiral Vego.'

'Putting you through, *Broadsword*.'

Vego appeared on the screen. Kausama started — the man looked exhausted. 'Admiral, we've had an extraordinary sabotage attempt —'

Vego held up a tired hand. 'I can guess, Fran. All hell has broken loose here too. You'd have received the alert call any moment. Details later. Just one question: is the *Broadsword* still operational?'

'Yes, Admiral. We sustained only minor damage, but what—'

'Fran, get the *Broadsword* under way *now*, and head for home port — pour on all that your stardrive will take. What's your ETA from Delta Epsilon?'

'Uh . . . About two days. I can check exactly —'

'No, just get here. Listen Fran, the *Broadsword's* on the active list as of this moment — in fact, as of this moment, she's the only functioning front-line ship we've got.'

Donal Robson rode the first truck of the convoy up the fault ridge, consulting the geological map display as he went. Now he knew what to look for, it was amazing he hadn't realized what was there before, though it was odd that he couldn't quite recall where his new knowledge had come from . . . Never mind.

The driver seemed to know when to stop without Robson telling him. He jumped down and pulled bundle of marker flags and a geo-scanner from the back. Rusty bounded after him, chittering excitedly. Robson scrambled up the slope, checking with the scanner every few paces. There it was. He took readings. The seam opened three metres under the surface and extended at least four hundred metres along the hillside from where he stood, rising slightly as it went. He drove in the first flag, paced out twenty metres, checked he was on the right line, then drove in the second.

By the time he had finished marking the seam, the first truck carrying the workers had arrived. It troubled him a little to witness their confusion and the way the soldiers had to herd them off the truck. Why could they not simply understand? This was a job that had to be done — even Rusty seemed to realize that, so why couldn't they?

He gave instructions to the bewildered people about the preparatory clearing of the slope for better access. There were not enough tools at the moment, but he knew more would be arriving in a few days. Till then, they could use their hands if need be.

Jon Amphipolis, Oberon Camp's doctor, tried to grab hold of him as he explained their task. Soldiers had to pull him back in line. 'Don!' he was shouting, almost sobbing 'This is madness — What has happened to you all?'

And for one terrifying instant it did seem like madness. What *were* they doing here? Why were his friends being treated this way? But the doubt faded and the wonderful feeling of order and place and purpose flowed back once more.

He could not quite remember what the ultimate purpose was — but he wouldn't let it worry him.

Chapter 13

Lyn Sorren stumbled along with the rest as they were marched along the rough track through the woods. Her feet moved mechanically, her mind still trying to distance itself from an unacceptable reality. Am I insane, she thought? The definition was always the prerogative of the majority, so by that standard I am sane, and it is the world that has gone mad, because most of those around me are frightened, confused refugees from a nightmare. She looked at their guards. But in this nightmare, she thought, the minority have the guns — and they set the rules.

Ahead of her, Holly Freyman started screaming and pleading with her husband again. Liam Freyman was one of their guards. Puzzlement seemed to spread across his face for a moment at the anguish of his wife's outburst. Lyn heard him say, in frighteningly reasonable tones: 'But we've got a job to do.' Then his face set once more into an impassive mask. His wife began to sob fitfully in wretched desperation.

Lyn wanted to put an arm about her, to offer comfort, but what was there to say? Only meaningless platitudes came into her mind. 'Don't worry,' and 'It'll be all right,' sounded very hollow at that moment. How could she say them when she did not believe them herself?

Fifteen hundred metres into the forest they heard the first crash of a felled tree.

Bernice looked around the half-empty Command Room. Outside it was mid-morning. With the apparent total withdrawal of the duplicates, the emphasis had turned to assessing the full extent of the thefts and sabotage. Many councillors were back in their departments or visiting the incident spots in person. Those left were planning Tairngire's response. Bernice noticed more uniforms in the chamber now.

She yawned and blinked at the growing lists of items stolen by the duplicates which were appearing on her chair screen. My, but they had been busy before they left — it would probably be days before a comprehensive list was compiled. Some of the items already listed seemed to be very odd choices. A variety of portable aerospace weapons-systems and munitions made sense, but manual digging tools, dozer/dumper vehicles and fifteen commercial air-blower units did not, as far as she could see. Maybe they would make more sense after she had slept . . . A regular drumming noise interrupted her thoughts.

Ace was softly pounding her fist against the arm of her chair. 'I should've been able to stop them,' she muttered, once again, through clenched teeth.

Bernice turned to her. 'For heaven's sake girl, don't keep blaming yourself,' she hissed. 'Against a squad of infantry, you were lucky to get out in one piece.'

'But they got the TARDIS.'

'Yes, and I resent that as much as you — it's my home too, remember. Don't get mad, get even, as you say. Now shush, it's the Doctor's turn.'

'I have a request to make of this Council,' the Doctor said, 'on behalf of myself and my associates, Professor Summerfield and Ms Ace. Quite simply, we wish to accompany the task force to Arden.'

'I feel that you are not offering your services out of pure altruism, Doctor,' replied the Prefect. 'You understand that I cannot allow this operation to become a private quest.'

'Certainly not. We have strong personal motives for going to aid the recovery of our ship which the duplicates stole. However, this is a case where our interests can be combined to our mutual benefit. May I remind you that I was made a special advisor to this Council while this emergency lasts — and it is certainly not over yet. To continue with that task, it is logical that I go to Arden and, of course, my associates must accompany me. Together we have already had first-hand experience of the duplicates' behaviour and mannerisms at close quarters, which may prove invaluable to such a mission. Then there is our knowledge of similar infiltrations in other parts of the galaxy. Did I mention the Daleks?'

'All right, Doctor.' The Prefect was holding up her hand to stem the flow, and managed a tired smile. 'I think you have made your point. I will recommend your accompanying the mission as special advisors. However, as the mission will be primarily military, Marshal Talevera must also approve your participation.'

The Marshal surveyed them thoughtfully for a moment. 'Doctor, a few hours ago you offered your services as a mediator between us and the duplicate controllers, should the chance arise. Now they have stolen your ship, would you still make the attempt? Do you still consider yourself unbiased?'

'The only thing I am biased against Marshal, is *war* — I have seen too much of it. Yes, I would still make the attempt if it was possible.'

'In that case, I believe they should go.' The Marshal smiled grimly. 'After all, they can hardly come to more harm than they have here.'

Bernice nudged Ace. 'Okay, you can breathe again. We're in — over our heads probably, but we are in.'

Ace gave a mirthless smile. 'Yeah. Think we'll live to regret it?'

'I'm more worried that we *won't* live to regret it, actually.'

O'Valle and Robson watched the ferry drop smoothly out of the sky and settle onto Oberon's landing pad. As its jets died and the dust settled, guards ran forward.

Its cargo hatch opened and the loading ramp unfolded. Slowly, blinking in the daylight, fifteen men and women filed out, looking dazed and uncertain. In the back of his mind, Robson knew they were from the skystation, and that the rest of its personnel were being taken to Touchstone. He would have liked more people for his work, but no doubt it had been decided fairly — somewhere.

As the guards ushered them away, O'Valle took a crate from his parked groundcar and carried it very carefully up the loading ramp, as though it were very precious indeed.

The ferry lifted off as Robson marched his strangely unenthusiastic new workers up the track. He wondered for a moment where it was bound, but the thought soon slipped from his mind.

Chapter 14

Lyn Sorren found the work hard but straightforward. They were simply cutting down a great swathe of forest — why, nobody knew. Presumably *they* knew, of course. 'They' were the overseers, mostly garrison soldiers but also some colonists, about eighty to ninety people, she estimated. The ones who had been touched by . . . whatever it was that caused the change.

She found the routine on the second day after the takeover identical to that on the first. Identical almost to the second.

There were two work shifts; hers was from twelve noon to twelve midnight. There were water breaks every two hours and a food break after six. The guards that escorted one shift into the forest took the previous one back; it was a very simple arrangement. Touchstone's social hall and storehouse had been turned into communal sleeping quarters, which each shift used turn about. A period for washing in the river was allowed — Lyn was thankful it was summer.

The work was exhausting, but it gave her plenty of time to think, and talk, when she had the energy. The guards did not seem to mind, as long as the work continued. That was probably the worst part of it, in a way, the most incomprehensible thing: there was no malice towards them, nothing to fight against. They were simply expected to work because — it was necessary. She felt that the ones who had been changed genuinely did not understand their attitude. Whatever had touched them had left a gulf of incomprehension in its wake.

They were divided into teams, with about twenty people in each. As a tree was felled, the larger branches were cut off and they dragged them clear by hand or with rope harnesses. The trunk was hauled away to one of the growing stacks by some of Touchstone's small fleet of groundcars. The branches were gathered and stacked between the piles of trunks. It was a very orderly arrangement. Slowly, a circular clearing was growing in the forest.

Lyn knew she should have cared more for this sensless destruction of the ancient woodland, exactly the thing the controlled colonization of Arden was intended to avoid. But every so often she caught sight of Holly Freyman, working like a zombie, dead-eyed, uncomprehending. And then she would see Liam Freyman, almost eagerly wielding a cutter — only *they* were allowed to use power tools, of course — to trim the branches of another tree, and then see his face go blank when Holly looked at him. In the midst of such madness, she could find precious little within her to pity the trees.

'I can't say it looks very impressive from here,' Bernice commented. 'If you tried to sell that to a viddy producer, looking for a design for the featured starship in his next space adventure series, he'd say it lacked visual excitement or something.'

'So what?' retorted Ace.

'Well, it doesn't exactly inspire one aesthetically, does it? Not particularly dynamic, no graceful lines. Basically it's just a big black egg with bumps on it.'

'Oh I don't know,' the Doctor put in, tilting his head to view the *Broadsword* from a different angle. 'I think its somewhat primitive form holds a certain sturdy and reliable appeal, don't you?'

'You two behave like a couple of total airheads sometimes, do you know that?' Ace exclaimed with exasperation. She pointed to the warship being loaded beyond the docking module observation window. 'That ship is built to do a job — no frills, no unnecessary trimmings, — just as strong and tough and undetectable as they can make it. I think it looks fine.'

'Now who's making aesthetic judgements?' asked Bernice.

Ace turned to Professor Strek for support, but he was intent on entering notes in his laptop computer. Beside him, Councillor York smiled. 'For what it's worth, I agree with you, Ace. The *Broadsword* is the first ship of its class and we expect great things of it. Technically, as I understand, it is classed as an assault ship, which means it can carry an armoured unit and their landing craft to a trouble spot and provide them with aerospace support with its own strike craft.' She gave a slightly nervous laugh. 'For strictly personal reasons I hope it performs as well as the designers claim − after all, we are going to be its first passengers.'

They watched the *Broadsword* in silence for a while as a twenty-five metre landing craft was gently edged through the open hatch of one of the ships' flight bays. The docking module they were in had been undamaged by the duplicates' sabotage, but beyond the bulk of the *Broadsword* they could see the intense repair work being done to other parts of *Olympus* skystation.

As the hatch closed behind the lander, Bernice said: 'Hello, I think we're going to get the full civic send-off.'

They looked round. Prefect Delray, Marshal Talevera and Inspector Quillon, and four other men had entered the observation lounge. They rose to greet them. 'I didn't expect to see Quillon,' remarked Ace.

'Well he's probably just pleased to see the back of us,' returned Bernice. She grinned. 'Especially the one with a penchant for explosives.'

Ace ignored the jibe. 'I hope they don't hang about too long − we're meant to be boarding any time now.'

'You don't like goodbyes, do you?' Bernice said. Ace shook her head.

'This is very kind of you,' the Doctor was saying.

'We are not all here just to wish you well, Doctor,' explained the Prefect. 'Some of us are going to be travelling with you.' She nodded towards Quillon.

The Inspector assumed a business-like air. 'A long list of civil laws has been violated, Doctor, and we have reason to believe those responsible are now heading towards Arden. I have been put in charge of apprehending them.'

'So the long arm of the law reaches out over the light years,' grinned Ace.

'Which reminds me,' Quillon said sternly, fishing into a pocket. He produced a crumpled bag. 'As you are leaving Tairngire, you may have the rest of your, ah, "sweets" back. I trust you will be more considerate of local regulations next time.'

'Next time, I'm not going to let certain people talk me out

of wearing my blaster in the first place,' she said firmly, patting the holstered weapon and eyeing the Doctor and Bernice.

The Prefect was introducing the others. 'Mister Chiminoe and Sergeant Santony will also be accompanying you. Mister Chiminoe is a hyperspace engineer, and he worked on Arden skystation on the hyperlink transmitter, so he has expert knowledge of the installation, and may be needed to reopen the link. The Sergeant's unit is part of the Arden garrison, but he was on leave when the incident occurred. His local knowledge should prove invaluable.'

Bernice looked at their two new companions with interest. Chiminoe had the appearance of a careful, practical man in keeping with his skilled work. He smiled at them as he was introduced in a friendly, open fashion.

Santony had the lean trained physique of a soldier, but his eyes were troubled and his smile tight and perfunctory. What is he bottling up? she wondered. 'Is he simply worried about his comrades, or is there something more? She watched Ace's reaction as they shook hands. Yes, Bernice thought, he's just your type — but watch out, girl, he's hurting inside.

The two other men were in Space Marine's uniform. 'Colonel Charters and Major Salsk,' the Marshal said, introducing them. 'They have been attending briefings while their unit was loading. You may rely on the Marines to see the job through, I think.'

Salsk nodded politely but remained distant. Charters shook hands firmly all round, a twinkle in his eye behind his reserved manner and the air of correctness lent by his greying hair.

'Excuse me . . . ' Bernice realized a smart young woman in naval flight lieutenant's uniform had appeared. 'Prefect, Marshal, ladies and gentlemen. Captain Kausama's compliments and would the supernumerary mission personnel please be prepared to board in five minutes.' Duty done, she walked up to the Marshal, said, 'Hello, Grandfather — you do look tired,' with a concerned smile and kissed him on the cheek.

'Excuse me for a moment,' the Marshal said, 'but I would like a few words with my granddaughter.' They moved away into a corner, he saying: 'It was kind of the Captain to send you . . . '

Bernice looked at them and smiled. No need to be a reader

of body language to see the respect and love between them. So, there would be another Talevera accompanying them. She caught sight of the Doctor's face for a moment as he watched grandfather and granddaughter. It reminded her of the expression he had worn in the TARDIS as he stood over the console.

Bernice looked at Ace chatting animatedly to Santony. The man already seemed a shade brighter. She sighed. Suddenly, there's so much emotion about this place it's hard for a disillusioned romantic to maintain her credentials, she thought.

The mooring grapples and docking tubes withdrew from the *Broadsword*. Its manoeuvring thrusters pushed it gently clear of the station, turning it slowly. There was a glow from its main engines and the ship gathered speed and headed out towards the stars.

Talevera and Delray stood alone in the observation lounge, watching even after the craft had disappeared into the void.

Chapter 15

Captain Kausama looked down the briefing-room table. The *Broadsword's* senior officers sat down one side, the special advisory team on the other, while Charters and Salsk sat at the far end.

Bernice felt the military were trying to outflank them.

'For the record, I will summarize our mission. The *Broadsword* is to investigate the situation of the Concordance citizens of the colony and garrison of Arden. Also the whereabouts and status of the Concordance cruiser *Adamant*, the Titan-class transporter *Atlas*, the frigate *Mercury* — last known to be on patrol in Arden system — and two fighter craft of the Devonport Field contingent. Upon reaching Arden, which is some five days away via hyperspace, we will reconnoitre the system in an attempt to determine the extent of duplicate activity. If feasible, we will attempt to make landings on Arden's skystation and Arden itself. This phase of the operation will of course be undertaken jointly with our Marine contingent.'

She paused for a moment and smiled slightly. 'What happens next will very much be in the lap of the gods.' There were nods of understanding from around the table. 'Meanwhile, we prepare ourselves as best we can, and this is where our special advisors come in.'

Now we are going to be organized, Bernice thought.

'We will have regular briefing sessions over the next few days to update ourselves on any further information from home, and discuss any other aspects of duplicate behaviour or motivation which may give us useful insights. But in addition, I have specific tasks I wish our advisory team to undertake.'

'Firstly, we must have a means of detecting duplicates at a distance. This is a special requirement of the Marines, who may have to be able to distinguish friend from foe under battle conditions. Doctor, I understand that the detector you built has been left on Tairngire for checking that there are no more duplicates in hiding there?'

'Yes, Captain.' The Doctor beamed in his most charming manner. 'However, as I assured the Marshal, I can build a simplified version of the device which should fulfil the requirements.'

'Then please start immediately. Professor Strek may also wish to advise on this, I understand. You have the facilities of the engineering workshop and any of Commander Stirling's team that can be spared at your disposal.'

The quiet, solemn-faced officer down the table nodded to the Doctor. 'Aye, Doctor. I'll be interested to see this gadget of yours.'

Ace pursed her lips to hide a smile. An almost undiluted Earth accent was rare these days — and for it to be a Scots starship engineer . . . Bernice looked at her, wondering why she was stifling laughter.

'Next,' Kausama continued, 'there is the physical situation we expect to operate in. Councillor York, Sergeant Santony and Mister Chiminoe, could you please assist our simulation department in producing and updating virtual models of the major Arden settlements and the skystation. These will allow the Marines to train in realistic settings.' The three nodded.

'Professor Summerfield, considering your xenocultural and archaeological background, can you continue the research I believe you started during the Emergency Council session, concerning the history of Arden and the possible nature of the duplicate controller's culture? All the information you require has been loaded into the ship's data base and any additional material can be relayed from Tairngire. Inspector Quillon may be of assistance in this, since it seems to me to be akin to detective work.' Bernice nodded; Quillon smiled.

'And last, but not least, Ms Ace.'

Ace looked up. 'Thought you'd forgotten me.'

'Not at all. We would like you to put your recent experience of close encounters with the duplicates to good use, by creating a briefing for the Marines about them. You have considerable combat experience of your own, so you know the sort of details they would find useful in planning one-to-one tactics.'

Ace thought for a moment. 'Yeah, right — I can do that.'

'In that case,' said Kausama, 'this meeting is adjourned. The next briefing will be at fifteen hundred, tomorrow.'

Chiminoe fell into step beside the Doctor as they left the room.

'Say, Doc. As I understand it, you know all about these hypergems. Now this is my field, but I've never heard of them, so just *how* do they work?'

The Doctor smiled. It wouldn't do tell the engineer to much, of course, but he could drop a few hints.

'The underlying principle is very simple . . . '

The conversation became technical.

The Doctor, Bernice and Ace sat for a while in the small lounge area assigned for the use of supernumerary personnel. The rest of the party had gone to their rooms.

Ace glanced at the Doctor with a twinkle in her eye. 'So, what did you think of our Captain then, Doc? Bit of a looker, eh?'

'She struck me as being most capable,' he replied midly. 'Her preparations seem most sensible.'

Ace snorted unbelievingly. 'We could see you giving her the eye, couldn't we, Benny?'

Bernice smiled. 'You did seem rather taken with her, Doctor. Personally, I would have thought she was just your type — thirty centimetres too tall, but otherwise you're perfectly matched.'

The Doctor dismissed the innuendos with a wave of his hand. 'I was more interested in *your* reactions, Benny. I noticed you were studying our military companions rather carefully, and I wondered what conclusions you had reached.'

'Yeah, not much material for you there,' agreed Ace.

'What are you talking about?'

'Your favourite pastime with the military.'

'Oh, brass-hat bating you mean. No, they all seem entirely reasonable types. Dedicated and verging practically on the sensitive. I fear I may have to give up the sport for the duration.'

'And any particular observations about the Captain?' the Doctor enquired.

110

Bernice frowned thoughtfully. 'Though she looks like an oriental Valkyrie, and could make a fortune on the viddys, I assume that the command of multi-million credit warships is not assigned solely on the basis of personal appearance. I would say that she feels her looks and youth are the greatest handicap to her career.'

On the evening of the third day, as the natural light was fading, but before the artificial lights were switched on, the routine changed. The clearing was by now a hundred and fifty metres across, a scarred tract of tree stumps and torn earth, dotted with neat piles of trunks and branches. Sorren had begun to wonder about the arrangement. There were stacks in the centre of the clearing and around the outside, close to the receding forest edge, but between them was a ring of open ground. It seemed deliberate but without reason.

'Stop work and move back to the perimeter,' the guard on her hauling team suddenly said, and Lyn heard his exact words being echoed by the other guards around the clearing. They left their branch where it was and did as they were told. She found Gil Enver, one of the colony administrators, walking beside her, rewrapping a ragged bandage around his hand.

'This must be important,' he said in an undertone. 'I thought the work didn't stop for anything.'

'Yes, but will they just add in onto the end of our shift?'

'Probably.' He tried to chuckle, but it sounded false.

'Wait a moment, can I hear a ferry coming in?' There was the growing whistle of jets from the sky, making them turn around trying to locate the direction. Some of those around them were also looking up, others were too tried to care and slumped to the ground, thankful for the unexpcted break.

'There.' Enver said, pointing as the ferry's landing lights appeared over the tree tops against the fading sky, the jet noise suddenly increasing in volume.

The craft set down neatly in the clear ring of ground in a cloud of blasted earth and leaf litter. As soon as the jets were cut, overseers hurried forward. The side hatch swung open and the loading ramp extended, work lights coming on. The figures disappeared inside and for a few moments all was still. Then four of them re-emerged, carrying something between them.

'What is it?' asked Enver. 'So black I can't make it out.'

Sorren squinted against the ship lights as they carried the thing clear and set it down carefully. 'A hemispherical dome, I think, but more humped — what do you call it? A beehive dome, that's it. A beehive dome about . . . two metres across, I'd say.' They watched while another eleven of the domes were unloaded with equal care; then the ferry's hatch closed, its jets came on and it lifted off into the night.

Working lights came on about the clearing and they were ordered back to their tasks. As she returned to hauling branches, Sorren watched the domes being positioned until they were evenly spaced around a circle perhaps a hundred metres in diameter. So that's why they left space clear, she thought — but what are the domes for?

A truck rolled into the clearing from the track leading to Touchstone and pulled up beside the dome ring. Sorren snatched glances as best she could. It looked as though they were unloading portable power packs. A length of cable was unrolled, connections made and the free end fed into what must have been a small orifice in the side of one of the domes. One by one, the connections were made around the ring.

There were puzzled murmurs from those about her who had been watching. 'What the hell do they want to power them up for?' somebody said nervously. There was a yellow glow of flame from in front of one of the domes. An overseer had lit a bundle of twigs and thrust it into a larger arched orifice in the base of the dome that Sorren would have sworn had not been there a moment before. There was a ruddy glow from inside the dome. More twigs were fed in. Then she realized that fires were springing up in the rest of the domes, casting fans of flickering light out across the trampled ground. Thin shimmering smoke plumes started to issue from lipped vents in the dome tops. She could hear the crackle of flames.

Memory stirred within her. 'They're like ancient beehive kilns,' she said.

The flames burned brighter. They started to feed in small branches . . .

Chapter 16

This really is somewhat macabre, thought Colonel Charters.

He looked again along the line of people standing, a little uneasily against one wall of the medical laboratory. As well as him there was Major Salsk, Lieutenant Anderman and Sergeant Grad from his technical staff — and a corpse.

No, he corrected himself, whatever the form in the life-support tank set against the wall between them was, 'corpse' was not an accurate description of its present state of being. While the tank functioned it was not truly dead, and when it had been animate it had not exactly been alive. It was the body of a duplicate pulled from the wreck of the *Skua*, one which had not self-destructed. Charters was thankful that the face and chest of the 'body' were bandaged. Even on a duplicate the injuries were not pleasant to look at. Appearances were not helped by the mechanical ventilator maintaining a steady breathing rhythm, or the intravenous tubes keeping it nourished.

Charters turned back to the workbench in front of them, where the Doctor, Professor Strek and Commander Stirling were huddled over a piece of equipment. 'Have you got it adjusted correctly *now*, Doctor?' he enquired, a little impatiently.

'Yes, yes, Colonel,' muttered the Doctor. 'One moment more . . . There it is.' He straightened up, looking pleased with himself. Strek and Stirling nodded in satisfaction and took their places amongst the others whilst the Doctor snapped a cover back into place. The device he was holding resembled a heavy-duty electric torch with a laser sight mounted on the casing. He swung it back and forth across the line of people and beamed. 'Smile please,' he requested.

'Oh, do get on with it, Doctor,' Charters said, beginning to sound a little exasperated.

'Have I mentioned that you remind me of a Brigadier I used

113

to to know?' the Doctor replied, and thumbed a button on the device. A steady tone sounded and a green light shone on the tiny display panel set on its handle. The Doctor waved it over the assembly again. Each time the laser spot rested on the duplicate body, the tone rose in pitch and the light blinked red.

'Most satisfactory,' concluded the Doctor, turning the detector off. The line broke up. Stirling, Anderman and Grad started discussing replication of the machine. Charters approached the Doctor.

'And how, in simple terms, does this thing work?' he asked.

The Doctor smiled. 'By heterodyning certain subsonic frequencies onto a low power force beam and detecting the resonances produced when it impinges upon a body. In other words, Colonel, duplicate's bodies do not vibrate quite as ours do, and this device detects that difference. It's not as sophisticated as the detector I left on Tairngire, but it will do the job you require of it.'

'What is its range?'

'Effectively up to about fifteen metres.'

Charters nodded and turned to the technical group. 'Well, Lieutenant, can you produce the quantity we'll need in time?'

'With the help of some of Commander Stirling's staff, yes sir, we can.'

'Then I won't detain you any longer. Start work as soon as possible.'

The *Broadsword* dropped out of hyperspace into the void of real space between the stars.

The Captain's voice came over the ship's speakers: 'Your attention. We are back in normal space for one hour for test firing of ship's weapons. All heavy portable weapons for testing to decks ten, eleven and twelve, please.'

From a port in hangar bay eleven, a target drone was ejected, inflating into a silvery sphere as it fell away. Weapons blisters in the ship's nose and tail opened and projector barrels extended, rotating to track the target. The drone suddenly glowed and puffed into vapour. Another target was released and the ship rolled to bring its other batteries to bear.

The main weapons retracted into their protective shells. The hangar doors rolled apart, opening the bays to space, their frames edged with softly glowing force curtains that contained the air within. Racks of heavy weapons extended through the curtains, and columns of smaller targets were launched and duly flared into nothingness. The Marines' self-powered guns rolled to the edges of the bays and tested their firepower in their turn. A few targets were missed, weapons adjusted and refocused, then tried again until they performed to standard.

Fifty-five minutes later the doors closed again.

There was a surge of power. The fabric of space twisted and the *Broadsword* appeared to blurr. Its image flattened, contracted and then was gone. The void between the stars was empty once more.

The growing roar of the *Atlas's* huge jets caused Sorren's work shift to jerk up their heads from where they were washing in the Titania River. For a few joyous moments they thought rescue had arrived — but the guards remained impassive and unperturbed as the massive craft touched down in a tornado of force-blasted air, tearing a great crater in the soil and flattening the experimental crop fields. When the air cleared, the massive craft could be seen dwarfing the ferries on the landing field beside it.

They watched as a stream of vehicles and containers was offloaded and dispersed into the surrounding woods or transferred to ferries, for transportation elsewhere.

'If they are using other ships as well,' said Enver, 'then we don't know how far this thing has spread.' His face suddenly became ashen. 'Oh God — we've assumed it's just here where this has happened, but supposing it's going on back home too . . .'

Later, when they were being marched to the clearing for their work period, they heard the *Atlas* take off again. Nobody spoke.

It was their third evening on the *Broadsword*. The Doctor, Ace and Bernice were once more sitting together in the lounge before retiring.

Bernice had been looking puzzled. 'Doctor, about the TARDIS, have you had any further ideas about why the duplicates took it? I can see how they became interested in us, but how did they realize there was something special about the TARDIS?'

He frowned and his manner became thoughtful. 'Now that we know more about them, I can make a guess. A fairly simply sequence of cause and effect can be deduced.' He raised an eyebrow. 'Can't you work it out for yourselves?'

Ace gave a stage whisper from the side of her mouth: 'He's testing us again.'

'I know, infuriating isn't he?' Bernice replied in the same manner.

'Oh, come on,' urged the Doctor. 'Think why we came to Tairngire in the first place.'

'For a holiday.'

'And why did we feel we needed a holiday?'

'Apart from celebrating Ace's birthday . . . Ah, well, we all got a bit depressed over the business with the telepathic circuit —'

'I've got you!' exclaimed Ace. 'The little rats that run the duplicates are telephathic. They could sense there was something special about the TARDIS through *its* telepathic circuits, maybe with those hypergems they're so fond of.'

'Their nature does rather suggest the possibility,' confirmed the Doctor, 'as we have already speculated.'

'All right,' conceded Bernice. 'That does reinforce the theory that we're dealing with a group mind, a sort of hive intelligence. They have a natural telepathic ability which they extend, shall we say, through the hypergems, and they could tell the TARDIS was something special. But that doesn't tell us *what* they want the TARDIS for.'

'Perhaps it was simply intense curiousity. In any case, we shall just have to find out, shan't we?' said the Doctor.

Ace grinned ironically. 'We do seem to find any trouble that's going spare, don't we? Or perhaps trouble finds us.'

'Like cosmic lightning rods,' Bernice suggested, then frowned. 'Have you ever wondered, Doctor, if it *is* just chance? I mean the number of these experiences you keep getting into . . . '

'Don't be coy, call them adventures,' Ace cut in.

' . . . these adventures, then. The number does seem to

stretch the rules of probability somewhat. Have you ever wondered if it *isn't* always chance?'

'Oh, I know my fellow Time Lords have occasionally directed my travels for their own purposes, but not often enough to account for the excess of my adventures.' He beamed boyishly at them. 'I think it's more likely that it is the nature of the universe that if you look long and hard about you, there is always something interesting going on. Louis Pasteur once spoke of chance favouring the prepared mind, with reference to scientific discovery. Perhaps it's the same with adventure. Though I don't seek it for its own sake, I admit my curiosity does tend to lead to it.'

'Of course, it also helps if you're highly mobile,' Ace pointed out.

'That too,' agreed the Doctor.

Bernice smiled ruefully. She too had an excess of inquisitiveness. 'Just remember what curiosity did to the cat,' she cautioned.

'Why do you think they have nine lives?' he replied. 'And why do you think Time Lords have twelve?'

The *Broadsword's* gymnasium had a banked circular running track following the inside curve of the hull around the entire deck on that level. Ace and Bernice had taken to using it twice a day. As Ace said: 'I'll be bloody amazed if we don't have to be pretty fast on our feet before this thing is over.'

Bernice had noticed that Santony also was keen to keep in shape, and by a curious coincidence, seemed to be there at the same time as they were − or rather, she amended, when *Ace* was there. The two were running ahead now, while she jogged with Kim Talevera. Kim, Bernice had decide, was a nice person.

'When are you going to let me give you both the guided tour?' Kim said. 'We're very proud of the *Broadsword* you know, even if the paint is hardly dry on her. And I want you to see my fighter as well − she's a sweet craft.'

'When we get time from this work your Captain has us doing. Hey, aren't you pilots keeping busy as well?'

'Regular simulator runs, briefings on likely mission scenarios − don't worry, we'll be ready.'

'Well, if we do find the time, I think you'd better include Santony in the party.' Bernice nodded to the two ahead of them.

'Sure, all welcome. We have a tradition of hospitality to uphold, you know.'

'Tradition? On a ship this new?'

'The name's not new; its goes right back to ancient wet navy times.'

'Even back to sail-powered warships?'

'I'm not sure. But actually, we've still got a sail on board.'

'A real sail?'

'Emergency solar sail. That's real enough. Works by the same principles, anyway.'

'Must be huge to move a ship this massive.'

'About ten kilometres across. All microfoil and gossamer fibre. Folds up incredibly small and only masses a few tonnes.'

'Now *that* would be something to see unfurl.'

'Listen, if things ever get bad enough for us to have to use the sail, sightseeing will be the *last* thing on your mind.'

'This will be our last regular briefing session,' announced Captain Kausama to the assembly in the briefing room. 'We are now only a little more than a day from Arden, so perhaps this would be a good time to summarize our findings. Then our civilian advisors can have at least a few hours' rest before we arrive, while we make our final preparations. After that,' she warned them, 'I cannot promise you much in the way of relaxation.'

Colonel Charters spoke. 'I think one implication of the items the duplicates stole is that they do not have weaponry or ships of their own, except what they have already captured from us, otherwise these replacement parts and munitions would be useless to them.'

'Perhaps these spares are just for what's already taken,' Ace suggested. 'Doesn't mean they haven't got armaments of their own, but just that they wanted to pick up some extra. You can never have too much hardware if you're expecting a war.'

'Possibly,' conceded Charters. 'But in my experience, the integration of dissimilar weapons systems can cause more trouble than they're worth.'

'I can say one thing,' volunteered Santony. 'Even adding all the surface combat equipment on this list to what my garrison already had in place, there's no way they could hold out for long in any stand-up fight.' Charters was nodding in agreement. 'They must be planning some sort of extended confrontation – a guerrilla war. With all the forest cover available, that's the only thing that makes sense to me.'

'It's the same for any space-combat scenario,' Commander Foss added. 'With what they've got, they might take us, but they must realize that the repairs to the fleet won't take forever. Latest estimates say we can expect the first reinforcements fifteen days after reaching the Arden system. Other Concordance ships might make it sooner. Unless they plan to run, their strategic situation will be hopeless.'

'If they are a group intelligence as we believe,' York speculated, 'and so think quite differently from the way we do, we may be trying to read deeper meanings into nothing more than a withdrawal of their infiltrators, who took whatever items they could get or thought might be useful.'

'No, Councillor,' Charters said firmly. 'I've seen a few retreats in my time, and this one was *very* well planned. From the reports, they took exactly what they wanted – nothing more nothing less. Their hand may have been forced prematurely, but I'm certain they were working to a precise list of requirements.' He tapped the print-out. 'The clue to their next move is probably here, if we can see the pattern.'

'I agree with Colonel Charters,' stated Kausama. 'They have been infiltrating us for over a year. They must know what our response would be in these circumstances, and have planned accordingly. Our greatest disadvantage is that we still know so little about the creatures controlling the duplicates. Professor, what news about the creatures recovered from the Command Room incident?'

'Not much I'm afraid, Captain,' replied Strek. 'As the Doctor intimated at the time, with the link to their communal mind broken, they exhibit as much intelligence as you would expect for animals for their size. Observation and tests are continuing, but I don't hold out much hope.'

Kausama nodded resignedly. 'And then, of course, there is

the motivation of these creatures. What exactly is their under-lying objective? Any suggestions?'

That sparked off a range of ideas of varying degrees of probability. The idea of a link with the Edonians attracted much support. When Bernice was asked, she turned to York. 'When you first arrived on Arden, you didn't happen to notice any "Trespassers will be Prosecuted" signs, did you?'

'None were reported,' the colonial officer replied dryly. There was scattered laughter.

'It's not that I don't take the proceedings seriously,' explained Bernice, 'but I simply don't think we have enough information to hand to reach any meaningful conclusions at present. For the moment, I think we should keep our minds, and our options, open.'

'And what about you, Doctor?' enquired the Captain finally. 'You've hardly said a word so far.'

The Doctor stirred from his reverie. 'I was just thinking about the one thing we *know* the actions of the duplicates have given them.'

'What's that, Doctor?'

'Time. Still another day until we reach Arden. Fifteen perhaps until reinforcements arrive. They must know this, which suggests that whatever they plan to do next can be accomplished within that period. This line of reasoning leads us on the rather interesting possiblity that they do not care what happens to them after that. Or, more disquietingly, that once they have achieved their initial goal, whatever it is, an entire starfleet will not have the power to prevent them.'

Sorren watched the tubes of the commercial air blowers being plugged into apertures in the kilns' bases.

They were feeding larger branches into them now, because the kilns were no longer two metres across, they were now five. Nothing had been built onto them, they were simply growing from the inside. Sorren shuddered. She tried not to get any closer to them than she had to.

With the new hand tools, the excavation of the seam proceeded at a faster rate. They were now undercutting a fair overhang of rock in places, as the black, glassy ore with the embedded nodules was removed. The ore was brought to Robson for sorting on the grading table. Rusty sat underneath, observing the proceedings with interest.

As Robson surveyed the progress, he wondered if he should not send a team to cut props for the deeper sections . . . but something kept telling him to wait until they were deeper still. A work team cutting props would cause delay, and that could not be allowed, because . . . The work was essential for Arden, because . . .

There was a deadline to be met — that was it. He just wished he could remember why.

Bernice rubbed her eyes and looked at the time display: 05:34 ship time. Today's the day, she thought.

Not feeling like lingering in bed, she washed and dressed. As she slid back her cabin door, the door of Santony's cabin down the corridor also opened. Ace, wearing a nightshirt, stepped out and quietly slid the door shut behind her. She blinked in surprise for a moment when she saw Bernice, then smiled and put her finger to her lips. Bernice beckoned and Ace tiptoed along to her.

They sat on Bernice's bed. 'Well,' she observed, eyeing Ace. 'You look remarkably sprightly for this early hour, rather like the cat that's just got the —'

'It's just for fun. Company, okay?' stated Ace. 'No strings, nothing serious. Just let's say he has a nice smile and felt lonely. I was feeling the same so we cheered each other up. End of story.'

'It's none of my business. It's none of anybody's business except yours and Santony's. But then, why leave so surreptitiously? Nothing wrong, I hope?'

'Oh, no. It's just that I don't want any early-morning pillow talks. That's when things *can* get serious . . . .' she became silent, chewing her lip, staring at nothing.

Bernice understood. She put a consoling arm around the younger woman's shoulder. 'Jan still gets to you, huh?' she said quietly.

'No.' Ace straightened up, gently slipping off Bernice's arm.

121

'Okay,' she said firmly. 'Let's get up and going. We'll be entering the Arden system in a few hours, and then I think we're going to be busy.'

The lip of rock collapsed without warning, sending a small avalanche of dust and boulders bouncing down the slope. Robson watched with distant horror as the workers clawed at the rubble and pulled out a woman's body. As they carried her down to the level ground, he heard Doctor Amphipolis shouting at the guards to let him attend to her. They let him through and he knelt beside her. She seemed semiconscious, groaning in pain. Her legs were badly crushed.

'Listen,' he said urgently to one of the guards, 'I must have my medical kit, do you understand? She must be taken to the camp surgery now!'

'Will she be able to work then?' the guard said flatly.

'Of course not — she'll die unless I can treat her. Donal, for pity's sake make him understand . . .'

Why didn't I have props cut? Robson thought. This isn't right somehow . . . The guard didn't move for a moment, as though listening. Then in one neat, efficient movement, he levelled his rifle and fired a laser bolt into the woman's head.

A man leaped at the guard, snarling in rage, but was rifle-butted aside with contemptuous ease. A body knocked Robson to the ground. Hands were at his throat, trying to strangle him. He was too dazed to fight back. 'Your fugging' digging!' the man was screaming in his face. Robson could only think how terribly wrong it all was. Why didn't the man understand? He was only doing this for the good of . . .

Then there was the buzzing whine of a stun beam and the man went limp. Robson pulled himself clear of his murderous embrace and staggered to his feet. For a moment he simply stared about him as though lost. Then he *knew* once more, and his face set and he straightened up.

'Remove this,' he said, pointing to the woman's body, and he returned to the grading table to sort through more ore. As he worked, a tiny cold analytical part of his mind was wondering why he hadn't been stunned with his assailant.

Chapter 17

Captain Kausama surveyed those gathered round the table, her smooth features creased by a serious frown. There was resolution behind her carefully chosen words.

'My original orders were to make an approach to Arden by stages from the outer part of its system, gathering intelligence data by passive surveillance methods as we went. However, due to the information we have received and our discussions over the last few days, I have decided we cannot afford the time for such caution.' She looked down the table. 'This decision is partly influenced by the observation you made about the duplicates' possible motives, Doctor, and the significance of the time factor involved.' The Doctor inclined his head in acknowledgement. 'I have communicated my decision to Fleetcomm and they have agreed to the change of plan. Therefore, I intend that we should make our re-entry into normal space at a point only a few million kilometres ahead of Arden in its orbital path. From there we may be able to detect lower-power surface transmissions on the planet, if there are any to be heard. Naturally, this increases the risk of our being detected, especially by the stolen ships, but I believe we have no other choice in the circumstances. Comments . . . Colonel Charters?'

'I concur with your reasoning, Captain. Besides, my Marines are beginning to feel restless. They wouldn't want the Navy to start thinking they were only here for the ride.'

The Captain smiled. 'Any other comments?' There were nods from around the table.

The Doctor looked unhappy. 'Captain, if there is any chance of avoiding conflict, any possiblity of negotiation, you will make the effort?'

'As I understand it, Doctor, you already made one such attempt in the Command Room back on Tairngire. If we encounter the *Adamant* or the *Atlas*, my orders are to treat them as hostile.' The Doctor nodded in a resigned manner.

Ace summed up the mood succinctly. 'Let's do it,' she said. 'Who knows, maybe they won't expect us to jump in at the deep end.'

'Thirty minutes to real space. Level two alert status is in force. Secure for combat manoeuvring. Pressure suits are to be worn. All fighter crews to stations. Power core to nominal, all reserve power cells to charge. Close all airtight hatches and ready secondary force curtains. Switch to independent lighting circuits. Ship's gravity will power down to combat level of point two five of standard on a one minute count . . . '

For the thousandth time, Fran recalled the moment when the Skavenger ship rose over the ragged limb of the asteroid. She felt again the impact of its energy bolts on the shields of the old *Farstar*. She, a junior officer, momentarily frozen in shock — and then Captain Lang's steady voice cutting through her panic, her hands moving across the controls once more, a tiny part of her mind wondering if she could ever remain as calm as he had seemed that day. Well, she was about to find out. She hoped she would do justice to her old Captain's example.

Kausama looked about the *Broadsword*'s bridge — her bridge: an arc of control consoles and screens with a low dais at its focus. Set on this dais, facing outwards, were four heavy command chairs, each appearing hump-backed with the bulge of a retracted interface helmet. There was a place for the Captain, Offensive and Defensive Weapons Officers and the Pilot. Together they would become the mind of the ship. She sensed the atmosphere: tense and expectant. But everyone went about their tasks with outward quiet efficiency. She was proud of them. For most it would be their first taste of combat.

Warwick was running through the final checks. 'Environmental systems?'

'All nominal, reserves ready to come on line.'

'Drive system?'

'Reaction drive on stand-by, capacitors charged and ready.'

'Sensor team?'

'All ready; sensor probes in launch tubes.'

'Bay ten status?'

'All fighters and strike craft ready for launch.'

'Weapons?'

'Charged and ready. First salvo missiles in tubes and armed.' Warwick turned to her. 'Reporting ship ready, Captain.'

She spoke, aware that her lips suddenly felt very dry. 'Sound warning for emergence. Initiate timing sequence — and, as our young friend said earlier, let's do it!'

The *Broadsword* dropped back into real space. Arden's sun showed a full disc on the bridge screens. The ship turned, orientating itself, pointing towards the speck of reflected sunlight that was Arden. Probes sped from their launch tubes and vanished into the darkness, accelerating furiously. Nothing else moved within the range of the ship's passive detector systems. Kausama set the ship moving away from the probe release point, until they were paralleling their flight paths. Should the probes be detected and their courses projected backwards, she wanted the *Broadsword* to be somewhere else.

'Captain.' Communications Lieutenant Le Paz was speaking. 'I believe we can just detect some surface transmissions on Arden, between some of the settlements I think. Not intelligible at the moment though.'

'Try to clean up the signals if you can. Anything we can find out about what's going on there may be important. Anything on the ship-to-ship channels, or the skystation relay?'

'Nothing yet, Captain.'

Time dragged by. Only thirty minutes since emergence, Kausama noted. It had felt like thirty hours.

Though the inter-space channels remained silent, the signals from Arden's surface grew stronger, and a few words began to come through clearly. Then Le Paz suddenly said: 'I think I've got a good link here . . . Yes, ah, I've picked up a communication between two settlements . . . One is asking if they are still out of touch with skystation relay . . . The other's saying no, what about Touchstone base . . . No contact with them either . . . They've sent a messenger to enquire, no response so far. That's it, they're signing off for now.'

'Keep listening, Lieutenant.' She turned to Warwick. 'That gives us something to work on.' She touched the intercom. 'Briefing room, you heard that?'

The Doctor answered first. 'Yes, Captain. That was most interesting. It does suggest the influence of the duplicates may be localized, at least so far.

'Let's hope so,' Kausama replied.

'Captain, forward probe has detected a ship. It's heading in our direction,' Warwick said simply.

Kausama turned to the tactical display simulation, which showed their position relative to Arden. From a point halfway between the *Broadsword* and Arden a new dot of light had appeared. It was moving on a course almost back along the path the *Broadsworth*'s probes had flown.

Warwick was scanning the displays. 'The probe sensed the ship's tail flare on its rear scanner once it had got past it. From the characteristics, it looks like the *Adamant*.'

Kausama frowned. 'Now, is this simply chance, or have they detected our probes and are backtracking them?'

'I don't think they can have detected the probes at that range,' Warwick said.

The Captain smiled tightly. 'Or perhaps it is *we* who have been detected by one of *their* probes.'

Warwick grimaced. 'I wish you hadn't said that, Captain.'

'However, there is nothing we can do about that possibility. How long to battle range?'

'At present course and speed, less than forty minutes.'

'Any other ships detected?'

'No other showing. Could still be ahead of the probes, of course.'

'Right.' She consciously drew in a breath, knowing this was the most important decision she had ever made. 'Relay tactical display coordinates down to bay ten. Tell Flight Commander Debly it's combat plan gamma two. Launch all fighters and strike craft immediately — and good luck.' She opened the shipcom channel. 'This is the Captain speaking. Move to alert level three. We are expecting to engage a hostile ship within the hour.' Kausama was aware of the knot of tension in her stomach and knew, at that moment, that Captain Lang had felt exactly the same. She was pleased at the even tone of her voice as she continued, 'Just do your job, everyone, and we'll have no trouble at all.'

The Captain of the *Adamant* could not remember who his enemy was.

He knew they were not expected for some days, but they patrolled anyway, as a precaution. Yet every time he tried to picture them, to actually put a *name* to them, his thoughts seemed to become confused and faded away until . . . What had he been thinking?

In the end there was only the *purpose* left. There was something on Arden, he could not quite recall what, that had to be protected at all costs. His duty was to patrol out here until the . . . work? Process? Whatever it was, had been completed. Then he could rest – though oddly enough he did not feel tired. He was aware that the ship did not have a full crew, but there were enough to fight her, and anyway, none of them seemed to be needing much sleep at present. That was strange, now he came to think of it. In fact, some very strange things had been going on lately. He could remember . . . No, the thought had gone.

He relaxed again. There was only the *purpose*.

'Battle range in four minutes, fighters in position. He'll be detecting us by then unless his systems are all off,' Warwick reported.

'Command team to positions,' ordered Kausama. 'Ready for computer interface, manual controls to stand-by.' Pilot Commander Esteval took her place in the fourth command chair. Kausama touched a control on her chair panel and a force-field shimmered into life around the dais. 'All right, helmets on.'

Power arms lifted the helmets over the back of the chairs and down over their heads, cutting off the sights and sounds of the bridge. Kausama felt the helmet automatically link with the terminal at the base of her skull. There was the expected moment of total isolation as her own body senses were bypassed and disengaged . . .

. . . her senses merged with the ship as the team found their places in the control matrix.

She could feel their thought processes accelerating beyond that of any unaided human mind, allowing them to control the combat functions of the *Broadsword* more precisely and more rapidly than any old-time commander could ever have dreamed possible. And if 'G2' doesn't work, she thought, we'll need all the edge we can get.

The long seconds of boosted perception-time ticked by.

'Multiple contacts, eighty-five degrees by one-three-oh relative, fighter class, four − no five − targets.'

'Engage countermeasures auto-systems; command team helmets on; computer interface on.' There was no doubt in the mind of the Captain of the *Adamant* now, only a desire to do his duty.

'Incoming missiles detected, anti-missiles away . . . ' The helmet shut out the bridge sounds and the Captain felt his mind mesh smoothly with the computer matrix. It felt good, it felt *proper*, to be part of a large mind. He had no need for words to communicate with his fellows now, he simply *knew*.

Kim Talevera was in the second wave of fighters.

They approached the *Adamant* a hundred and twenty degrees around from the first wave as the ship was busy intercepting the first wave's missiles. Fifty kilometres from target she locked on and loosed two multi-warhead anti-ship missiles, then twisted onto her escape vector. The third wave was due in under twenty seconds.

The *Adamant* was at the centre of a halo of fire. Incoming missiles blossomed into swelling spheres of incandescence as the ship's beams tore into them. Some warheads intentionally broke up before they were hit, shedding their multiple loads of bomblets and decoys. Laserbombs vaporized themselves as they converted their nuclear charges into focused beams of energy that stabbed against the protective fields. Hypervelocity hail vaporized against its hull shields, buffeting the ship as though it were ploughing through a rough sea.

128

Nothing could stand such a bombardment unscathed. Temporary shield overloads fused sections of hull. Some compartments were penetrated and lost pressure. But it was a warship, braced and powered for such conditions. Leaks were sealed, and damage contained by a crew working with inhuman vigour and efficiency. And it retaliated by sending its own projectiles out after the tiny craft that harassed it from beyond the range of its beams.

Kim 'heard' the missle's scan beam lock on as she finished her second attack run. She pulled a tight evasive loop and strewed her wake with chaff bouquets and radar decoys. The missile ignored them, still closing. Damn thing's got me on visual tracking, she thought. She engaged maximum boost and dropped a spread of micromines. Fireballs erupted behind her and she heard the pseudo-sound of explosions. She looked back — it was still there, still closing. In accelerated time, Kim scanned the projectile closely. It was no simple interceptor missile but a multi-function homing torpedo — shielded! Time for Plan B, she thought, cutting her drive and tumbling through one hundred and eighty degrees.

Thank you vacuum, she elated, where flying arse-backwards doesn't matter. All her forward projectors now zeroed in on the torpedo. She poured fire into it until its nose cone glowed, burning out its control systems, and it veered away from her. Its drive flickered and failed.

Kim left it falling uselessly out into infinity and headed back towards the battle raging around the *Adamant*. It was vital that they keep the ship's attention focused on them. The *Broadsword*'s normal complement was fiften strike craft. If the duplicates on the *Adamant* had time to count, they would find only fourteen attacking them.

Flight Commander Debly fought to control his craft as he flew through the battle wake of the *Adamant*.

Two thousand kilometres behind the accelerating ship, the plume of expanding reaction gas, vaporized metal and fragmentation debris it trailed behind it was still dense enough, at his velocity, to give a bumpy ride. Every few moments his craft shuddered as a larger particle impacted on its shields, but he held his course. Battle wakes were detector blind-spots for the ships that made them, and his cargo was intended to make full use of that fact.

He could feel the massive projectile underslung beneath his own craft. At present it was known only by the uninspiring reference code 'G2'. If it worked, Debly thought it would be better named 'Fire Eater'.

The wake curved as the *Adamant* made a course change to confuse the targeting of massive hypervelocity weapons intended to crash its shields head-on. Debly followed the curve, holding his place in the heart of the wake. They would not be expecting an attack from this direction. Checks had been made. 'G2' was still experimental, and the *Adamant*'s captain would not have heard of it — they hoped.

He felt the projectile's internal tracking system lock onto target. It detached automatically, cutting in its own drive, and vanished up the battle wake at twenty gravities. Debly slowed and gratefully curved away into clear space. He would know in a few seconds if 'G2' could really eat fire.

Kim did not see the projectile strike the *Adamant*, but all the fighter pilots witnessed the result.

A brilliant point of light blossomed on its aft section as one of its drive stacks exploded, the compression wave tearing open the hull halfway round the engineering decks and along the entire length of the ship. The unbalanced drive force tumbled the ship wildly then cut out. Reaction mass and nuclear fuel tanks split open, enveloping the ship in a spreading cloud of vapour. Megawatt power cells ruptured, discharging artificial lightning bolts through the gashed hull. Munitions started to explode, blowing out glowing craters that filled with oxidizer-fed fires.

The *Broadsword* arrived, drive flaring madly as it braked the ship to match *Adamant*'s trajectory, weapons at the ready. They were not required.

They watched the *Adamant* die on the briefing room screens.

It tumbled through space, burning, disintegrating. Fitful explosions sprayed debris out into the void. Then a ruddy glow started to diffuse through what had been the stern of the ship. It grew brighter; yellow then white hot. The screens darkened against the intensity. The carcass of the warship began to flare and boil away in multicoloured waves. In minutes there was only the minature, short-lived star of the *Adamant*'s power core left to mark its passing.

The room was still silent when Warwick entered, rubbing his eyes and blinking. 'The Captain will be with you in a moment,' he said, sitting down heavily. He poured a beaker of juice and sipped it in a slightly distracted manner, still disorientated after coming out of fast time. 'We were bloody lucky,' he said, to no one in particular. 'One fighter lost; pilot ejected and he's being picked up okay. Otherwise just minor damage.' He shook his head in wonderment.

'What *was* that that blew them away?' demanded Ace.

'Oh, something new – experimental. Only had one available, unreliable. Well, not this time obviously.' He realized an explanation was due. 'The only parts of a warship that cannot be protected by force shields are the reaction drive exhausts. They don't need them. At full thrust the exhaust speed is measured in thousands of kilometres per second and is white hot. Nothing had been found that could survive those conditions *and* get close enough against the drive-field repulsion – until now. "G2" penetrates right into one of the drive stacks itself and, well, you can see what happens then.'

'A ship is destroyed,' the Doctor stated bleakly.

'They'd have done the same to us,' Ace said simply.

If they had watched the sky carefully, the work shift that came on at midnight might have seen the pinpoints of light that marked the track of the battle. But they were too busy feeding the kilns. They were taking split tree trunks now, as fast as they could be fed into them. They were growing faster. Now their bases were almost ten metres across.

The blazing power core fell onwards, out of the system. It would grow cold somewhere between the stars.

Chapter 18

The Doctor surveyed the magnified image of Arden's skystation on the main screen. 'It looks as though your expertise with hyperwave transmitters will not be needed after all, Mr Chiminoe,' he commented.

Chiminoe scowled angrily. 'Now why the hell did they do that?' he exclaimed, slamming his hand down on the table.

The station was still and dark. There was no light from its viewports or regulation warning beacons. Ragged holes showed where hull panelling had been removed. Some of its service modules were missing, and the boom which should have carried the station's power core now ended in a stump trailing a spray of disconnected cables.

Bernice smiled sympathetically at the engineer. He loved finely made machinery, and the sight of something he had helped build now torn apart for no discernible reason clearly touched him deeply.

The Doctor was examining the image with interest. 'Can we increase the magnification? We might learn something if we know what's been taken.'

'It's at maximum,' replied the Captain. 'And I'm not bringing the ship in any closer.'

The Doctor smiled. 'Very wise. A probe then?'

Kausama considered. 'Yes, I suppose we must check anyway in case there is still someone on her, though I have a feeling it's quite deserted.' She opened a command channel. 'Prepare and launch a flying-eye drone to examine the skystation. Advise on approach.' She surveyed the assembly again. 'I suggest there is no point in speculation until we get a closer look at it. Meanwhile, you may be interested to know that we've been making two-way contact with some of the outlying surface settlements, now that we don't have to conceal our presence from the duplicates.'

'Can they tell us what happened?' asked York.

'I'm afraid they don't know much. The intelligence section is still gathering details, but the reports so far seem to fit the same pattern. Nine days ago they lost contact with Touchstone and the skystation relay links also went down. They tried to contact Oberon Camp, it being the nearest settlement to Touchstone, but with no response. A few settlements sent people in aircars to find out what happened; they never returned.'

'What have you advised them?'

'Basically, since they seem safe at the moment, to stay calm, stay put, and let us know if anything unusual happens. We're working them into a regular check-in rota as we make new contacts.'

'And what about Touchstone and Oberon?'

'We'll be dropping spy probes to take our first detailed look at them on the next orbital pass in . . . ' She checked the displays. ' . . . about fifty minutes from now.'

Bernice glanced at her watch, realizing that it had only been a little over four hours since the destruction of the *Adamant*. 'Any sign of the *Mercury* yet?' she asked.

'We're keeping our eyes open for it, you can be sure − and for the other station ferry ships. Unfortunately they have a lot of room to hide in. They could simply be hanging dead in space beyond the range of our detectors. Or, since they are all capable of planetary landings, they could be somewhere down on Arden, in which case a full scan must wait until we have dealt with the skystation.'

There was desultory conversation while the drone made the five-hundred-kilometre orbital transit between the ship and the skystation. Bernice watched the globe of Arden roll beneath them, wondering what plans the duplicate controllers had down there. She looked at the Doctor, but he seemed to have fallen into another of his meditative trances. She turned to Ace. 'Bored, impatient, angry − want a game of ping pong?' she ventured.

Ace grinned. 'Some of those,' she admitted. 'I don't like this hanging about, twiddling our thumbs, letting other people do the job for us.'

'It's *their* job too,' Bernice reminded her. 'we're lucky to be here at all.' She frowned wryly.' If "lucky" is the word I want.'

'Yeah, well you know what I mean. If there's going to be action I feel better being part of it. I'm taking root in this room while all we're doing is *talking*. Sometimes you've got to go in and *do* it, you know, instead of waiting for drone probes.'

'Perhaps we have all been luckier than we know,' said Bernice, now observing Ace closely through narrowed eyes.

'None of your body-language reading, Summerfield,' Ace warned her.

'I knew it!' Bernice exclaimed. 'You were hoping to go with the Marines to liberate the station — laser blazing and all. Only now it looks like there is no one to be liberated . . .'

'All right. So one of the squad leaders said I could ride in the backup shuttle — so what?'

'Nothing,' said Bernice with a grin. 'Nothing.'

They started watching the screens as the drone neared its target.

Arden skystation resembled a smaller version of the *Olympus* orbiting Tairngire, as though built from the same basic kit of parts. Bernice recognized the forms of some of the units, especially the station's single docking module. The drone spiralled around the main tower structure, its camera zooming-in to pick out details. Chiminoe started muttering as he noted missing items. 'Transformer units . . . scanner array . . . Hell, they've hacked out the emergency power cells . . . No sign of the workshop module . . . Shield generator . . . '

'There,' the Doctor said suddenly. 'An open airlock. Can the probe get inside?' Kausama gave instructions to the drone controller, who steered the little craft into the airlock. The drone's remote manipulator arms unfolded and delicately worked the manual test valve on the inner airlock door. There was no air pressure on the other side. The drone turned the emergency release handle and the door slowly slid open.

The corridor revealed was pitch black. The drone's lights sprang on, casting brilliant beamless circles around the interior. 'Straight ahead,' said Chiminoe, 'and you come to the central access shaft. The control room's three levels up from there, if you want to try it.'

'As good a place as any,' agreed the Doctor. The drone moved forward, drifting easily through the nul-gravity structure, cameras swinging from side to side as it passed open doorways. Bernice anticipated the sight of decompression victims' bodies hanging grotesquely in nothingness as they passed each room, but there was nothing to be seen but a few 'floating' microfile discs, a pen, a couple of beakers and a desiccated pot plant. The open central shaft was reached without incident, and the machine rose smoothly past the empty lift tubes.

As the drone reached the control level, the operator's voice came over the intercom. 'Detecting something faintly, Captain. Power circuit still working, I think.'

'Track it down,' said Kausama.

The drone moved slowly into the control level, turning to find the strongest signal. It glided down a corridor until it reached a closed door. A red light was flashing feebly on the control panel beside it. 'Emergency pressure chamber,' exclaimed Chiminoe. 'Still sealed − there could be somebody inside!'

The drone opened the outer door and manoeuvred inside the small airlock. It worked the manual controls again. The outer door closed. As the inner started to open, a swelling hiss of sound was suddenly audible over the drone's microphones. The machine rocked slightly as the inrushing air buffeted it. It floated into the chamber, dimly lit by failing emergency bio-luminescent tubes. Lightweight pressure suits, oxygen bottles and leak repair kits were racked neatly around the walls. Lying face down on the floor was a space-suited body.

'Is he human or duplicate?' asked Strek. 'We should have fitted the drone with one of the duplicate detectors.'

'If I could see his face, I . . . might recognize him,' Chiminoe said with a catch in his voice.

'Thermal reading?' Kausama asked the drone operator.

'Body heat, Captain, allowing for suit insulation.'

'Try to turn him over.'

The drone moved forward, arms extended, gently sliding under the body. 'No − wait!' the Doctor said sharply, but the body had started to lift. The drone camera blanked in a burst of static.

On the screen showing the telescopic view, a perfect white globe of searing light sprang into being where a moment before the station had hung. The screen dimmed as the globe swelled and grew, its outer boundaries gradually dissolving into a lace-work of filaments and streamers. As the central core of the nuclear fireball gradually faded, the Captain turned to the Doctor.

'All right, Doctor, what did you spot that we didn't?'

The Doctor contrived to appear modest and superior at the same time. 'Too late, I'm afraid. I wondered why a body in weightless conditions was apparently pressed so firmly to the floor. Of course, it was attached there in some manner so that its release would trigger the booby trap. Fortunately we only lost a drone.'

'Yes,' Bernice said enthusiastically, looking at Ace. 'Isn't it lucky that nobody went there without checking first. But then, that's the advantage of not rushing in with lasers blazing.'

'Just watch it, smart arse,' Ace advised coldly.

'But what's happened to the crew?' demanded Chiminoe. 'Damnation! I *knew* most of those people.' His face was flushed and he looked ready to strike out at something. 'Were they on that?' He stabbed a finger at the cooling cloud of gas that orbited where the skystation had been. Bernice saw that York and Santony also appeared moved. Of all of them, these three had the closest personal links with Arden.

Santony put a hand on Chiminoe's shoulder. 'Okay, Vince,' he said quietly. 'We'll find them.'

York was nodding reassuringly. 'I'm sure they're all right. They've probably just been taken down to the surface.' She looked at the others for support and reassurance. There was a murmur of encouraging noises. The Doctor's face was sympathetic, but his words did not encourage false hope.

'Perhaps we shall know more when we see the next reconnaissance pictures,' he said simply.

The probe transmissions came through live to the briefing room, the images being computer enhanced and stabilized in real time as they were received. Bernice thought them remarkably good quality for something taken from a satellite one hundred and fifty kilometres up, moving transversely at several kilometres per second. What was also remarkable, in the circumstances, was how long the probes survived — almost a minute before they were blasted by interceptor missiles.

But that was sufficient to show them the mine working near Oberon with its pinhead shapes of workers and watchful guards. The spreading clearing in the trees near Touchstone, with its ring of kilns at the centre, was completely unexpected. 'That's what they wanted those blowers for,' said Bernice, indicating the snake-like tubing connecting the kilns. They watched the work-teams hauling the felled trees for a few seconds until the images were lost in bursts of static.

There was a moment's silence. Kausama looked at them thoughtfully. 'Would anybody care to make any comments?'

'I suggest that we view the recordings again, plus all the ancillary data,' said Colonel Charters slowly. 'Then we can work out an operational plan. I would like to confer with my staff to develop a military strategy, and perhaps while we do so, the specialists can work out their scientific objectives.' He gave a half smile. 'I recommend everybody takes a few minutes to refresh themselves — this could take some time.'

'I would advise the same,' confirmed the Captain.

Ace slumped in her chair. 'I swear I'll take root here,' she muttered.

'Complaining again?' queried Bernice.

'Not really. Now we've got a *target*, at last. There's twelve somethings in the woods, and a bunch of slave-drivers to be taken care of. No problem.'

'To summarize,' said Colonel, indicating the map of the target area on the screen. 'An open landing on any of the few clear areas of any size in the operation zone would be prohibitively dangerous; we already have evidence that the enemy are prepared to use the weapons at their disposal. Touchstone, Oberon and the adjacent foothills of the Phebe Range are undoubtedly protected, and they have had time enough to camouflage their emplacements from aerial observation.

'The least risky of the options we have considered is to send in two lightly armoured parties of platoon strength under cover of darkness, making their planet-fall by unpowered glider landings: hopefully undetected if the weather conditions are as we expect them to be. The two platoons will make their way from their landing point here −' He indicated a place in the forest about ten kilometres from Touchstone and Oberon. ' − to their respective objectives. One will reconnoitre Oberon Camp and the mine workings, to confirm, if possible, that they *are* digging for hypergems as we suspect, and to ascertain the condition of the hostage workers and the position and numbers of duplicates guarding them. The second platoon will make for Touchstone and these "kilns", or whatever they are. They will also determine and relay the positions of the hostages and duplicates and, if feasible, investigate the nature of the "kilns" more closely. Depending on their initial findings, both platoons will then attempt to locate the enemy's air defence emplacements and relay the information back here. With this knowledge we can then plan the major landing on Arden. At the commence-ment of that phase of the operation, the personnel already *in situ* will attempt to disable as many of those emplacements as feasible to reduce the threat to the landing forces.'

The Colonel paused. 'I am not happy about civilians partici-pating in such a primary operation. However, I have been swayed by the arguments of three of our specialists that the circumstances require their presence, and that they *also* have sufficient experience in such affairs not to jeopardize the mission. I hope they will excuse my frankness. The aforementioned does not apply to Sergeant Santony, of course, who will accompany the first platoon to Oberon. With him will go Ms Ace.' Santony and Ace exchanged quick smiles. 'With the second platoon bound for Touchstone will go Professor Summerfield and the Doctor.' Ace gave Bernice a thumbs up while the Doctor bowed his head slightly.

'The rest of the specialist team will remain on board to advise as required as the mission proceeds. Depending on the circum-stances, they may be able to follow the others down to the surface after the main landings have been made.' He looked around the room. 'If there are no further questions, I suggest those concerned get some rest − the landing parties leave six hours from now.'

Bernice examined the landing craft waiting for them in bay eleven critically. Like the fighters, they had dull black, non-reflective, non-detectable skins, but were half again as long, with somewhat fatter basic delta forms, though still with the same flowing contours that the requirements of physics demanded of stealth craft. Their most notable features were huge folded wings, which, to Bernice's eyes, appeared alarmingly filmsy, possibly because they were not black, but transparent. 'I've seen sturdier wings on a dragonfly,' she commented. 'Are you sure there isn't an easier way down — back stairs or something?'

'I think somebody would have commented if there were,' smiled the Doctor.

Ace stretched up and thumped the leading edge of the wing with her first. 'Lamaplex C, I know this stuff. Don't worry, Benny, this is tough enough for the job.'

'I just wish it weren't transparent, that's all.'

Ace grinned at her. 'If you think these look flimsy, just wait till you see the chutes.' She patted a small pack on the Marine-issue harness she wore over her combat suit.

Bernice examined the corresponding pack on her own harness with horror. 'That's the parachute? I thought it was a lunch pack.'

'Didn't you do any jump training at that fancy academy of yours?'

'I missed the practical,' Bernice replied coldly.

'With any luck we won't need them,' Santony reassured her. 'As long as the wings hold out, of course,' he added.

'Very amusing,' Bernice responded heavily.

As they prepared to board the landers, Kim Talevera came up to them. 'I just wanted to wish you all luck. My flight will be escort for you until you're well down in the atmosphere. From then on you're on your own, so take care.' And she was gone.

Ace turned to the Doctor and Bernice. 'As she said, take care of yourselves. See you on the ground.' She and Santony boarded their craft.

The Doctor took off his hat with a flourish, ushering Bernice ahead of him. 'After you,' he offered with mock gallantry.

Bernice pulled a face.

Their craft carried the command teram and first squad of Blue Platoon, together with their heavier weapons. Squads two and three flew in the second lander. Ace and Santony were flying with Red Platoon in the first of their two landers.

Platoon commander Lieutenant Paak indicated their seats. 'Strap in please, Doctor, Professor — launch in five minutes.'

Bernice watched the Doctor as they fastened their belts. Reluctantly he had been persuaded to wear more appropriate clothing for the mission than his cream linen suit, and was now clad in military-issue battle dress, boots and helmet. But, defiantly, he had tucked his red-handled umbrella into his backpack. The most jarring thing, Bernice thought, was to see the holstered pistol hanging from his belt. It had been a condition of their participation that, having proven their military aptitude, they should not prove defenceless liabilities to the rest of the platoon. This, of course, did not bother Ace who, once having proven her familiarity with weapons, had been given the run of the armoury and was now, Bernice guessed, the most heavily armed person on the mission.

Bernice looked at her companions, receiving a few polite nods, but conscious of the gulf between soldier and civilian. Their minds were on the job to come; the dangerous game they were trained to play. She listened to their banter and private jokes, meaningless to an outsider. She watched them automatically run through the final checks of weapons and kit — and noted the few who were silent, staring at the opposite bulkhead with sightless eyes.

She felt a chill of anticipation within her and turned to the Doctor for distraction. 'About the duplicates . . . '

'Yes?'

'Well, I was wondering why they haven't made use of the hostages as something more than forced labour. They know we're here, so why not signal us threatening to kill a few of the hostages unless we keep off Arden? I know it's an unpleasant thought, but it would make sense. They've already shown they're willing to kill for their cause.'

'That's a good question. I think it might be due to the nature of the duplicate controllers. If they are part of a group mind or hive entity as we believe, then they would not value individual beings highly. What is the death of one drone to a beehive? The idea of hostages to bargain with may simply not occur to them.'

'But surely they've been infiltrating Tairngire long enough to learn that humans generally *do* value individuals?'

'Perhaps,' mused the Doctor. 'It's hard to understand the workings of a really alien mind.' He paused. 'Of course, it is possible that they don't care whether we land or not.'

'I thought that bomb on the skystation was a sort of hint that they didn't.'

'Oh, I don't take that so seriously. At the most it was meant to delay or discourage – or possibly *en*courage.'

'Come into my parlour . . .'

' . . . said the spider to the fly? Maybe.'

'The informed money tends to be placed on the spider in these circumstances.'

'True. But remember what happens when a spider thinks she's caught a fly – and finds it's a wasp.'

Chapter 19

The invisible docking-field beams carried the four landers and their fighter escort gently out of the hangar bays.

Once clear of the ship, the craft swung around until they faced back along the path of their orbit. Their engines flared and they dropped away and down towards Arden. The *Broadsword*'s hatches closed and she continued her endless orbital fall, heading towards the darkness that lay in the cone of Arden's shadow. By the time the landers reached them, it would be night over Touchstone and Oberon as well.

The bridge screen displayed a schematic of the landers' descent path. 'Is the weather still good over the target zone?' Kausama asked Warwick.

'According to the meteostats, there's nice thick cloud sheet waiting for them, Captain.'

'The thicker the better as far as we're concerned,' she agreed. 'Thank goodness Arden's moonless.'

The descent continued uneventfully for the next few minutes, then one of the sensor team called Warwick over to his screen.

'Something odd here, Commander. About fifty k's behind us, I'm getting an intermittent reading on some of the skystation debris — it's spreading some way along the orbit now — as though something which doesn't register is getting between us and it.' The operator looked puzzled.

'Any direct scan reading?'

'Nothing. Commander — and I also think I saw a star occultation. Now I'm sure none of the fragments is big enough to do that at this range . . .'

The Captain joined them and examined the readings. 'Keep an eye on it,' she instructed. She conferred with Warwick. 'Worth a probe, perhaps.'

'Couldn't hurt, Captain, though I don't see how we can miss detecting a ship of any size this close.'

'Hmm, you know what the Doctor said to me just before he went down to the lander bay? "Be prepared." I asked for what in particular, and he said, "Almost anything." And he looked at me in that intense way of his, as though he was expecting something . . . ' She trailed off thoughtfully. For a moment they were both silent.

'I'll ready a probe,' Warwick said suddenly, turning to his command position.

Kausama moved to her chair and opened the shipcom channel. 'Attention please. As a precaution, we are moving to alert level two. Initiate standard proceedures.'

'Captain!' It was the planet scan operator. 'Fast moving contact coming over from polar region . . . In stratosphere and rising — I think it's the *Mercury*.' The main screen lit up with the grid of Arden's surface.

Kausama watched the new trace for a moment. 'That heading — it's not coming for us.'

'No, Captain. I think . . . Yes, trajectory curving — it's making a sub-orbital hop. Target's the landers.'

'Communications: warn landers and escort. Weapons: missile intercept — at least try to slow it down. Fighter Bay: stand by for launch.' She turned to Warwick. 'Can we intercept ourselves?'

'Marginal in the time, we'll be in the upper atmosphere.'

'Captain! Something's coming at us.'

The concussion reverberated through the ship, knocking Kausama half out of her chair and flooring those standing. The air seemed momentarily to thicken as the pseudo-grav fields moderated the impact effect. Alarms sounded, warning lights lit up panels and voices gabbled damage reports. 'Beam strike: forward section. Main antenna damaged — pressure curtains up. Shields on full. Projectors ready — no target acquisition . . . '

She clawed her way back into her seat and pulled the restraining web over her. '*No* target! At beam range?'

'No, Captain. Star occultations only. *Something* passed us — coming in again!'

'Evasive!' She felt the fields counter the sudden tumbling of the ship. There was another jolting impact.

'Damage — level thirteen and fourteen outboard, stardrive module two . . . '

'Initiate random fire programme on projectors, star mines: broad pattern. Command team take your places; prepare for computer link.'

The fields kept gripping them as the *Broadsword* made sharp evasive turns. Foss staggered as he tried to reach his command chair and almost fell into it. On the screen that showed tumbling stars there was a vapour flare. 'We hit something!' shouted a detector operator, and another said: 'Momentary contact: it put shields up then down again — lost it now.'

'If it needs shields it can be hurt, we're not fighting a ghost,' said Warwick.

'Never doubted it,' replied Kausama. 'Ready? Helmets on.'

'What about the landers?' he said as the helmets descended.

'For the moment they're on their own.' Then the helmet cut off her voice.

'Come in *Broadsword*, come in *Broadsword* . . . ' There was only static on the channel. There had been *something* up there in orbit watching them, passing on their entry path data to the *Mercury*. Knowing that and guessing their target gave it a good idea where to look for them. Kim swallowed. They were on their own now. For all she knew the *Broadsword* was already gone. What to do? She thought coldly for a moment then changed channels. 'Did you copy that, landers?'

'We did. Any suggestions?'

'Yes: continue with mission but change to secondary landing zone. Start your unpowered descent phase now and pull some evasives. Your only option is to get down somewhere; you're dead meat in the air or in orbit. Maybe they'll assume we'd abort the mission. Anyway, the secondary site won't be as closely watched so you'll have more chance of making it safely. Meanwhile, we'll see if we can head off the *Mercury*.'

Pause. 'Understood, escort, we'll try it. Good luck.'

The landers' engines died and their almost invisible wings extended slightly, into the thin air of Arden's upper atmosphere.

They sideslipped and faded into the darkness. If they can just get down into the cloudsheet, they'll have a chance, thought Kim.

The three escort fighters banked, turning onto an interception course for the projected flight path of the *Mercury*. Back in fast time, she considered their tactics.

How do we play this, Kim? enquired Dag Felden.

I'm taking first crack. You and Nick hang back and open out. If I miss or it changes course you're the backstops. Copy that, Nick?

Understood, chief, came Cort's steady reply. *Don't hog all the fun for yourself.*

She allowed herself an instant of fast thought to feel cheered by that little quip. Nick had been brooding over the business of the Toni Pandril duplicate. Maybe he was starting to come out of it.

They spread out, detectors wide open, ready for the first sign of the approaching ship. Kim knew that nothing the size of the frigate could travel through the atmosphere at speed without leaving traces. She strained her boosted senses impatiently, knowing that in real time only seconds had elapsed since the warning had come through.

There it was! Her first missiles were locked on, armed and away almost before she realized she had initiated the sequence. She followed her missiles in, ready with the next salvo. There was a distant explosion, too early to be her missiles; the *Broadsword*'s interceptor, of course, but it had been stopped by an energy bolt. Her missiles detonated in orange blossoms of fire but the *Mercury* was still coming. She loosed a second salvo, and felt an interceptor lock on as she did so. She banked hard — feeling the stress on her airframe and cursing the air that limited her manoeuvrability — dropped a radar decoy then sideslipped onto a new course. The blast was frighteningly close. There was a wash of heat and the shockwave sent her spinning wildly for a moment until she regained control.

The *Mercury* was a fast receding speck in the darkness, already on the edge of her atmosphere-attenuated detector range. Kim tore after it as fast as air resistance would allow, heedless of the bow-wave of friction-heated air glowing before her nose shield, or the supersonic shock-waves radiating thunderously in her wake.

There were bright pinpoints of explosions. Good, Nick and Dag were on it. Hell, they were close in. She saw searing threads of energy-cannon fire, made visible by the atmosphere — and something was falling out of the sky trailing smoke and flame. She felt the telemetric link with Dag's fighter snap as he ejected. *Just keep it busy Nick, I'm nearly with you.*

Missile on my tail. Can't . . . A ball of fire erupted and dropped tendrils of flaming debris. Nick was gone.

Kim detected smoke billowing in the *Mercury*'s wake, and realized that their efforts had not been entirely futile. I hope it was Nick who got you, and I hope it hurt, HURT, *HURT!*

The fighter flew on at maximum speed, aware that the body inside itself was crying.

It was amazingly peaceful inside the lander. Gliding without power or lights through the deep blackness under the overcast, drifting silently through the air, trimming its course delicately as it checked its position by the navsat net orbiting Arden.

This can't last, thought Bernice.

Harsh light suddenly blazed into one side of the cockpit and she could see the clouds illuminated from below as though by a continuous bolt of lighting. 'Sun-flare,' said Lieutenant Paak simply. 'They can see us now. Brace yourselves.' The lander's power surged on and they were pressed back into their seats. Brief splashes of orange light shone into the cockpit followed by rumbling explosions. The craft banked sharply, fragments spattering the fuselage like hail. They dropped sickeningly as something huge roared past them and they rocked in its wake.

Then it seemed to Bernice that they were struck by lightning. White light illuminated the interior and she felt the shock wave try to punch its way through her as her seat bucked wildly, jarring her spine and snapping her head back so that it rebounded from the rest, leaving her dazed. She felt the craft tumble into a spin and start to fall out of the sky, the rising shrill of air tearing at its no longer sleek contours announcing its doom.

'Ready to jump, weapons packs first.' Paak's voice seemed remarkably calm. The lander's rear hatch opened and there was a sudden rush of air through the craft that sucked her breath away. She was aware of the Doctor unfastening her seat belt and that the rest of the soldiers were standing, leaning against the torque of the fall and moving towards the rear.

'Your 'chute opens automatically, remember,' he was saying. 'When you're down, home in on the beacon.' Suddenly they were the only ones left and a big rectangle filled with spiralling, strangely lit clouds was before her and she fell out into space, wanting nothing more than to hug the ground and have nothing further to do with a sky full of missiles and artificial lightning.

The air blasting through her facemask cleared her head. By the time her transparent, almost invisible para-wing billowed open a mere three hundred metres up, she had only a few seconds to take in her surroundings before landing.

There was the sun-flare, too brilliant to look at, drifting down under the clouds. There were smoke trails in the sky and something burning out across the sea of foliage that was rushing to meet her. A vessel was hurtling across the sky, like a smaller, more streamlined *Broadsword*, and it was firing energy bolts at something on the ground. Then there was a fighter arrowing towards the other craft, itself spitting fire . . .

Bernice was amongst the tree tops and crashing through the upper branches, jerking to a halt, swinging on the end of her rigging lines. Golden fire blazed through the forest canopy. Unconsciously she started counting, like a child in a thunderstorm. She had reached eleven when the sound came: a wall of noise that pounded in her ears, slowing fading. A blast wave washed through the trees, tearing loose a few leaves and setting her swaying again.

Slowly the sound died. The sun-flare spluttered and went out. There was only the distant glow of the *Mercury*'s funeral pyre to hold back the darkness of Arden's forest.

They saw the distant brilliance of the sun-flare lighting the clouds from as far away as Touchstone and Oberon. Workers stopped, suddenly anxious and hopeful. Sorren was roused from her sleep by the distant rumble of sonic booms and explosions.

From the foothills of Oberon, the mine workers could see the battle as it took place far out across the great forest, starkly lit by the flare.

Robson saw, astonished, the fire trail of something falling to earth burning. Lances of artificial lightning struck at the ground. Then a huge fireball blossomed into being, rolling upwards and through the cloudsheet. From its core, a blazing mass tumbled down and burst amongst the trees. Over a minute later, the long drawn-out roar of that explosion reached them.

A column of black smoke was still rising from the remains the next morning.

Chapter 20

The missile came out of nowhere, as had the others.

The composite mind of the command team that controlled the *Broadsword* rolled the ship, bringing its undamaged forward projector battery to bear. The missile vanished in a star-hot fireball. Kausama saw stars flicker briefly as something with a hull far blacker than their own crossed in front of them. The computer melded with her, calculated a probable cone of trajectories, and through her mind link with Foss she said, without words: *Fire*. The invisible energy-beam lashed out and, for a moment, burned something in the darkness.

The black ship's shields went up to deflect the worst of the beam, reacting once more with astounding speed. There was an instant when its strange outline could be seen, then it turned aside, dropped its shields and disappeared from even their boosted senses.

Kausama turned the ship onto a new course, feeling the relative slowness of its response. One of the main thruster domes was damaged — among other things. She directed another spread of mines to be discharged. Had they done as much damage to the black ship as it had done to them? No, she decided coldly. They had grazed it a few times, but it still accelerated faster than them, turned more tightly and, crucially, could see them when they could not see it.

They could not hide, they could not run — and they could not jump. Hyperdrive module two was ruined. They should have been able to shut down its opposite pair and still jump with just two, but the synchronization linkages had been fused by the hit. Until they were cleared, the ship was locked in real space, pursued by an almost invisible enemy.

Black ship coming in head-on, said Warwick's pseudo-voice.

Has it ever seen a Catherine wheel? she wondered.

Only one way to find out.

The *Broadsword*'s drive cut and the ship tumbled, propelled by the undamaged thruster domes, its internal force-fields bracing them against the rotation. The drive cut in again at maximum, a white-hot flare of gas licking out before them, spearing towards their adversary. *Tail batteries: random fire. Mines: broad pattern now,* Kausama ordered.

Something shimmered in the lash of their tail flare and was sent tumbling through space, pounded by the thousands-of-kilometres-per-second particle wind of the exhaust flare impacting on its shields. They saw it fall past them, temporarily slowed by the encounter. A mine detonated close by it, sending it spinning again, shields still on as it fought for control. For the first time, the *Broadsword*'s beams had a chance to lock onto the black ship for almost a full second. Its shields glowed cherry red, flickered, started to fail − and the ship disappeared at full drive acceleration.

For an instant Kausama felt sheer elation. This time you ran from us! she wanted to shout. But over the matrix they only heard her say: *Well done all.*

Then Kausama felt the opening of control circuits and Commander Stirling's slow-time voice saying, 'Limited stardrive now operational, Captain.'

Pilot, deep space jump, any direction, now, she ordered. The *Broadsword* vanished into hyperspace.

They came out of the forest darkness in ones and twos, homing in on the locator beacon carried by Lieutenant Paak. Nobody used lights, but their night goggles turned the forest into a strange world of infrared shades, populated by the glowing heat-ghosts of fellow survivors.

Bernice was once of the last to arrive. The Doctor, an odd figure in his combat suit and thick visored helmet, stepped forward and clasped her by the shoulders. 'Are you all right, Benny? I was beginning to worry.' His voice was deep with concern.

'Oh, I'm fine,' she replied wearily. 'I only parachuted into the top of the tallest tree in the forest and have just spent an enjoyable hour climbing down it, that's all.' She looked about her. 'How are we doing?' she asked more seriously.

'Not so well, I'm afraid. It looks as though we've lost about half the company. Three of the landers were hit in the air and the one that did get down was rayed by the *Mercury* before they could all get clear.' She could hear the bitterness in his voice. 'Red Platoon — what's left of them — are forming up a few kilometres to our west. The plan is to join up with them in the morning.'

'Ace and Santony — are they okay?'

'Santony is. Ace hasn't come in yet, though we know she bailed out all right. She probably got hung up on a tree as you did; as most of us did, come to that. There are a few broken bones because of the trees — that was the idea of the special landers, after all. Those wings you found so alarming were designed to fold up on landing and cushion the impact. Oh, well. The best laid plans . . . '

'Doctor. Just before I hit the trees I saw a fighter heading straight for the *Mercury*, then there was an explosion. Did it deliberately crash into it?'

'I think so. It was a very brave act. That ship would probably have wiped us all out had it not been stopped.'

'Did you see if the pilot ejected?'

'I don't think there was time.' He looked at her closely, as though trying to peer through her visor. 'You think it was Kim Talevera, don't you?'

'Yes. I've only known her a few days, but I think that's the sort of thing she would do. Oh, dammit! Why does it have to be like this?'

The Doctor put his arm around her shoulders for a moment. 'My dear Benny. If you feel like this after your short life, imagine how I feel after all *my* years.' He looked about him at the temporary encampment under the trees and the injured soldiers receiving first aid. Bernice felt his hands ball into fists. 'I hate war. I will do everything I can to avoid it. But sometimes there is a dreadful inevitability about it. And then you know that good people are going to die for the lives of others. And all one can do is to try to build something worthwhile from their sacrifice.' He turned to her again. 'There now — not a terribly original observation to make, was it? But I'm afraid that is the

151

best I can offer at the moment.'

A grey morning light filtered thinly through the tree tops. Bernice flipped up her night-vision goggles and looked at her surroundings properly for the first time.

The trees were mainly venerable and massive, throwing out huge boughs high above them thick with summer foliage, forming an almost continuous canopy, resounding with the first bird calls and the buzz and click of insects. A botanist would probably have noticed significant differences in the vegetation around here, but as far as Bernice was concerned, she could have been standing in any temperate forest on Earth. Except, of course, that this forest covered most of a continent.

A deer-like creature bounded out of the underbrush and into the aisle between the trees fifty metres from them, startling the sentries. It regarded them curiously for a moment, then disappeared as suddenly as it had come.

An hour after dawn the survivors of Red Platoon appeared through the forest. Two of their number were being carried. Ace was not with them.

Santony greeted the Doctor and Bernice sombrely, looking worried. 'I know she got out of the lander okay, but the thing was throwing itself all over the sky at the time, so I guess she could have fallen well clear of the rest of us. A few hours ago we tried activating the tracers of those still missing. You understand we didn't want to risk it earlier as tracers can't be as secure as the other comm channels. Well, there was no response. So either she's somewhere shielded, or her tracer's busted.' They looked at each other with troubled faces.

After a few moments, the Doctor said resolutely: 'A ground search is clearly impractical in the present circumstances. There is no other course for us but to press on with the mission — whatever remains of it. If Ace is still alive, the best thing we can do for her is to resolve the situation on this planet as quickly as possible so that a search with full facilities may be mounted.' He looked at Bernice and Santony. 'Don't give up on her yet. Ace is an extraordinarily tough person: a born survivor. You can be certain that she won't give up on herself.'

Chapter 21

Ace reassembled her consciousness painfully slowly, one piece at a time. It felt like building a house of cards whilst wearing boxing gloves; every so often she would disturb the stack and have to start from the bottom again.

TARDIS . . . holiday . . . Arden . . . No, not Arden. TARDIS . . . holiday Tairngire. What was a 'Tairngire'? Oh, yes. Holiday . . . statues . . . TARDIS. Stolen! Yes, she remembered that. *Broadsword* orbiting Arden (this was better), landers, going down, *Mercury* attacking them, bailing out, falling, hung up in a tree . . . Climbing down, there was a rotten branch, it broke, she fell, hitting other branches on the long way down, bouncing like a pinball, then the ground — *Pain!*

Her eyes were wide open, staring at something white, softly luminous and intermittently far away. She had been wimpering, thinking the pain was coming back and that she could not move without it hurting more. Then she realized the pain had gone.

Her whole body felt gloriously warm and whole, supported by something spongy that cradled her as though it had been molded to her individual form. For a few moments she luxuriated in not hurting, trying to get her mind out of first gear.

Somebody had done a good job of fixing her up. Where was she anyway? What was this white thing over her — an oxygen tent? She tried to reach up and touch it — and could not lift her arm.

Oh no, please no. Don't let me be paralysed. Wait a minute . . . She could *feel*. Her arm *had* tried to move; her muscles *had* been working.

Her wonderful form-fitting sponge support was gently but firmly holding her fast.

Lieutenant Paak, as senior surviving officer, held a brief council of war, seated on the great splayed roots of the Ardonian equivalent of a beech tree. He spoke bluntly:

'We've got thirty-five active people left out of the seventy-six military, lander crew and specialist personnel we started with. We have seven non-mobile casualties in our care at present, five confirmed dead — we had to leave them where they were — and the rest are missing. We have rations for ten days and our weapons status is good.' He surveyed the faces around his. 'We are at present some twenty-five kilometres from Oberon and over thirty from Touchstone. How long we shall be safe here I do not know. The question is, when we move, which way do we go, and with what objective in mind? I hesitate to divide our forces further, but we could still send two groups to continue the original mission, though the chances of success would be slim in the circumstances. This also assumes that contact will be re-established with the *Broadsword*. Until then we are on our own — no backup or air cover in an emergency. Anybody care to make an observation at this point?'

The Doctor spoke quickly, clearly with a plan already in mind. 'Yes, Lieutenant. I suggest the following: firstly, that we leave the wounded here, in some suitable place of concealment, tended by the surviving lander crew-people. They will not be in any greater danger than anywhere else in the forest and probably much less. I think the duplicates are too busy with their activities at Touchstone and Oberon to spend much time searching for a force they know is scattered and diminished. We can leave a beacon at some point observable from the hideway for any of our companies who have been delayed in regrouping.' Santony and Bernice looked hopeful. 'But we leave it where it will not be a liability should the duplicates find it first.'

Paak looked thoughtful. 'Okay. And the rest of us?'

'Unencombered by the injured, we can make our best time to Touchstone.'

'And then?'

'An investigation of the "kilns", naturally. I think we will find the answers to a lot of questions if we know just what their purpose is.'

'Or we may simply find more questions.' Paak thought for a few moments. 'All right, Doctor. We'll give it a try.'

154

Ace tried raising her head, feeling the stiffness in her neck. At least the sponge pillow was not adhered to her the way the rest of the 'bed' seemed to be. She looked around.

The whiteness above her resolved itself into a semi-circular tube with closed ends that covered the pallet of green sponge on which she lay. Hesitantly, she looked down at herself. Will you look at all those tubes and things, she thought. I've got more plumbing than a washing machine.

Besides the tubing, and wires she took for medical sensors, there were casts — apparently made of solidified green gelly — on her left leg from ankle to knee, right ankle, left forearm, right wrist and a broad band encircling her ribcage. In addition, there were glossy translucent green patches covering the worst of her sizable collection of bruises and deeper contusions. She observed the resultant colour scheme with bleary distaste; lime green over purple bruise set against pink flesh clashed, she decided. Her head began to feel heavy and she dropped it back onto the pillow. Good thing I was wearing my combat suit, she thought, or else I *really* might have got hurt.

Suddenly she found tears running down her face. Her suit — they'd have had to cut it off her, it would be ruined. Pull yourself together, she told herself firmly, half aware that she was probably dosed with painkiillers making her mind wander. Selfish bitch, worring about your suit! What about the Doctor and Benny and Santony! Were they all right?

Where was she? Was this the *Broadsword*'s sick bay? Had she been delirious? Was the bed holding her down to stop her injuring herself? How long had she been out? Hell, why wasn't there a nurse around, now that she'd come to — a nice reassuring starch-white-uniformed nurse who would tell her everything was fine. Even better, a nice hunky male nurse . . . Hey, you're feeling better Ace. She shook her head. Stop that. Get your mind together and *call* for someone.

'Hello . . . ' she croaked. That was no good. She licked her lips and tried again. 'Hello?' That was better.

'Hello,' said a flat, toneless voice from the beyond.

Lieutenant Paak traced their route on the map display.

'We'll head out on a bearing of two eight five relative from here. That'll keep us south of Touchstone and any traffic between there and the mine near Oberon. A bit under forty k's and we should strike the Titania River where it curves here, below Touchstone and the "kiln" site. We can approach along the edge of the river valley, hopefully from a direction the duplicates won't expect and then, well, we'll have to see what happens then.'

'How long will it take us to get there?' enquired Bernice.

'In this country, keeping our eyes open, a day and a half, two days, maybe. It depends.' Paak looked around.

Platoon Sergeant Ashton approached. 'Shelter's finished. Lieutenant, and we've moved the wounded inside.' Paak inspected the work. A pile of boulders was half hidden by brushwood. Tenting material had bene stretched over a cleft between the rocks and camouflaged, enclosing a room-sized space. He exchanged a few words of encouragement with the injured and those being left to tend them, checked they had sufficient supplies, then rejoined the others.

'Pass the word, Sergeant. We're moving out in five minutes.'

Ace swallowed. The voice had a curious quality to it. Nothing she could quite place, but definitely *not* the reassuring tone of the expected medical person. She gritted her teeth, but there was no other way to put her next question: 'Where am I?'

'You are on the world you call Arden,' came the flat reply.

Okay, she thought, not exactly chatty, but it's a start. 'Can you tell me where more precisely?'

'You are in our . . . habitation. You might also call it a nest, or burrow or city.'

'Are there many of you?'

'There is only one of us in this habitation, though we have many of what you would call "bodies".'

I know who you are, she thought — and I wish I didn't. Why the hell am I still feeling so calm? Is it the painkillers, or have they given me something else? Still wondering, she asked the big question. 'Why did you make the duplicates and send them to Tairngire?' Well you might as well, she told herself.

'We did not.' Huh? she thought. 'We sent only *one* duplicate to Tairngire,' the voice continued. 'We are not sure, but we believe that you saw it there.'

'Ostman!' she exclaimed. 'Gerry Ostman – you made him?'

' "Gerry Ostman" would be how you would identify him amongst your kind.'

'Uh, sorry, I tried to save him but the other duplicates got there first.'

'We understand. If you are troubled by the incident, do not be. There was no great loss.'

'But one of your people died!'

'This is where your kind and ours differ. The loss to us was as if, as if you lost the end of one of your fingers, but you knew it would grow quickly back again.'

Oh yeah, she thought, the Doctor had suggested something of the kind. Hard to accept so causally though. That reminded her . . . 'Thank you for taking care of me. You did bring me in from the forest, didn't you?'

'Yes. We understand that if your body dies, all that is you dies. You are a nest-of-one. We wonder, how do you survive being so vulnerable?'

'Well, we're just used to the idea, I guess.' Let's leave souls and religion out of the discussion for the moment, she thought.

'It is good that you are so well adjusted to your condition,' the voice continued. 'But it was not just to preserve all that is you, nest-of-one, that we brought you here. We believe there is mutual benefit to both our kinds if we now openly communicate with you. We both face a common enemy.'

'Well I'm all for mutual benefit and such, but before we go on, can you do a few things please?'

'What do you wish?'

'First, can you get this bed thing to let go of me so that I can move a little?'

Pause. 'You must understand that you are a very large being, compared to ourselves. You could do great damage within our nest.'

'Hey, aren't we all friends here? Why should I want to hurt you: I'm grateful for what you've done for me.'

'From what we have seen, you are a violent species. The possessions we found with you included many weapons.'

'Because things have got dangerous around here lately, as

157

you've already admitted. But you don't use weapons against friends,' she said fiercely.

'Are we friends? We are very different.'

'You judge friends by how they treat you, not what they look like. Anyway, how much damage can I do in my condition? The most aggressive thing I can do is pick my nose at you.' The 'bed' released its gentle grip on her. She squirmed carefully. 'Oh, that feels good. Uh, is there something to drink, please?' A tube extended itself from somewhere behind her pillow like a bendy straw. She sucked from it cautiously; it tasted of sweet spring water. 'That's great. Next thing: what are you called? My name's Ace, by the way.'

'Called? We do not have names like you, nest-of-one-called-Ace. We know who we are amongst ourselves.'
Telepaths would of course, she realized.

'Well, the name of your race, then?'

'We call ourselves people. What else would we?'

Ace laughed and winced — her ribs hurt. 'Sorry, silly question. Everybody does, of course.'

The voice seemed to consider for a moment. 'The sound to your ears of something of what we are might be "Shenn".'

Well that's easy enough to say, thought Ace, trying the name a few times. 'Okay, one last thing before we get back to talking: is this canopy thing over me essential? Is the air in your, er, nest, harmful to me?'

'No, but we thought your surroundings would disturb you until you had completely recovered.' Ace felt surprisingly touched by their consideration; she wished some people she'd known were as thoughtful as the Shenn seemed to be.

'Thanks, that's very kind. But I'll be okay now, so if you could open this thing up so I can see who I'm talking to . . .'
For a moment she thought of asking for a sheet, but she was quite warm enough already, and in the circumstances, modesty would be ridiculous.

The canopy opened up over her head and folded down like a bellows towards her feet. Warm air smelling of furry bodies washed over her. She had an impression of rows of small, soft lights and looking up at a wall of tiny balconies. She turned her head.

'Oh *shit*!' next to her bed a Shenn creature sat on a stumpy green column. Gerry Ostman's head was mounted beside it.

They advanced slowly but steadily through the forest, moving silently over the moss, last year's leaf litter and the occasional grassy knoll that carpeted the ground between the great trees. In other circumstances, this could be a magical place, thought Bernice. Forget *As You Like It*, she thought. What a setting this would be for *A Midsummer Nights Dream*.

She looked about her, hoping for unicorns. What she saw were soldiers in full battle dress, sinister in their sense-boosting helmets with lowered blast visors. They were scanning their surroundings as she should have been: alert for danger, fingers on triggers. Can't you see how lovely this place is? she wanted to shout. She didn't, of course. First rule of the march: no unnecessary talking or radio traffic.

Bernice acknowledged the priority of the moment and dutifully turned back to watching her surroundings with a more cirtical eye. When this is over, she promised herself, I'm going to come back here for an idyll — maybe drink a few bottles of something potable to the memory of Kim Talevera. She shuddered. And maybe to Ace as well, for all I know. She looked about her regretfully. Perhaps it was her morbid thoughts, but the place already seemed to be losing some of its charm.

The canopy rapidly folded back up to enclose the bed again.

'It's all right,' said Ace, more positively than she actually felt. 'I'm okay. It was just a surprise to see that . . . thing there. Just tell me, why do you need it?'

The Shenn managed to inject a trace of surprise into its flat voice. 'To translate our thoughts into your spoken language, of course. Then to translate the sounds of your words back into a form we can understand.'

'Right, I can understand now. But why did you have to take off his head?' She felt sick.

'Take? You do not understand as you think you do. This is not the actual head of the being called Gerry Ostman, it is what we believe you call a "duplicate". In this case, not of the whole body, but only the head and those organs necessary to supply

159

blood and air for it to speak and hear.'

'Oh, wow. Sorry. You had me worried for a moment there . . . But what about Ostman's real body then?'

'It is still within our nest. But it sleeps. Its mind was shocked by the death experience of its duplicate. We tried to revive it afterwards, but it did not function correctly. It needs the healing skills of your own kind, we think. For the moment it is safe and while it sleeps, we can use it in this manner.'

Ace sighed. 'I really do understand now. Okay, pull back the cover again and we can talk properly.' The canopy retracted. Ace looked very deliberately at the immobile head beside her. Its eyes were closed, she noted, and actually appeared almost serene. The supporting column was also a container, she realized now, made of another variation of the apparently multi purpose translucent green material. Inside she could just make out various organs suspended in fluid. Okay, I can get used to it she told herself. She looked at the Shenn sitting on what seemed to be a tiny beanbag beside the head. It looked exactly like those retrieved from the duplicates in the Defence Building, except that they had scuttled around like rats. This one clearly was animated by intelligence. It had purpose. She thought for a moment before saying: 'That Shenn beside the head, it's just one of you, isn't it?'

'That is correct,' The duplicate head said, eyes still closed. The Shenn pointed to itself with its tiny, dexterous hand. 'This is just one part of us. We are all around you. Our consciousness is not trapped in one body as is yours.' Ace thought she could almost sense pity in its words. 'This one is here to relay this conversation to the mind we all share and contribute to. When this one needs to rest, another will take its place, but you will still be talking to us, the nest.' The Shenn spread its tiny arms in an oddly human manner.

Ace looked about her properly for the first time. The chamber she was in was lined with stepped-back balconied galleries and burrow-like openings, with Shenn scurrying busily along them apparently taking no notice of the 'giant' alien being in their midst. The lighting was gentle — bioluminescent, she guessed — while the overall atmosphere reminded her a little of the lofty atrium of a prestigious office development, but in miniature.

160

On a Shenn scale, she realized, the space was six or seven storeys high. If she stood up in it, she would hardly have headroom.

She turned her attention back to the head. 'Now,' she said firmly, 'if we're going to help each other, you're going to have to tell me what's been happening on Arden that we don't know about.'

'The story will take some time to tell,' warned the Shenn.

Ace shrugged as well as she could in her position. 'I'm not going anywhere.'

Chapter 22

'. . . and that is the total of repair work required, Marshal.' Kausama paused from her report to take a sip of water. The images of the Marshal and the Prefect on the briefing-room screen could be seen conferring for a moment.

'How long do you estimate for the work?' the Marshal asked.

'According to Commander Stirling's estimates, between thirty-six and forty-eight hours using every available hand. Then the *Broadsword* will return to Arden space. Next time we will be ready for this "black ship".'

The Marshal smiled gravely. 'We appreciate your determination, but have you considered waiting for the reinforcements?'

'I don't think we can afford to, Marshal. Apart from the safety of the landing party, the more I think of it, the more I am convinced that the Doctor was right: the duplicates are playing for time. I do not believe we can allow them to have even a few days more.'

'Very well. Proceed as planned. Is there anything else?'

'Only that . . .' Kausama hesitated. 'I'm sure Lieutenant Talevera is all right, Marshal.'

The Marshal's face softened for a moment. 'Thank you, Captain. Good luck to you all.' The screen blanked.

Kausama turned to the people around the conference table. 'That is all, ladies and gentlemen. Please continue with your scheduled repair work. Could the remaining special advisors stay a moment please?' The *Broadsword*'s officers filed out. Quillon, York, Strek and Chiminoe waited expectantly.

The Captain managed a tired smile. 'I have a special task for you. Not exactly one you might have envisaged when you volunteered to come on this voyage, but it arises from a connected problem: the black ship. We evaded it last time by an unorthodox manoeuvre; that will not work again. When we next face it I need an edge to work with: perhaps an insight into its tactics, a possible weakness, ideally a means of detecting it. *Something*. We in the command crew will of course be working on the same problem, but I believe a fresh viewpoint from outside the strictures of military thinking may be vital in this situation. If the duplicates are manning that ship, as we believe, then they are familiar with Concordance military practice from the minds of the naval personnel they control.' She encompassed them all with a sweep of her hand. 'You have knowledge and experience between you in widely differing fields. You know the situation on Arden and have all the information we could gather on the black ship to hand, in addition to the not inconsiderable resources of this starship. Use them. That is all.' She rose, nodded to them and left the room.

There was silence for a moment.

'We're not combat tacticians,' said York, frowning.

'The Captain said as much,' cut in Quillon. 'But that is not what the situation requires. They have all the tactical knowledge they need on the bridge. What the Captain was asking for was that most challenging of intellectual feats: *original thought*.' He smiled quickly. 'Almost like detective work, I suppose. I suggest we exert ourselves, because the stakes are rather high.'

'Yeah,' drawled Chiminoe, 'our lives. Okay, Inspector, let's give it a try. Why don't we see if the simulation department can put together a composite of the black ship. Maybe that'll tell us something.'

I wish the Doctor was here, thought Ace. Or Bernice; she'd love listening to this chunk of history. 'Okay,' she said aloud to the Shenn, 'let's see if I've got this straight.' She took another swallow of water from her 'straw'. 'Communities of Shenn have been living in burrows under Arden for thousands of years, quite peaceably. You link telepathically to form group intelligences, but the effect is limited: a single Shenn too far from its nest isn't smart. Your ancestors used the carapaces and hides of various animals for disguise and protection outside their nests, and got better at the trick with time. Then they found the hypergems, which could extend your telepathic links and range of movement. Also, they could allow the minds of the original creatures to more naturally animate the duplicates you made of them, which helped when you wanted heavy work done or to travel a long way beyond your nests and so on. And you've been living like that very happily for ages — correct so far?'

'That is an accurate summary,' replied the Shenn.

'But about thirty years ago, the big nest of Shenn living under the mountains north of here, suddenly started hearing a god speaking to them —'

'Not a "god",' the Shenn corrected. 'That is your word. We do not understand the concept as you have explained it. And it was not a voice; it communicated in thought to the nest mind as a whole.'

'Well, it sounded pretty godlike the way you told it. Okay, so not the genuine article, but the implication is of something claiming to be pretty powerful. It said it lived in the sky, yes?'

'That is true.'

'And it "spoke" to them loudest at dawn, you say?'

'Yes.'

'Hmm . . . Anyway, the nest started listening to this "voice" and started a big project under the mountains which you think had something to do with developing space travel. But because you go in for bio-engineering — which I think is pretty neat stuff by the way — instead of mechanical engineering, this was probably going to take a long time.'

'That is correct. Even from here we could sense the displeasure of the sky-entity, but there was no way to speed the progress of the work.'

'And then humans came to survey, then settle Arden, and you kept your heads down. And since you'd had the sense not to foul up Arden by over-population or pollution, nobody knew you were here. Then, after a while, the mountain Shenn's project was cancelled, and they started watching the settlers closely and making the first duplicates of them. And when the military came along, they turned their attentions to them and started infiltrating Tairngire with duplicates, so you made the duplicate of poor old Ostman to try to find out how far they had got.'

'Doing this troubled us. Even though you are unlike us, in your way you are intelligent beings. But we had no choice'

Ace could not decide if the Shenn was being complimentary

or not, and skipped the point. 'However, it didn't work out too well, did it?'

'No. Although we know much about concealment, we have no talent for what you would call "spying". Our duplicate was detected in some way even before he reached Tairngire.'

'Yeah, well I know what happened then. And now the duplicates run by the mountain Shenn are clearing and burning the forest in those kiln things, and digging up hypergems by the tonne in that mine near Oberon — and you don't know why?'

'No, but this is their new project. We sensed this when the sky-entity announced it had taken a name from your speech.'

'Huh? What name? You didn't mention that before.'

'It did not seem relevant. It is now to be addressed as Umbra.'

They took a rest after six hours' uneventful march. Bernice flopped down thankfully against a tree trunk next to the Doctor and Santony. She glared at them as she drank from her flask. They both seemed a lot fresher than she did. Bernice thought of herself as pretty fit, but her pack and weapons made a substantial load.

'Are you sure I'm not carrying some of your kit?' she enquired suspiciously.

Santony grinned at her good-naturedly. 'Feeling a bit tired are we?'

'No "We" obviously aren't; *I* am. You two look disgustingly chipper. You I can understand, Mister Professional Soldier — you probably do this sort of thing every day before breakfast — but as always, Doctor, you surprise me.'

'Oh, it's nothing special,' said the Doctor. 'I've had some practice with routemarches in the past, that's all.'

'Somewhere I've heard of, Doc?' enquired Santony.

'Probably,' the Doctor said absently. 'Marco Polo . . . Hannibal over the Alps . . . Mao's long march . . . ' Santony's eyes were widening.

Bernice grinned. 'Well I could do with an elephant or two right now. Why couldn't we have brought some powered transport?'

'Because, my dear Benny, power drives or force-field jets are too easily detected: especially in a largely unmechanized

165

environment such as this.'

'True,' added Santony. 'So far nobody's found any better way than foot-slogging to do this sort of job.'

'Well my feet aren't going anywhere for a while yet.'

Two minutes later, Sergeant Ashton came along the column. 'Rest time over,' he was saying cheerfully. 'Up and at 'em, troops.'

'Ace. Wake up, nest-of-one Ace.'

'Huh? what? Okay, I can hear you.' Ace realized she had fallen into a doze whilst trying to assimilate what the Shenn had told her and plan something constructive.

'We have found one of your fellow beings in the forest.'

'What! Who is it? Are they hurt?'

'We do not know the name of the being. It is a female of your kind, like yourself. It is injured, but we have brought it into the nest and we belive we can keep it alive.'

'Can you take me to see her?'

'If you wish, though you may find it . . . disturbing.'

'It doesn't matter.' 'Oh shit, this is going to be something bloody bad, she thought. 'You have to face this sort of thing — this is war, you know.' She realized she was almost shouting. 'Sorry. Just get me to her, please.' Silently, her mattress-like pallet rose slightly and with the faintest of rippling motions, headed for a low arched tunnel opening in the wall. Ace twisted round to see the container bearing the head gliding along behind her. This is a seriously weird procession, she thought. She frowned and leaned over the side of the 'mattress' as best she could, to see how it was moving. Thousands of tiny sucker-ended legs rippled along underneath. She settled back into place gingerly. 'I know it's a silly question,' she called out. 'but this thing I'm on is *alive*, isn't it?'

'Of course,' came the Shenn's proxy voice. 'It is a hybrid of useful characteristics from several plant and animal species.' There was a thoughtful pause. 'Does it trouble you?'

'Oh no, just a little unusual, that's all,' she replied lightly, revising in her mind the probable nature of the 'tubes' and 'wires' intimately associated with her at that moment, and swallowing queasily.

166

The tunnel was a good fifty metres long — a couple of city blocks on the Shenn scale, Ace realized. They passed several branching tunnels on the way, busy with purposeful Shenn and other creatures only briefly glimpsed, possibly more hybrids or other domesticated nest animals. As before, the Shenn appeared to take no notice of her, making way to let them pass without a second glance, then continuing on their way.

She emerged feet-first into a high-ceilinged chamber. From her ground-level viewpoint, her first impression was of a chemical plant crossed with a mad scientist's laboratory of the sort popular in period horror films. On a Shenn scale, this is a factory, she thought. Cylindrical vats, again built of the translucent green material, lined one wall. They were enmeshed in lattice-like gantry structures and connected by a mass of pipe-work to other retorts and jars, containing vari-coloured liquids, some bubbling in a traditional manner. Unidentifiable bio-mechanical forms were set about the room, performing their functions soundlessly, except for occasional gulping sounds and the odd pulsation along their linking tubes, which Ace found uncomfortably sensuous.

The mobile 'mattress' stopped before the vats and the 'pillow' obligingly lifted her head. Suspended in fluid within the first was the naked body of a man connected to a familiar array of tubes and wires. It was the real Gerry Ostman. Inside the next vat was . . .

Ace turned her head away sharply, telling herself she was not going to be sick. After a moment she forced herself to look again.

It was a woman's body, terribly injured, twisted and broken, swathed in Shenn medical tubes and wires. Half her face as burned. Her right arm finished in a stump below the elbow and it seemed a great bite had been taken out of her torso above her right hip. Her left foot was missing. There were gashes and burns all over her, disfiguring her smooth flesh. Ace screwed up her eyes, wanting to shout out all the obscenities she knew — and knowing it would be a pointless gesture. Now was the time for planning, coldly and practically, a suitable revenge.

She watched the Shenn creatures working about the open top of the vat. They were lowering strangely articulated manipulator arms down into the fluid. The clamps on the ends of the arms closed about the woman's obviously broken left upper arm and gently pulled and twisted until it was set true. A wrapping of the green cast jelly was applied about the limb. Well, she told herself firmly, the facilities are not standard but the care is first class.

She was about to turn away when she realized suddenly that the woman in the vat was Kim Talevera.

'Are you better now?' The Shenn almost managed to make the flat voice issuing from Ostman's head sound concerned.

'Yes . . . I'm going to be okay. I don't usually break down like that, you know. Not at my best at the moment.' The mattress's manipulators finished cleaning her. Ace felt ashamed and angry at her . . . weakness, there was no other word. And she called herself tough! 'This is war,' she'd said. And then when she realized who was in the tank — friendly, bright, brave Kim — the reality had hit her. All her flimsy resolve had gone. She had vomited and cried and tried to move so that the mattress had had to hold her down again to prevent her doing more damage to her own injuries.

'It is understandable,' the Shenn said. 'You have suffered yourself, your mental processes have not yet recovered fully, your surroundings are strange to you and now you discover the injured one is what you would call a "friend".'

'Only known her a short time . . . But she's one of those people you get to like quickly. Will she be all right?'

'We are certain now that she will not die. How far her other injuries can be treated we cannot yet say. What skills in repairing bodies do your people have?'

They probably had limb cloning at least, she thought. But Kim's whole body was so mangled it was a miracle she was alive. And if there was radiation damage . . . Hell, she must have ejected her cockpit module as she hit the *Mercury*, Ace thought. The thing must have had automated emergency medical systems to keep her alive long enough for the Shenn to have found her. 'I'm not sure how much she can be helped.' She thought of the missing *Broadsword*.' I'm not sure there will be any help for some time; being in a war zone doesn't help.

168

This thing must stop *now* — which means stopping the duplicates run by your mountain cousins. Otherwise we'll never get Kim back together again.' Ace paused and was silent for some moments, turning an idea over in her mind. It was far out — but then, wasn't she already in looking-glass land?

'Now listen,' she said. 'you're going to tell me about all the resources you have and all the help we can expect and everything about duplicates and the mountain Shenn. Then we are going to make plans.'

Chapter 23

Quillon sat down in the empty chair of the simulation department. All hands were on repair duties, of course. His investigating 'team' found seats and watched with interest as he called up options and parameters on the main computer. 'Yes, I think I understand these,' he said. He opened the interface with the main ship's computer and loaded the information gleaned about the black ship into the system.

Various images of the ship appeared, caught in the brief moments it had been visible when its screens were resisting the *Broadsword*'s bombardment. Ancillary technical data recorded in those brief moments flashed onto secondary screens.

Chiminoe whistled. 'Even now I can't see anything but an outline: there's no sense of it being three-dimensional at all.'

'All warships have dark, non-reflective surfaces,' said York. 'I suppose the duplicates have gone one better.'

'I can combine the images,' said Quillon, 'and synthesize a probable surface configuration from the different angular views we have of it.' He played on the controls. A blurred, angular shape appeared, as though several forms had been overlaid.

'Is that it?'

Quillon frowned. 'Its surface changed shape as we fought it,' he said incredulously. 'Look, there it had extruded something almost like a tail structure. but in the next view it's gone.'

'Neat trick,' admitted Chiminoe. 'Makes sense, too.' He looked at the others. 'A ship's exhaust flare is trackable at high velocity. The black ship would be no use if you could detect its drive and thruster nozzles, which I guess would still be warm even when the power was off. So maybe they've got something that acts as highly mobile baffles to shield them when they're side on to us, then close over them entirely like a . . . What's the word?'

'Sphincter?' suggested Strek.

'That's it. The stuff, whatever it is, would have to move fast, but I don't see that it's impossible.' The others considered the idea.

'Well, I would still like to see what the core of the ship is like; I assume that is constant,' said York. 'Inspector, can you subtract the, uh, "skin" to show the solid parts?' Quillon nodded. The images appeared to fade away, leaving a single stable wire-frame model, rotating slowly on the screen before them. They stared at the angular and irregular form.

'Rather an untidy looking thing,' observed Professor Strek. 'No lines to it. Looks almost as though it were put together out odd parts, like something a child might make from a construction set.'

Chiminoe smacked his hand to his forehead. 'Of course. Inspector, can you load up the external simulation of the skystation I made for the marines?' A second image appeared beside the black ship. 'There,' said Chiminoe, stabbing his finger from one image to the other. 'That's where the pieces of the station went! Look: power core there, spar there, ferry drive units angled out for manoeuvring around here, sensor array there. Those are reaction-mass tanks; energy cells. And that big drive stack at the tail is −'

'Those drive rings taken on the *Atlas*!' said York. 'Now we know where they got to.' She frowned. 'As Colonel Charters said, the duplicates took *exactly* what they wanted. Obviously they had been planning to build this well in advance. And they did it in what, seven, eight days?'

'But why go to the trouble?' asked Strek. 'They stole ready-made ships from us. Why build this as well?'

'For a start, it outperforms anything of its size,' returned Chiminoe. 'We learned that the hard way. It may look odd, but it's customized to serve a particular function: planetary defence. Look, no stardrives to carry around because it doesn't need them, so less dead weight, making it more manoeuvrable. Whereas its opposition − us − still carry them but can't use them close to a planet because of the gravitational gradient.'

'There is also,' Quillon said quietly, 'something else this black ship seems to lack which may also account for its surprising

171

performance.' They all stared at him. 'Well,' he continued, 'it has no life-system or control modules, does it? It has no provision for carrying *any* crew.'

The aircar with the military markings drifted over the forest on whispering jets, its twin side-mounted energy cannons angled downwards, following the sweep pattern of antennae rotating within its nose scan-dome. As the sky flushed with sunset, the car completed a five kilometre track and made a long banking turn to begin the next one.

When the sound of its jets had completely faded, shapes moved out of concealment from the hollows of trees roots and bushes, throwing off their thermal camouflage blankets and tying them back over their packs. The Lieutenant waited until the platoon had reassembled. 'Okay, that was good. But stay alert in case it makes another pass during the night. IR visors down now. We can make another couple of hours until camp.'

There was a distinct groan from one of the specialist members of the company, raising a few light chuckles from the professionals. They formed up into close-country advancing order again and in moments had disappeared into the growing gloom beneath the trees.

The Factory, as Ace now thought of it, was a hive of activity; which, she decided, was a wholly appropriate metaphor.

Spread out on the floor around her were her kit, weapons and combat suit salvaged by the Shenn when they had found her. A little team of Shenn were pulling the things around so that she could examine them with her one good arm. 'No, that goes there. Yes, that's it.' The combat suit was being reassembled. They had cut it off her to treat her, now they said they could rebond it again. Ace thought it would be a good trick if they could manage it — but, she had to admit, they must have pretty clever tools to have removed it so neatly in the first place.

She looked around. Two extra vats had been installed in one corner and were even now being filled. Teams of Shenn were working around the room on the different projects she had initiated. Isn't it wonderful what you can do with a bit of cooperation, she thought.

'Ace,' said the Shenn voice, 'we have received a response from the nest we contacted to ask for aid.'

'Great. Will they help?'

'They will not participate directly, but they will supply what we ask for.'

'Well, that's better than nothing; more than you thought they'd do, anyway.'

'That is true. We believe your words . . . interested them. We relayed their meaning as accurately as we could.'

'I never knew I had it in me to stir the people.' She twisted around to look at the vats. Shapes were already beginning to form in the ones next to those that held Kim and Ostman. 'Are they . . . growing okay?'

'They will be ready when we planned. But, Ace, this is not the way it is done.'

'It's never too late to change; look on it as a learning experience. You've been stuck in a rut on this planet for years. Now it's a very nice rut to be in, and you've got everything running smoothly and if it was up to me I'd say good luck and keep on as you are. But it isn't up to me. There's a big universe out there and it's knocking at your door and you've got to start thinking flexibly and be ready to change or you'll go under. Life isn't fair or just or kind, and sometimes you've got to fight simply to stay in the game.' She paused for a moment to take a sip of water.

'Remember earlier, when I woke up, you thought I was something from pretty low down the evolutionary scale to be packing all those weapons — I could feel it.'

'We were, cautious of you.'

'Understood. But you have to learn to distinguish between readiness to use force when you *have* to, and using force for the hell of it or to swipe something that doesn't belong to you. I don't mean that everybody should go around armed all the time: they don't on Tairngire and they seem to have a decent sort of life from what I've seen. But they are ready to fight if they are pushed.' She looked at Kim's body suspended in the vat. 'And pay the price. Well, like I said, life's not fair.'

'Ace, the message is about to be dropped to your friends.'

'Oh, fine. Those pet birds of yours have managed to keep

track of them okay, then?'

'We have used their kind for many years. They are perfectly capable of performing such tasks.'

'Hey, I just thought, what if the mountain Shenn are also using birds to look for the recon party?'

'It is unlikely. Since the influence of Umbra fell on them, they have turned in upon themselves, becoming more mechanistic in their thinking and using what you would call "domesticated" creatures far less. They have been using human duplicates and their aerial machines to search, so far without success.' The Shenn voice paused, then added, 'It seems that sometimes the old ways are still the more effective.'

Ace blinked in surprise, then chuckled. 'I think you're developing a sense of humour.'

'It must be the company we are keeping,' the voice replied. Ace would have laughed louder, but it hurt her ribs.

The glowing streamer fell out of the sliver of dark sky between the branches and into the middle of the platoon's encampment. There was a stirring as blankets were thrown back and weapons snatched up. But only the endless ranks of trees faced them and only the usual night sounds of the forest could be heard. The Doctor cautiously approached the streamer as it lay on the grass. What appeared to be a glowing marble was fastened to a long strip of filmy plastic-like material, on which was written in luminous letters:

TO: THE DOCTOR/ BENNY SUMMERFIELD/ NAT SANTONY/ PLATOON LEADER. HOPE THIS REACHES YOU SAFELY AND YOU'RE ALL OK. THIS IS BEING SENT BY LOCAL EQUIVALENT OF PIGEON POST – DIDN'T LIKE TO USE RADIO IN CASE OF EAVES-DROPPERS. HAVE TAKEN SOME KNOCKS BUT STILL PITCHING, SO IS KIM. MADE SOME NEW FRIENDS AND WORKING ON CUTTING THE OPPOSITION DOWN TO SIZE. IF YOU'RE HEADING FOR TOUCHSTONE AND KILNS, *BE CAREFUL*. DON'T KNOW WHAT THEY ARE YET, BUT PART OF SOME BIG PLAN. TAKE CARE. *Ace*.

Bernice, Santony and Paak were looking over his shoulder as the Doctor read the message. 'I knew she was too mean to get herself killed,' exclaimed Bernice. 'And Kim is with her — she must have ejected in time.'

'Why doesn't she say what she plans to do?' complained the Doctor. 'Really, she is quite impossible sometimes.' And he strode back to his bedroll with every sign of annoyance.

'He is really *very* relieved to get that message,' Bernice commented.

Santony laughed. 'Yeah, I know,' he agreed.

'So is it a drone ship?' wondered York.

'Could be,' agreed Chiminoe. 'Or completely automatic.'

'I thought it was considered too dangerous to make purely robotic warships?' said Strek.

'The duplicates may not think so,' countered York. 'Of course, in a way the ship might be seen as a duplicate in itself.'

'You mean these hypergems linked directly into the control systems? But is that possible? We know they can act as a mind link, but will they connect too with artificial electrical circuits?'

'I remember the Doctor suggested they could form part of a hyperwave transmission system,' York said thoughtfully.

'Then I could build you a control relay set up with them,' Chiminoe stated confidently. 'But that doesn't help answer the reaction-time question. Even allowing for instantaneous hyperspace transmission time, there would still have to be another interface at the other end, then allowing time for the little creatures to react. No, it still can't explain how they can react faster even than our ships *autonomous* systems. And if they had a computer that was so much better, then you wouldn't think they'd need to cobble up a spacecraft to carry it.'

There was a thoughtful silence. Then Strek said. 'We may be making an unwarranted assumption here. We know the creatures who built the duplicates are very capable bio-engineers; well perhaps they have created a specialized quasi-living form to control that craft, one that interfaces much more immediately with the hypergems.'

'If only we knew what it was made of,' remarked York.

'Almost pure carbon,' stated Quillon. They looked at him in surprise. 'There was spectrographic data recorded on the material vaporized from those hits — I don't think anybody on the ship has had time to look at them yet. I fed the data to an expert analysis programme from the main computer and it's just putting up the results now.' They watched the secondary screen he indicated.

'Should have known,' muttered Strek 'Carbon: most versatile element there is. Look, fullerine forms, spheres, helixes, the involutes . . . Tell me, Inspector, was there any energy discharge recorded in excess of that from the weapons?'

Quillon searched the data. 'Yes, definitely on two of the hits.'

'Charge carrying as well.' Strek rubbed his hands together. 'There is complexity enough for a synthetic form of life. And its surface is so hard to detect because it is formed in a micro-conical texture; super matt, you might call it, with an underlying charge to hold it together and perhaps negate other detector frequencies. I wish the Doctor could see this, he would find it fascinating.'

Chiminoe was nodding. 'Yeah, that makes sense. Wait a minute.' He looked thoughtful. 'We're saying this whole ship is run effectively by one, ah, controller?'

'That seems reasonable.'

'And we've got a pair of those hypergems the Doc made back home.'

'Yes,' confirmed York.

'Then thinking of something the Doc said when I asked him about the uses of these things, I think I can put together a gadget that might give a shock to anybody on a hypergem link.'

'Then go to it, Mister Chiminoe,' said York. 'The Captain would be very —'

'Wait a minute,' interrupted Quillon. 'The kilns on Arden, burning of trees, carbon. Could they be making *more* of this material?' They all paused for a moment.

'But think of the *scale* of the burning,' York said slowly. 'What can they want hundreds, thousands of tonnes of the material for?'

Chapter 24

'Doctor, those kiln structures are definitely bigger than when we saw them on the satellite pictures,' said Bernice.

The Doctor adjusted his position on the branch next to her and focused his field glasses. 'Yes, I believe they are,' he agreed after a moment's study.

They were sitting high in a great blue oak on a slight rise of ground, looking out through a rift in the foliage. The edge of the cleared area was now little more than a kilometre away. The shadows cast by the kilns were lengthening across the expanse of scarred earth and tree stumps as the afternoon drew to a close.

Paak, who was astride a branch on the other side of the trunk, said: 'According to my scope scale I make them as least twenty metres at the base now.' He looked across at the Doctor. 'How does a kiln grow? I don't see any bricks around.'

'I think these structures are a little more advanced than that,' he replied. 'It is not burning alone that is taking place inside them. Remember the infrared images? They have an internal structure far more complex than ordinary kilns. They are *processing* what they consume as well, and presumably storing the end product inside them.'

'But what *is* their end product?'

'That I don't know — yet.'

'However they're doing it, it's not surprising they've grown,' Santony growled. 'Look at how they're driving those poor bastards to keep 'em fed.'

They could clearly see the teams of colonists being driven by armed guards to drag branches from the expanding perimeter of the clearing to feed the ring of kilns, supplementing the larger trunks being hauled by a miscellaneous collection of military and civilian vehicles. 'They must be desperate to keep the supply going to resort to slave teams. Dammit! It's just really sinking in now. I must *know* many of those people down there: both the ones pulling logs, *and* the ones standing guard over them,' Santony said.

'If they're carrying guns,' Bernice said firmly, 'then they are *duplicates* — remember that.'

'I know it,' he responded thickly. 'But I can't *feel* it. I'm not sure how easy it's going to be to blast someone . . . something that looks exactly like a close friend. I'm not sure . . . '

'Sergeant Santony,' Paak said with iron in his voice, 'if it comes to it you *will* pull that trigger. It is your duty to *all* of those people down there. Do you understand?'

'Yes, Lieutenant, I hear you,' he replied dully.

'Doctor,' Bernice said, changing the subject, 'do you see that line leading away from the kilns and into a pool by the trees. I noticed it on the satellite view. Is it a trench? The pool it feeds looks like black mud.'

'Distillation wastes,' said the Doctor, after a moment's examination. 'If they are doing something akin to charcoal burning down there, which they certainly appear to be, then the by-products include turpentine, creosote, resin oil, a little methyl alcohol, pitch — all of which might contribute to that stream. They are probably burning off the inflammable gasses from the top vents on each kiln, but the rest they seem just to be throwing away, at least for the moment.' He trailed off, muttering to himself: 'Pool might be lined . . . charcoal . . . carbon . . . '

Bernice and Santony exchanged glances and suddenly grinned. They both had the same idea. 'Might be a useful diversion,' Bernice agreed, pleased that Santony had brightened.

There was a low call from below: 'Scouting party back from Touchstone, Lieutenant.'

They slid down the grapnel lines that had aided their ascent and into the half light of the forest floor. The party reported to Paak. The situation in Touchstone appeared unchanged, with the central dome still being watched. A forced labour party had been observed being taken back to a guarded outlying building to rest, while a fresh party was returned to the kiln site.

Paak unfolded the map display showing Touchstone and the

kilns and rested it against the tree trunk. They clustered round as he started marking in additions with the stylus. 'This was based on the last satellite info. The clearing has expanded now to about here.' He extended the perimeter line. 'The guards are still circling the main dome here; this building seems to be where they are housing the workers; and here's the pathway linking the clearing with Touchstone.' He looked at the ring of faces.

'My original orders were to scout the area, ascertain the strength of the enemy, locate weapons emplacements and prepare to sabotage them if feasible. Investigating the nature of the kilns was only a possibility. But that was when we had the rest of the task force in orbit above us. Now I must consider how to use the limited force at my disposal to do maximum damage to the enemy and delay his plans if possible until either the *Broadsword* or the rest of the fleet arrives.' He tapped the map. 'Now I've seen these kilns directly, and witnessed the obvious importance — for whatever reason — the enemy assigns to their continued functioning, there is no doubt where such action would have most effect. Do you agree. Doctor?'

'I hate to destroy what I don't understand, but yes, Lieutenant, that is the only possible target.'

'Right. Now we decide how.'

'Wake up Kim.' She was drowning . . . No —

It was her seventh birthday and her grandfather had given her a radio-controlled model plane. Delighted, she had flown the tiny craft — though it had seemed huge to her — around the garden, its micro-jets hissing merrily. The instructions had said that with practice you could make it fly a complete loop. Kim tried it after just five minutes. The plane crashed into the ground and came to pieces. She did not know that it was meant to break up and that it could easily be snapped back together again. She cried: she'd lost her wonderful plane and it was worse because it was from her grandfather, and he was somebody important as well, though she was not quite sure how. Tear-streaked, she had approached him. 'Sorry, Gran'pa —'

'Come on Kim, time to move.' Her chest was heavy.

She graduated from the Academy; she had her military pilot's wings. Her grandfather, *Marshal* Talevera, was waiting for her with her parents. 'No crack-ups this time, Grandfather −'

'Rise and shine.' She was choking.

She hit the *Mercury* at full boost, all her remaining missiles armed to swell the bang. She was not planning suicide, she was ready to eject just before impact, but she had to be *certain*. At accelerated thought speed she had plenty of time to realize she had left it just too late as the shockwave caught her. There would be tears again. 'Sorry, Gran'pa −'

'That's better. Cough it up, we've got work to do.'

Kim was coughing and spluttering and drawing in wonderful deep breaths of clear air. She blinked her eyes and her surroundings swam into focus: a softly lit room filled with pipes and tubes and containers, half partitioned by suspended sheeting. She could see organically formed machinery that seemed oddly out of scale, somehow. She was lying on something soft and spongy with Ace kneeling beside her. Ace was naked. She looked down: so was she. 'What is this,' she asked weakly, 'nudists' convention?'

Ace grinned. 'The tailors haven't quite finished our costumes yet.' She jerked a thumb in the direction of the sheeting, from behind which Kim could hear a rustle and patter of quiet sounds. 'Don't worry, skin doesn't matter round here.'

Kim sat up carefully. 'Would I regret asking where "here" is?' She frowned. Ace was watching her intently. 'Something wrong with me . . . Oh, dammit − the smash. Am I?' She touched her face, but there were no scars. The rest of her looked okay.

'How do you you feel?' Ace asked. 'I mean, inside.'

Kim climbed uncertainly to her feet, leaning on Ace's arm. 'Uh, well, fine I guess. Hell's teeth but I must have been lucky. How long have I been out?'

'Bit less than two days. Kim . . . you *weren't* lucky.'

Kim took a few experimental steps, looking about her in a puzzled way. 'What do you mean?'

'You were smashed up mega-bad; you almost didn't make it. I got pretty bust up myself: fell out of a tree, broken legs, arm and stuff, but nothing compared to you.'

Kim stared at her. 'And I suppose you just heal fast.'

'No, I'm still mending. Some way to go yet. So have you.

Look, I haven't got long to explain, we've got be moving in under an hour.' She took a deep breath. 'Kim, you're just going to have to trust me.' She tapped her chest. 'This body and yours are both duplicates.'

Bernice followed Santony's lead through the darkening forest, making sure she placed her feet exactly where he had stepped. He was good at this, she could tell.

He held up his hand for her to stop, swinging a detector to and fro before them. She waited patiently; they had been expecting traps. He stepped forward and drew a line in mid air, passing between two trees at waist height. She nodded. He crouched down and slid under the invisible beam. Bernice followed, trying to think of limbo dancers.

Once past the beam they continued their stealthy progress.

Kim stared at the body floating in the vat wreathed in tubes and wires. Even with the eyes covered she could see that it was Ace. The duplicate Ace beside her touched her shoulder. 'How do you think I felt when I first saw her, uh, me, I mean?'

Kim nodded dumbly, then pointed to the vat next to it which was draped with a sheet. 'And . . . I'm in there?'

'Yeah. Don't bother to look, you'd find it depressing. Wait until they've fixed you up some more.'

Kim swallowed. 'But you are sure there are none of these Shenn creatures inside us now. Inside *these* bodies, I mean?'

'None,' Ace replied positively 'We are, as you might say, independent duplicates. Like the ones they make of animals that don't need Shenn inside to control them, except we control *ourselves*, with a voluntary link to the nest mind. Actually, it was hard for the Shenn to accept. They don't like changing their ways, but I convinced them to − well, you'll see.'

'Okay. But how do they do it?'

Ace chuckled. 'You're lucky, you missed the yucky bit. I was awake. Not that it hurt, but knowing that a hole is being cut in the top of your head, however neatly . . . Anyway, they slip one of a pair of the hypergems into the middle of your brain and the other is already implanted in the duplicate they've grown. It's a sort of clone from your cells, with some plant hybrid organics thrown in — the Doctor could probably tell you how they manage that trick — and then you get into the vat. Well, they had to carry me in. And then you breathe in the fluid — it's something super-oxygenated — and then you *stop* feeling as though you need to breathe . . . '

'Must feel strange.'

'Fairly weird. Then with your eyes covered you're in sensory isolation, and you sort of wake up in the duplicate body. The process is obviously more complex than that, but I haven't had time to find out more details.'

'Hold on,' said Kim. 'If it takes over a day to grow a duplicate, how were all the substitutions made without arousing suspicions?'

'The same way they did it here for Ostman, I should think. Took two goes at it. Got a tissue sample one day: trick thorn or ''insect'' bite or something. Grew the duplicate. Then waited for the target to appear again, when they put him to sleep with gas and made the substitution. As soon as they got a few duplicates in charge they could probably use other methods; you can guess the sort of thing.'

Kim managed a shaky laugh. 'Just as long as there's not going to be two of me running around at the end of this.'

'That worried me at first, but apparently the duplicate brain just sort of resonates with the mind pattern transmitted through the hypergem. It doesn't *hold* any memory after the link is broken.'

Kim took a deep, deliberate, breath, just to reassure herself — she felt so, so *normal*. 'Okay, I believe you. Maybe you'd better fill me in on this plan of yours.'

'Right, but first you should meet our hosts, who have been considerate enough to wait out of sight until I clued you up.' Ace drew back the hangings — and Kim jumped. She had been prepared for a group of the little creatures whose pictures she had seen in the briefings, but Ace had neglected to warn her about the five two-metre tall Shenn waiting with them.

The platoon waited in the gloom of the forest. The sun was still up, but its low rays did not penetrate to the forest floor Lieutenant Paak consulted his watch; five minutes and they would be setting out. 'Final weapons check,' he instructed. He walked among them as they checked power cells, magazines and chamber actions, making a few light remarks to ease the tension, letting them know he was there. He stopped before the Doctor, who was staring with distaste at the preparations going on around him.

'We have to do this properly, Doctor, you know that. So we must take good care of the tools of our trade.'

'Even when your tools bring death?'

'We respect these weapons' abilities, Doctor, but we do not glory in their function. We are facing an enemy who will not hesitate to use their weapons, as we already have ample evidence to prove. I understand your obvious unwillingness to use weapons, but —'

'Oh no, Lieutenant,' the Doctor interrupted bitterly. 'You do not understand at all.' He sighed. 'I wish I was as pure as that. My problem is that I have used entirely too many weapons.' He gestured at Paak's own rifle. 'A Fleming Duo mark seventeen, twin barrel heavy assault rifle. A variable frequency energy projector ranging from stun to vaporize, with firing rates from pulse to continuous discharge. Underslung, a thirty-millimetre micro-grenade launcher, force powered, firing a range of projectiles including smoke, armour-piercing or high explosive . . . Need I continue? Lieutenant, that is an ingenious and awful piece of equipment, but it is a pea-shooter compared to the devices I have handled.'

He stared at the ground for a moment, then said bleakly: 'I once triggered a weapon that destroyed an entire world. And knowing it "had to be done" does not make the memory any easier to bear.'

Paak unconsciously stepped back from the little man. Suddenly there was something very frightening about him.

'You might have warned me that they'd made enlarged duplicates of themselves as well,' Kim admonished, again, as they dressed. She was donning a remarkable close copy of Ace's repaired combat suit, identical right down to the distinctively shaped helmet, thought it did not mimic all of the original's functions. But apparently she would not be needing them.

Sorry, Ace replied. Her lips did not move but Kim heard her clearly. All right, she told herself, it's just like the interface with my fighter computer. Well, almost. She glanced again at the vat holding her real body. A small Shenn creature was sitting motionless on the gantry-like structure slung across its open top, from which depended the life-support connections. Another creature was similarly stationed over Ace's vat. They formed a link, via their hypergem implants, for non-telepathic human minds to talk through the mind web of the nest. If she concentrated, she could hear the distant multiple whisper of the composite nest mind. Perhaps this is a dream, she thought. It's crazy. Maybe I'm crazy . . . She realized Ace was looking at her intently.

No, Ace told her firmly, *you are not crazy. I know this is far out — and believe me I'm an expert in far out experiences — but it is real. As the Doctor says, the impossible is only something that hasn't happened to you yet.*

They finished dressing and distributed Ace's salvaged weapons between them. Kim slung her copy of Ace's pack, loaded with the unusual armaments they were going to use against the mountain Shenn nest, realizing as she did so that the giant Shenn duplicates were also wearing packs. They followed the giant Shenn duplicates as they led them towards the surface, via the only passageway large enough for beings their size. Ace called it the goods entrance.

Kim looked about in fascination at the complex burrow of the nest and the busy, apparently indifferent Shenn multitudes swarming around her, then ran to catch up with the others and fell into step beside Ace. *All right,* she said, practising the paratelepathy, *I've got the general objective straight, but what about transport? As I understand it, we're about thirty kilometres from this mountain Shenn nest place. Are we going to walk?*

Transport's been laid on — wait and see.

The nest entrance was concealed by a reinforced stone slab that pivoted silently closed behind them as they passed through. They were standing on a wooded ridge of ground with the great Ardonian forest rolling away before them, the tree tops sinking into purple shadows as the crimson of sunset faded from the sky. Kim looked up. A few early stars were appearing through a tattered blanket of cloud. They could hope for more of that.

Ace drew in a deep breath of fresh air and exhaled loudly. *That feels good. Been under this planet for nearly two days but haven't set foot on its surface yet. At least, when I did touch ground, I was going too fast to appreciate it. Same with you I guess.*

They are coming. The deep, powerful, not quite toneless mind voice of the Shenn made Kim flinch; she hadn't got used to the 'sound' of it yet. One of their Shenn companions was pointing out across the tree tops. Kim peered in the direction indicated, aware that her eyesight was sharper than it had been, as Ace had warned her it would be. Why not treat this body like a fighter, augmented senses and all? she thought. This altered mind-set seemed to help and she focused her attention more easily. Yes, she could see something. Seven large birds were flying low over the trees towards them. Large birds — *very* large birds indeed.

Kim began to feel she was beyond surprise. *There appears to be a flock of miniature zeppelins with wings coming towards us. I would say their wingspan was about ten metres.*

That about sums them up, replied Ace. *They're our transport.*

I knew you were going to say that. I suppose natural selection played little part in their design.

That's right. They're bio-engineered transportation animals, on loan from another Shenn nest who specialize in building those kinds of creatures.

Kim watched in fascination as the beasts made their landings in a clearing in front of the nest entrance. They had no distinct heads or necks, their eyes being set on the forward end of their tubular, presumably gas-filled bodies. Their beaks did not appear to be hard, but flexible, somewhere between an anteater's snout and an elephant's trunk — not a beak belonging to a predator, she was pleased to note. The birds extended long legs with broad splayed feet and settled neatly onto the grass, folding back their huge wings in a complicated fashion, and regarding the party with large, slightly soulful eyes. Kim noticed what appeared to be bunches of tendrils hanging from the underside of their bodies.

Come on, said Ace.

How do we uh, steer them?
Telepathically. Don't worry, the Shenn'll do that.
And we ride them, do we? Kim said hopefully.
No. See those tentacle things . . .

Chapter 25

Robson himself drove the ground truck carrying the latest load of hypergem ore down the track to the ferry pad. He was feeling the satisfaction of a job well done. Two ferry loads of ore had been the target for this first phase of the operation, and they had made it with a few hours to spare. For a moment he felt a twinge of guilt, but it was hastily buried. Yes, there had been losses, but that was necessary for . . . Odd that he couldn't quite remember what for. Something important, something *good* for Arden, he was sure. Otherwise he wouldn't be working on it — would he?

As he turned onto the side track leading to the pad and saw the lights of the waiting ferries, he looked across at Rusty squatting in the passenger seat. 'We've done well, haven't we, boy,' he said, trying to reassure himself. The bushtail regarded him with bright, intelligent eyes.

I'm a *pilot*, Kim kept telling herself. I really ought to be taking this better; after all, I'm not that high. She watched the tree tops roll past below, and sometimes beside, her. She felt that if she reached out she could almost pick leaves from some of the more isolated branches. Fifty kilometres an hour was nothing for a spacepilot, she thought, but suprisingly impressive when experienced whilst hanging beneath a hedge-hopping giant pseudo-bird.

She tried to relax within the lattice of tendrils that supported her, wishing the animal looked more substantial. The body of the creature was slightly translucent, as were its wings, so she could see the shadowy outline of its skeleton. The bones must be incredibly light, she thought, and the muscles amazingly strong. Nothing this size should be ably to fly *and* carry my weight. Aerodynamically this is unbelievable. Maybe I'm dreaming —

You're thinking out loud again, Ace's mind voice said. *This is all real, merely very, very improbable. Don't forget or we might really end up dead.*

But even if something happens to these bodies, our actual bodies will be okay. We'll just wake up in them again, won't we?

Yeah, but as I understand it, getting your duplicate body killed is the hard way of doing it. So I'm going to try not to get careless. Now look sharp, we're getting near the target.

Over the trees, in the last glow of twilight, Kim's augmented vision could make out the mass of the forest breaking against the foothills of the Phebe Range.

Bernice and Santony crouched behind a tree ten metres from the edge of the clearing. The radiance of work lights was slatted by the ranked trunks and faded into the darkness of the forest behind them. They could hear the hum of engines, the swish and crack of branches, and the terse, toneless orders to the labourers. To their right a power cutter buzzed sharply then stopped. There was a rush and crash as another tree came down.

Santony consulted his watch, then touched his helmet to hers. 'One minute,' he whispered. She nodded.

To their left, under the trees, a stream glistened blackly in the reflections of the worklights. The air was heavy with the vapour of tar and spirit. The stream was the overflow of the pool in the clearing, which was fed in turn from the discharges of the kilns. Some attempts had clearly been made to dam the lower side of the pool to reduce the seepage. Bernice remembered the Doctor muttering about the pool. Was its contents needed for later? She wished the Doctor would be more open about his suspicions.

'Ten seconds,' whispered Santony. Bernice clutched her small incendiary grenade tightly.

Lyn Sorren watched the branch she had just helped haul being fed into one of the smaller coal-red orifices in the base of the kiln. She eased the rope harness about her shoulders. Only time for one more before the end of the shift, she thought, then longed-for rest. She had become practised at judging these things over the last few days.

No, no, no, she told herself. Get a grip. Life has not resolved into simply working and sleeping. You're a scientist; observe and keep alert, be ready to take a chance if you can. She thought of the others who had tried to run. No one she knew of had yet escaped. Her shoulders dropped. She looked at the branch disappearing into the kiln, shielding her eyes against the furnace radiance, and saw again that as it was almost inside, it seemed to be *pulled* from the hands of the feeders.

This is a nightmare. And there's no way —

With a rush and thump, the overflow pool burst into flame. She watched a tongue of blue and yellow fire race along the stream towards the kilns, setting the grass along its edges crackling merrily. It reached the point where the overflow pipes from each kiln opened into its roughly dug channel and licked about their ends, igniting the flammable vapour trapped insde them and making little popping explosions.

Overseers ran forward and kicked earth over the end of the trench. One of the makeshift pipes came away from its plug point in the kiln side and both ends started to burn. Orders were shouted to the working teams to quench the fires. She ran forward, kicking and scraping at the earth with every show of enthusiasm, trying to splash the burning stream further across the grass. She found herself laughing. It was a dangerous, ridiculous game, but if *they* wanted to put out the fire for whatever reason, then she wanted the opposite. For the first time in days, she felt she was fighting back in some small way. Then she realized that the guards were also trying to put out the fire — and that there seemed to be more of them than she had thought.

The guard beside her had frozen for an instant, staring at the battle-suited figure opposite him, and the other man levelled his rifle and shot an energy bolt through the guard's chest.

'All workers get down!' an amplified voice bellowed across the clearing. Sorren dropped to the ground. Beams and energy bolts cracked and hissed over her head, and grenades thumped and cracked. Somebody was screaming. A guard was firing one-handed — her other arm was gone — then a stream of energy bolts crashed into her chest, lifting her off the ground, tearing her apart in midair. Sorren shut her eyes and scrabbled forward, half on her belly, half on hands and knees, trying to find some shelter.

Suddenly there were roots under her hands and she pressed against a broad tree stump — and there was a small, battle-dressed figure kneeling beside her. He made a strange gesture, as though raising an invisible hat. 'Hello,' he said, 'I'm the Doctor.'

Robson felt the wave of panic strike as they were loading the ferry. For a moment they all seemed to stumble, feeling loss and pain — not their own, but shared. The disruption of the order. The unexpected. From the direction of the workings he heard shots. Someone had taken advantage of that brief distraction. A rising clamour of shouts came from the camp domes, then more energy weapon discharges. Then order reasserted itself in his mind and he *knew* once more what had to be done. He started heaving at the crates of ore.

The 'birds' landed silently amid the shadowy forms of the evergreens that dotted the hillside. Their passengers slipped out of the embrace of their carrying tendrils and vanished into the darkness.

Ace could feel the knowledge of 'her' nest mind guiding her steps as they headed towards one of the entrances to the Umbra Shenn nest. It beats memorizing plans, she thought.

The giant Shenn duplicates moved silently with a naturally hunched, slightly bounding run. It looked odd, but it covered the ground. After a few minutes they halted behind a pile of rounded boulders. *Beyond this,* said the Shenn mind voice. Ace nodded.

Kim stepped up beside her. *Ready?* Kim had her blaster ready. *Yeah, let's do it,* Ace replied.

They stepped into the open. Ace shouldered the launcher and fired an armour-piercing missile at the very centre of the apparently blank slope of rock and scrub before them.

Beams and bolts of energy hissed and cracked across the ferry pad. One of the guards fell; the other two dived for cover and started to return fire. Robson heaved at the last container of ore and almost fell into the cargo hold. Rusty sprang in after him and the hatch started to close. He ran forward through the linking airlock and into the control cabin, impelled by the absolute need to get the cargo to the kiln site on time. Then? No, nothing mattered beyond then.

The pilot was punching buttons. Robson heard the force jets start up. There was a crack — a fused hole appeared in a panel of the cabin window. The pilot jerked back in his seat, a seared hole in his forehead. The stench of burned flesh filled the cabin. Robson hauled him clear and took his seat. He had flown nothing larger than an aircar before, but somehow the knowledge he required was there. The other ferry lifted off with blasting jets. He heard shots striking the craft; another hole appeared in the window; and they were off, jets howling, the landing pad lights falling away below them.

Robson banked and headed out across the forest.

Sorren tried to take in the scene around her whilst answering the Doctor's insistent questions about the growth of the kilns. The site was veiled in a slowly drifting haze of smoke, lit by the work lights and the still burning tar stream. Bodies littered the ground and dazed workers stumbled amongst them. A line of Marines covered the entrance of the track from Touchstone, while others were moving purposefully from kiln to kiln, laying demolition charges.

A man and woman, also in combat dress, appeared out of the smoke, calling for the Doctor.

'Hello, Benny, Sergeant,' he replied absently, tapping the black swelling curve of a kiln. 'Thanks for the diversion. This is Lyn Sorren, Touchstone's science coordinator. She's been telling me about the kilns.'

The man lifted his blast visor. 'Hello, Doctor Sorren.'

She blinked at him for a moment. 'Sergeant . . . Santony? Thank God you've come back. It's been a nightmare.' It was the simple truth, she realized as she spoke.

'Doctor!' the woman with Santony said with exasperation. 'It doesn't matter now, they'll be blowing them up any minute. We've got to get clear!'

'But we must know *what* we're destroying,' he complained, sounding petulant.

'Tell us later,' said Santony. 'Now we move.' Sorren ran with them, stumbling, exhausted. The Doctor took one arm, the woman the other. Energy bolts cracked from the direction of the track. The Marines returned fire. 'Get down!' the Sergeant commanded. 'Keep low. Head for the forest.'

They were crawling forward when the Doctor suddenly stopped and rolled on his back, looking up into the night. 'I can hear something.' There was the rising note of powerful force jets. A flare of light appeared and a jet-wash blasted the smoke away and sprayed the remains of the fire stream over the turf. A huge shape was dropping out of the night into the clearing.

Santony shouted over the scream of the downrushing air: 'It's the *Atlas*!'

The Umbra Shenn nest was like the one Ace had woken up in, but much more extensive. They ran along the main thorough-fares, the Shenn scuttling away before them into their side galleries and burrow holes. Seven Gullivers invading Lilliput, Ace thought.

She and Kim fired at anything that looked threatening, throwing occasional micro-grenades down side tunnels. Their Shenn duplicate companions dispensed their long-range arma-ments. Grenades issuing a fine dust and drifting vapour were methodically cast into chambers and passengers as they passed them. They were the Shenn equivalent of tear gas and itching power. The nest mind had assured her that nothing would better disrupt the concentration of the Umbra Shenn — itching was a serious business for a furred animal.

Ace headed on in the direction in which her new knowledge told her the duplicating chambers lay.

The spray of dirt and debris thrown up by the *Atlas*'s landing fell to ground; the sound of its jets died. Its great splayed landing pads sank deep into the earth. Bernice raised her head from behind a sheltering tree stump. A port opened up high in the craft's side and a mounted heavy-calibre blaster rifle started picking off the Marines. They stared returning fire. More shots came from the direction of the track.

Bernice started firing at the ship, trying at least to disturb their aim. Santony was crouched beside her. Below his visor she could see a mirthless grin. He snapped off a couple of shots at the ship gun. 'Crossfire gauntlet if we break for the trees, or go up with the kilns if we hang around,' he shouted over the gunfire. 'Do you want to choose?'

'Well at least it can't get worse,' replied Bernice. A hatch in the *Atlas*'s side opened, a ramp unfolded and an armoured personnel carrier rolled out, its turret-mounted blaster swinging towards them. 'On the other hand . . .'

Ace stared at row upon row of bodies floating in isolation vats. Most were human, but some contained animals and a few things she couldn't even describe. The Umbra Shenn's duplication chamber was *big*. And over each vat sat a Shenn creature, linking the mind of the body below with its duplicate.

Okay, she said, *let's break some concentration here.* The Shenn behind her threw a tear-gas grenade.

Bernice saw the APC swerve, it's blaster fire going wild. It bounced crazily over a tree stump and slewed to a halt. The ship's gun stopped. The fire from the guards along the Touchstone track petered out.

Bernice put her head cautiously over the top of the stump, looking about her. 'Was it something I said?'

The door of the armoured vehicle swung open and a figure lurched out, dropping to the ground on all fours, rolling over, twitching feebly. Santony levelled his rifle, but the Doctor's commanding voice rang out: 'No! They're harmless.' He was on his feet, waving his hands in calming gestures to the rest of the Marines. 'It's all right now, their control's gone,' he said clearly. Lieutenant Paak ran over to them.

'Are you sure, Doctor?' he said, looking suspiciously at the figure beside the APC.

Bernice suddenly laughed loudly. 'This is Ace's doing — she's thrown a spanner in somebody's works, mark my word.' A second soldier appeared at the door of the vehicle, seeming dazed but on her feet. 'She's still going,' said Bernice.

'The shock of losing their controllers will affect them in different ways,' the Doctor said confidently, walking towards the confused figure, the others trailing after him.

'Soldier!' Lieutenant Paak spoke with parade-ground authority. 'Report to me.'

The soldier saluted by reflex. 'Trooper Flyn, Lieutenant. I don't understand what has been happening . . . ' She trailed off, looking hopelessly about her. Bernice stepped forward, searching for the best explanation to give, when a movement caught her eye. The chest of the duplicate soldier fallen beside the APC was twitching and pulsing unnaturally. She spun round. The chests of all the duplicate bodies she could see were doing the same. The controllers were trying to leave their hosts.

Robson could see the lights of the clearing and the squat, truncated cone of the *Atlas* before him when he felt the panic. Many voices seemed to be calling out in the back of his mind, their words just beyond his understanding, but their underlying message clear. Disturbance! Confusion! Order failing . . .

For a moment he sat rigidly in the pilot's seat, locked in fearful terror of losing something quite alien but infinitely precious. And then a tiny but vital link seemed to snap.

His memory of the last few days lay clear before him, with nothing to twist its meaning. He knew what he had done had been madness. It was a lie. It was not for Arden at all. The alien touch had left him, and he knew what he must do. The other ferry was ahead of him. He banked towards its, accelerating. Whatever their cargo was intended for, he could ensure it did not reach its destination.

The bushtail was squatting of its haunches beside his seat. 'Sorry, Rusty,' he said. He straightened the craft, the display projected on the windscreen showing the outline of the second ferry swelling before them — and Rusty sank his teeth into Robson's wrist, pulling his hand off the joystick. Robson saw the unnatural light in the creature's eyes and shouted in rage: 'Not him *too*! It's not fair. He's only a pet.' He grabbed at the stick with his other hand and pushed it forward.

The two ferries smashed together and fell out of the sky.

* * *

Flyn writhed and kicked on the ground. The Doctor grasped her head and turned her to him. 'Look only at me,' he commanded. 'Hear only me. You will feel nothing.' Her chest heaved unnaturally. Bernice fumbled at the fastenings of Flyn's flak jacket. Santony suddenly understood and helped. Bernice tore open the seal of Flyn's tunic top; Santony pulled a knife from his belt and ripped open her singlet.

A line had appeared from her sternum halfway to her navel. As they watched, the lips of flesh parted bloodlessly, a tiny dexterous hand appeared, then a furry head. Paak swore fluently. Then the whole creature was clear of its host and scuttling away across the grass in a half stooping, bounding run. Around them in the clearing, other small creatures were squirming free of their hosts' clothes and hopping and bounding away into the darkness.

Bernice hesitantly pressed the sides of the wound together, and found they seemed to rebond as they touched. In a moment there was only a faint line left, like an old scar. Flyn stopped struggling. The Doctor released her head and smiled. 'There now, that was better out than in, wasn't it?'

'Doctor!' exclaimed Bernice. 'That was awful.'

'Lieutenant!' Sergeant Ashton was standing by one of the kilns, pointing. 'This thing's starting to crack open.' The Doctor locked eyes with Paak for one moment of understanding, then they were hauling the still confused Flyn to her feet and Bernice could hear Paak's orders over her helmet radio.

'Clear the area! Take any duplicates who are alive with you; they're not dangerous anymore. Head for Touchstone.'

The Marines, a few stumbling and confused duplicate guards and overseers and a ragged company of labourers, ran for the track. Paak was in the rear, checking the last had got clear. A hundred metres down the track he shouted: 'Everybody down!' He dropped flat himself, pulled the remote detonator from his pocket and pressed the button.

The entire clearing seemed to explode.

Chapter 26

There was little room in the sensor module compartment. Stirling and Chiminoe crouched over a sensor projector array, installing a complex piece of equipment of makeshift appearance to a two-metre projector dish. Finally, Stirling straightened up and glanced enquiringly at Chiminoe, who nodded. 'Yes, I think that's it. It'll probably burn out the whole assembly when it's activated, but there's nothing we can do about that.'

Stirling communicated with the bridge. 'Kindly inform the Captain that Mister Chiminoe's device is as ready as it ever will be.'

Captain Kausama turned back to Quillon, York and Strek. 'As I was saying, thank you for your efforts. At least we know something of what we are up against now. With what you have deduced about the black ship, our experience from our first encounter — and Mister Chiminoe's device, of course — we have a fighting chance next time.'

Quillon smiled. 'Well, it wasn't exactly the kind of detective work I had envisaged when I came on this mission. I just hope it proves useful. But we can't take credit for Mister Chiminoe's invention.'

'As I understand it, Inspector, it was jointly inspired by your discussions and something the Doctor told him. However it is, we'll know if it all works a few hours from now.'

Ace looked about with satisfaction at the duplication room. All the Shenn were gone from their posts above the isolation vats; hiding in confusion and some discomfort in their burrows, no doubt. In the back of her mind she could just 'hear' their myriad fragmented mentalities buzzing and twittering in the deepest recesses of the nest. Yes, a good neat job, she thought.

She turned to the giant Shenn duplicate waiting patiently beside her. *Now, you're sure they can't take control of the duplicates again, or try to kick us out of here or anything?*

We are quite sure, Ace. Do not worry, this nest will not recombine its higher mind structures for some days.

And have you heard anything from Mister 'Voice-from-the-sky' Umbra about all this? No rude comments from above?

We hear nothing. It is possible it has turned its attention away from this nest.

Okay, we'll have to leave that for now. She indicated the rows of suspended bodies. *How are they taking reality?*

Some are badly shocked by the death experience of their duplicates; it is best that they sleep. Some are still with their duplicates, but unbalanced by the realization; they should be attended to as soon as possible. A few are coping with their situation. Ace, you humans exhibit such varied reponses to the same situation.

It comes with the original specifications, I guess. Okay, can you sort of keep an eye on things here? Kim?

I hear you Ace. This level's clear.

Fine. I'm going up top to try to contact the Doctor or somebody — they should be started on the mopping-up by now.

The patter of falling debris faded away into the night. Bernice cautiously raised her head, brushing twigs from her helmet, and looked towards the clearing. All the work lights had gone out and the only illumination came from the track-side beacons behind her. She switched her visor to image intensify and the clearing partially resolved itself into a smoke-filled hollow. Had the kilns — and whatever they contained — been destroyed? She turned to thermal imaging, piercing through the drifting smoke. She could dimly see the bulk of the *Atlas* on the far side of the site and a swathe of still-hot fragments around the perimeter, but the distinctive beehive forms had gone. She heard someone laugh in relief.

A woman's anguished sobbing cut through the night. Bernice turned to see one of the labourers kneeling beside the form of a very dead duplicate. Lyn Sorren got stiffly to her feet and went over to her. 'No, Holly, that's *not* him.' Bernice heard her try to explain the improbable truth. There is going to have to be a lot more of that, she thought, and it's not going to be easy.

As she got to her feet, she noticed the Doctor. He was stalking forward in a curious manner, peering intently towards the clearing. Bernice frowned and followed his gaze, switching back to thermal imaging. In the center of the clearing, where the kilns had been, there was something . . .

The Doctor spun round and raced back towards them. 'Everybody on your feet! Make for Touchstone. Move!'

'What is it, Doctor?' demanded Paak.

'We were too late, they had already become self-sustaining. Now get everybody clear.' The urgency in his words permitted no further questions. Paak started issuing orders and confused survivors started retreating, urged on by the Marines.

Bernice was staring in horrified fascination at the clearing, where a black shadow seemed to be rolling across the ground towards the mouth of the track, building up speed. The Doctor grasped her arm. They turned and raced towards the tail guard of marines. She realized that Sorren was still beside the anguished woman, trying to get her on her feet, but the woman seemed beyond reason. The Doctor grabbed Sorren and hauled her up. Bernice tried to lift the woman but she jerked free, eyes stark and wide, clinging to the duplicate's body. Santony and a Marine ran back to help. Bernice looked over her shoulder: the shadow was on the path and bearing down on them, washing over the track-side beacons as it came, blinking them out. It was half a metre deep and it rustled and whispered as it rolled over the ground. The thought that shadows should be silent flashed through her mind. Bernice tugged at the hysterical woman. The soldiers levelled their rifles.

'Fuse the edges with your beams,' shouted the Doctor. 'It's the only way to slow it down.'

The beams lashed out and the matt-black wave glowed redly as they struck, its substance fusing and cracking, glowing shards falling away. The mass swirled behind the leading edge, extruding a tendril that arched into the air over their heads. A bolt of electricity cracked from its tip. The Marine was knocked off his feet, outlined in blue fire. Santony burned through the tendril and it fell back, reabsorbed in the body of the shadow. The thing rolled forward again over the charred fragments of its skin. 'Run!' bellowed the Doctor to Santony. 'You can't stop it.'

The Doctor was beside Bernice, dragging the woman up, starting to run her along between them. She started to scream. Santony was beside them, firing back at the wave that poured after them, enveloping the body of his companion. The woman suddenly tore free of them, turned and fell. The black wave washed over her.

Energy bolts and micro-grenades whistled dangerously close as the main body of the Marines turned to fire at the shadowform. It slowed a little; they gained some ground, Bernice running as hard as she had ever done. You were right, Ace, she thought: those jogging sessions in the gym were needed. They reached the Marines and together they pounded on down the track. Behind them the beacons blinked out inexorably, one by one.

Ace stood on the hillside above the gaping hole that now marked the entrance to the Shenn nest. She keyed her suit radio into the Marines' frequency. 'Hi there,' she said. 'Ace calling. Doc, Benny, Nat — how's everything?'

The trees thinned and they ran out into the open ground that sloped gently down to the bank of the Titania River. Lights picked out the domes of Touchstone and figures moving cautiously around them. The figures fell back uneasily as the crowd of panting, stumbling people appeared out of the night.

'It's all right,' Sorren called out breathlessly, 'they're friends.'

They reached the outer domes. A few people came forward to greet them. Paak addressed them: 'I am Lieutenant Paak of the Arden Expeditionary Force. Please stay where you are. Sergeant?' Ashton stepped forward, swinging the beam of the duplicate detector across the group. Bernice noticed other Marines covering him. They've rehearsed this, she thought, and they're not taking any chances.

'There's no need for this,' said the Doctor impatiently. 'What happened here was the same as at the kilns: the ones who had taken over collapsed. Some are dead; Some mad; a few terribly

199

confused. You saw creatures come out of their chests, yes?'
Nobody contradicted him.

'Now, how many people have you here and what transport is available — shuttles, aircars, boats? It won't be safe here very shortly.'

Paak interjected, 'Will that thing follow us, Doctor?'

'At least one of them will, possibly all twelve. It depends how much of a threat it perceives us as.' He turned to Sorren 'Well, how many and what transport? You can help too,' he said, pointing to a still dazed Flyn. They went into a huddle. Paak was ordering a watch to be kept on the edge of the forest. Bernice felt at a loss for a moment, then she saw Santony gesturing to his ear. She switched her radio on.

' . . . anybody hear me? Come on guys —'

'Hello, Ace, we can hear you now.'

'Well where have you been?' Ace responded impatiently.

'Oh, just breaking the Arden all-comers record for the fifteen-hundred-metres dash over difficult ground whilst being pursued by an animated killer shadow thing that popped out of the kilns.' She paused for breath, wondering how she could sound so flippant.

'So, not quite over yet then?'

'That happy state still eludes us.'

'About the usual in fact, huh?'

'You could say that.'

'Are the Doc and Nat okay?' Bernice could hear the half concealed concern in Ace's voice.

'Nathan's here; the Doctor's organizing things.' Bernice looked over at him. 'There is no justice: he doesn't even look winded. I hope I'm that fit at his age. How are you — and Kim?'

'You could say I'm not feeling myself and Kim's about the same, otherwise fine. Look, we thought we'd got the duplicate problem corked at this end, so what's this new thing?'

'I think the Doctor knows but, as usual, he's forgotten to elucidate. I'll try to put him on, then he can explain it to all of us at the same time.'

'Great. I've got some info for him too.'

Paak had joined the Doctor, Flyn and Sorren. 'With only one aircar and two flightpacks we cannot evacuate in time,' the

Doctor stated. 'We can risk proceeding on foot and hope that it loses interest, but you know what our position would be like in open country if it maintained its pursuit. Remember, it will not get tired. Here we have a defensive position we can sustain for some days, with luck. But can we hold out until reinforcements arrive? Both options have their drawbacks.'

'That is an understatement,' Paak remarked dryly. He considered for a moment. 'We'll stay. Doctor Sorren, move everybody and all the supplies you can into the central dome complex. Sergeant Ashton . . . ' The walkways between the main and outer domes rapidly filled with hurrying people. Bernice got the Doctor's attention and put him in contact with Ace.

'Listen up, Doc, − I've got the inside line on what's been happening here . . . '

The Doctor appeared delighted with Ace's news. 'Of course, of course,' he kept repeating.

'But, Doctor,' said Santony, 'what *are* these shadow things?'

'Tools, devices, cat's-paws −' The Doctor gestured wildly. '− puppets, servants of this Umbra entity. Just as the duplicates were tools of these Shenn people, so they were *its* tools.' He gazed blankly into space. 'Until they had fulfilled their function . . . '

'But *physically*, what are they?' demanded Bernice.

He looked at her in surprise. 'Why, what you would expect them to be, considering their origins: mainly carbon, plus certain impurities of course. Heat, electricity, wood combusting under controlled conditions − directed by a hypergem "seed" no doubt, brought in with the original kilns. Carbon is the most versatile element, you know. Under certain conditions it can form very unusual structures, and some of these can conduct and store charge. Building blocks, you see, for synthetic life forms. Remember the "black ship" the *Broadsword* reported; well that was probably a similar form made from pre-existing material.'

Ace's voice cut in. 'But what *for*?'

'Why, to grow and spread of course. What more basic drive is there?' The thoughtful silence that followed was broken by a blaze of light from the forest. A tongue of red fire licked upwards into the sky, throwing a section of the intervening trees into stark silhouette. As they watched, a second fire started beside it. They could hear the distant rush and crackle of the burning trees. 'It's started, I'm afraid,' said the Doctor. 'The shadowforms do not need kilns any more. They'll convert the new material when they're ready and spread and burn again.'

'But how much to they, it — Umbra, want?' asked Bernice. 'Who knows? Perhaps all the trees on Arden.'

Chapter 27

Kausama felt the power to the *Broadsword*'s star drive cut out, and real space shimmered into being around them. Arden's sun was a distant brilliant disc, while Arden itself was a mere speck of light to her telescopic sight.

Right, this time we're coming after *you*, she thought.

The ship got under way.

'Touchstone calling Oberon. Science Officer Sorren calling. Come in Oberon . . . '

The screen lit to show the pinched and unshaven face of the Oberon operator. What could be seen of his shirt was torn and grimy. Don't suppose I look much better myself, thought Sorren. 'Officer Sorren, is it really you?' the man asked hesitantly.

Sorren grunted. 'I can understand your doubt, if you've experienced the same as us. But help has arrived. Now, can you put me through to O'Valle?'

'No. He was one of them that . . . changed. He's dead. And something came out of his chest — and the others, and some of them are mad . . . '

'All right,' Sorren cut in firmly but gently. The operator seemed on the verge of a breakdown himself. 'Then who else senior is left? I have important instructions for them.'

'Is it to do with the fires? We can see them from here.'

'Yes, and other matters. Now, who is there?'

'Well, there is Mister Jefferson from the skystation. He was brought down here to work in the mine and now he's helping organize things. Then there's Doctor Amphipolis . . . '

'Either of them, please, as quickly as you can. You'll be receiving some unusual visitors shortly, and I want you to be prepared for them.'

From a gallery, Bernice watched the main hall of the central dome fill with colonists and salvaged stores and equipment. She saw Santony greet some people, obviously old garrison or colonial acquaintances. He must have mixed feelings, she thought, but at least he's among friends again. As she tried to spot the Doctor amidst the throng, she noticed there were some figures who were trying to press into corners out of the way, shying clear of the glances of hate, puzzlement or pity the others were casting towards them. They were the surviving duplicates. Lyn Sorren was going round to them, Bernice realized, presumably to offer comfort or explanations. But what good were words against the guilt they must be suffering, however blameless they actually were?

Beside her, Trooper Flyn was looking in the same direction. 'She won't stop us feeling gutted about what we've done,' she said in a dull voice, echoing Bernice's thoughts. '*I* still remember what I did, most of it anyway.'

'How does it feel?' asked Bernice.

'What? To behave like a nutter or to be inside a copy of myself?'

'Well, both I suppose,' Bernice said, with what she hoped was a sympathetic smile.

Flyn sighed, then tapped her chest. 'This just feels like me – real. It would have to be if you think about it, else the trick wouldn't work. As to what I did, *that's* frightening. Everything seemed so bloody reasonable. I mean, I remember searching for your friend in the park back home and, except for a moment when I wondered why we were after her, it was just the job, you know: what we were trained for and all proper and correct.' She looked troubled. 'I think you can get people to do anything to anybody, as long as they think it's the right thing to do. Not having any doubt and uncertainty just, *knowing*. Believe me, it's easy to go along with.'

Bernice led the way around the gallery, trying find the Doctor in the confusion. Why wouldn't he answer his helmet radio? Flyn followed her, asking hesitantly: 'This sounds odd, but can I stay around with you and the Doctor? I don't know if the Marines'll want me close to them yet, and none of the rest of my unit made it and I want to help, and I think you and your friend are the ones who really count at this moment . . . ' She trailed off, looking embarrassed.

'Of course you can,' responded Bernice, trying to sound as welcoming as possible. She glanced at Flyn's rifle, which the young soldier had been clutching firmly to her since she had arrived. 'In fact, you can help me keep an eye on the Doctor. He's sometimes careless about his own safety, you know? Usually it takes both Ace and myself to watch out for him, but with her doing her bit up in the hills . . . '

Flyn looked relieved and almost smiled for the first time.

They almost ran into the Doctor coming out of a room on the gallery level. He was talking earnestly to a colonist in engineer's coveralls who had a large coil of wire slung over his shoulder. The man nodded and headed for the stairs to the lower levels. 'Doctor,' Bernice said reproachfully, 'why can't you keep your helmet on? We lost your radio link and couldn't find you.'

The Doctor took his old hat off and examined it in surprise. 'I didn't realize I'd removed my helmet. Must have put it down somewhere. Force of habit, I suppose. Not really comfortable in a helmet.'

'And what have you been doing?'

'Arranging our defences, of course.' He frowned. 'I wish we had better *offence* though.'

'We've got plenty of these,' said Flyn, slapping her rifle.

'Yes, but they are not powerful enough. Until Ace can find those heavy weapons we think are hidden in the hills . . . You didn't help place them by any chance?'

'No. Sorry, Doc. I was sitting in the *Atlas* under camouflage up north somewhere most of the time. I know we unloaded a lot of gear here, but what they did with it I don't know.'

The Doctor brightened for a moment. 'You don't happen to know what they did with my TARDIS — the blue box you took from the park?' Flyn shook her head. The Doctor scowled again in concentration. 'What we really need is something to —'

'Gum up their works?' Bernice said casually.

The Doctor started, then mouthed the words to himself a few times. He beamed. 'My dear Benny, that is *exactly* what we shall do.' He turned and almost ran for the stairs, legs twinkling.

Bernice and Flyn dashed after him.

'I have these moments of genius,' Bernice said modestly over her shoulder as they followed the Doctor.

The two birds flapped their way out of the darkness with disconcerting silence to land on Oberon's deserted ferry pad. A dishevelled group of former mine workers stepped forward warily as the huge wings folded back and their passengers slipped out of the mesh of carrying tendrils. The two figures in black combat suits with slightly sinister helmets slipped out from under the birds.

'We and a few friends of ours are the Seventh Cavalry Irregular Reserves,' one of them said brightly. 'And you've just volunteered to help us find some serious hardware.'

In the dome's workshop, the Doctor busily mixed chemicals in a variety of improvised containers. Bernice, Sorren and Flyn were assisting. They had raided the storeroom and returned with a collection of sealants, dome repair solvents, laboratory chemicals, lubricants and other more obscure fluids, the purpose of which Bernice did not know, but which seemed to please the Doctor.

Just like a schoolboy with his first chemistry set, she thought.

'And now,' said the Doctor, still mixing, 'one of those spare stolen compressor/blower units.'

'Yes?'

'Take it up to the observation gallery, will you.'

'That's right at the top of the dome,' Bernice pointed out.

'Wouldn't be much use if it wasn't,' replied the Doctor.

'Come on,' said Flyn, 'we'll manage it. I'll say this about being a duplicate, you don't seem to get tired easily.'

'Some of us do not have that advantage,' Bernice replied caustically. Flyn grinned.

Cassal paced around his section of the perimeter of Touchstone's cluster of domes. The work lights behind him cast his long shadow across the broad stretch of open ground to the forest, where it merged with the shadows of the forest thrown back by the glow of the fires. He fingered the trigger of his rifle, preset for a broad beam burn, and eyed the distance to the first line of scrub at the forest edge. A good clear hundred and ten metres at least; nothing was going to cross that before he could burn it.

His helmet radio broadcast Ashton's voice: 'Five minute check' perimeter: Brant?'

'All quiet.'

'Cassal?'

'Yo.'

'Kwon?'

'Here, Sarge.' The check ran down the list.

Cassal reached and end of his section, turned and paced back again. There was still activity behind him between the outer domes and the main one, but he didn't let it distract him. His eyes didn't leave the edge of the forest and the open ground and his shadow marching across it with giant strides. Funny, it was darker than it had been. He heard the whispering rush of the shadowform as a thin tongue of its substance raced along his own shadow. 'Sarge!' His rifle was burning into the stream as it flowed over his feet and up his body.

There was an electric flash.

They heard the commotion in the workshop: running feet, the heavy thump of doors, shouted orders. 'It's started,' said the Doctor to the others. 'Help me with these.' They gathered the miscellany of containers and made for the stairs.

The tongue of the shadowform thickened as more of its substance flowed out of the forest. Beams burned and fused its leading edges, but it rolled on. It was massive enough now to ignore such ablation. Grenades blew temporary holes in it, but the loss of stored charge was minimal and coherence quickly re-established. Its vital core was out of range, still back in the forest. It flowed on until the last of the soldiers retreated into the central dome. It licked around the edges of the structure, encircling it, probing, seeking some crack through which it could penetrate. But the dome was solid: stormproof and weather-sealed. Slowly the black tendrils started to climb upwards.

* * *

Ace wished the people of Oberon had not been quite so thorough in their retribution when they retook control from the duplicates. There was nobody left who knew for certain where the heavy air-defence emplacements were sited. So they were doing it the hard way: following vehicle tracks by torchlight, scouting with a couple of aircars and people in flightpacks. Former labourers were trying to remember which way transporters had gone on the day the *Atlas* had brought the new tools. Such was human nature that they remembered the improvement the tools had brought in their lives more clearly than the disposition of weapons. The Shenn nest mind, she could feel through her link with it, was fascinated by this further display of human contrariness.

From the ports of the observation gallery at the very top of the dome, they poured beam-fire down on the questing shadow tendrils. Chunks and crusts glowed, fused and fell away, rattling like clinker down and curve of the dome to vanish in the blackness that spread out from its base for twenty metres. But as fast as one tendril was cut away, another took its place.

The Doctor, Bernice, Flyn and Sorren clattered up the last flight of stairs to the gallery. Marines ringed the circular room, firing out into the darkness. Lieutenant Paak stood in the centre, directing the defence. 'We're holding it back, Doctor, but nothing more.'

'Well, we must try to give you an edge then,' the Doctor replied briskly, laying his burden of pails down by the air blower. Santony and the colonial engineer came up the stairs, paying out lengths of cable.

'All well earthed Doctor,' said the engineer. He disappeared down the stairs again. Santony started to lay the cables across the floor.

'What is all this, Doctor?' asked Paak impatiently, as the engineer reappeared carrying several three-metre lengths of plastic piping.

The Doctor beamed in an almost juvenile manner. 'Neutralizing and offensive weapons, of course. Wait and see.' The Doctor started fitting a nozzle to the end of a length of compressor tubing. The nozzle was also connected to a length of smaller-gauge flexible tube he fished out of his pocket. The other end of this Bernice dipped into one of the containers of peculiarly odorous liquid.

Paak began to look interested. 'What are you going to spray at it then?'

The Doctor smiled modestly. 'Oh, just a little concoction of my own. It should bind the surface of that thing rather effectively, and since it also contains conductive molecular chains, it should help to dissipate its stored charge. And without *that*, the shadowform is just so much exotic soot.'

'And the cables and pipes?'

'It uses electricity as a weapon.' He nodded to where the engineer and Santony were threading cables with bared ends through the semirigid pipes. 'This will deflect and earth the discharges.' Paak began to look enthusiastic.

The Doctor attached the nozzle to a spare earth cable, then donned a pair of heavy insulated gauntlets the engineer handed him. Bernice pointedly held out his helmet, which she had rescued, and he exchanged his hat for it with a smile. Sorren stood by the pails of fluid and the compressor, which had been dragged to the centre of the room. Santony, the engineer, Bernice and Flyn flanked the Doctor, carrying the earthing rods as he pulled the nozzle end of his oversized spray gun to one of the panoramic view ports and slid back a window panel opening out onto the fire-lit night. Sorren turned on the blower.

A shadow tendril reared up over the curve of the dome and was met by a hissing blast of fine spray. Blue-white bolts of electricity cracked from its tip and were earthed harmlessly through the rods jutting from the windows beside the spray gun. The tendril tried to withdraw. Sparks were discharging across its surface and onto the dome. It collapsed like a deflated balloon and slithered down the side of the dome. The Doctor gave a final blast of spray out onto the main bulk of the shadow, then dashed around to the next quadrant of the gallery, the others following in a tangle of cables.

Before they reached the third quadrant, the shadowform had flowed back down the wall and there was clear ground around the base of the dome.

'Hello, Ace. Can you hear me?'

'I hear you, Benny. How's things?'

'Looking up. The Doctor has just been using a king-sized spray gun to shoo away our sooty friend, so it's a stalemate at the moment. How are you doing?'

'Not bad. We've found a launcher and a self-propelled blaster cannon. We're getting a convoy together. Look, what about the stuff they must have hidden around the kiln site or Touchstone itself? Can't you get to them?'

Bernice laughed ironically. 'If you'd seen these things close up, you wouldn't say that quite so lightly. Anything around the kiln site is right out of bounds. The Lieutenant's considering sending people in the aircar or in flightpacks to look for them, but again, nobody around here is sure where they were concealed amongst all this greenery. Maybe we'll try it when it gets light.'

'Yeah. You know, we can see those fires from here and they're spreading. What happens when they reach you?'

'We should be all right; we're far enough back from the tree line and a grass fire won't hurt the dome. Oh, I've just thought of something . . . '

'What?'

'Can these shadowforms use launchers and blasters and such? If they find them first, they might think to use them against us.' There was a mutual silence.

'I think the cavalry had better mount up pretty quickly then,' said Ace.

In the main office they watched the picture relayed from the masthead camera on the dome top.

A pearly grey pre-dawn light was flushing the sky and tinting the clouds of smoke billowing from the still spreading fires. Through gaps in the smoke, the clearing and the *Atlas* could be seen, standing in the middle of a growing circle of destruction. Dark forms flowed across the open ground and into the ship's gaping hatches. The camera turned slowly, showing the shadow still encircling the base of the dome, then out across the river to the still and silent trees on the opposite bank.

Lieutenant Paak turned from the screen and regarded Santony

and Flyn thoughtfully. 'You'd be taking a considerable risk.'

'We know that, Lieutenant,' Santony admitted. 'But it makes sense. I know the area and have some ideas about where they might have hidden the heavy weapons. I can handle them if we get the chance, or disable them if need be, and Flyn here has also had some training on them and —'

'Hasn't anything to lose,' Flyn continued. 'Also we need to know if the shadows will follow us across the river. And if there's any delay in the weapons coming from Oberon, it wouldn't hurt to know if there are some close to hand.'

'All right, you can do it. Just be careful.'

Ace steered the leading heavy, caterpillar-tracked vehicle along the twisting forest track towards Touchstone. A blaster cannon and a multi-function missile launcher, she thought; well, they hadn't time to wait to find more. They'd just have to do.

Okay Kim?

I'd rather be in my fighter. This thing steers like a concussed crab.

Ace didn't need to check on their respective gunners — she knew they were all right. Two of their giant Shenn companions had arrived as she and Kim had been puzzling out the targeting and firing sequence for the weapons. Very shortly, the Shenn knew all that they did, and she was sure they would not forget. Funny how quickly you learn to trust some people, she thought. Her only objection had been that it was not their fight. *But it is, nest-of-one Ace*, the Shenn insisted firmly. *This threatens all of our planet*. And that was that.

They had left Oberon digging in. Any further weapons they found they might need themselves. If the shadows were not stopped, Oberon was too close to the hypergem seam for comfort.

Santony and Flyn skimmed across the river on flightpacks and turned to look at Touchstone. The dome, with the aircar perched precariously on its apex beside the camera mast, was still surrounded by the black skirt of the shadowform. If it had senses to register their departure, it gave no indication of the fact.

As they watched, a fireball rose over the trees from the edge of the burning forest, throwing blazing fragments into the air which shot away, flaring and exploding in turn. For a moment they hovered uncertainly as the sound of the multiple detonations reached them, then Santony laughed. 'They've just burnt up one of the mobile launchers,' he said over the radio. 'I think those shadows are really dumb.'

'Hope it hurt them,' replied Flyn.

The distant explosions jerked Bernice out of her uneasy doze. She'd hunched down in a corner of the main office because there were no spare chairs and she must have dropped off. She shook herself again, blinking. She was so tired. She fumbled in her pack and found a stim-tab. Was anybody going to be making any real food? she wondered. The alternative was Marines' issue rations. She got up and made her way out onto the first level gallery. The main hall was littered with the sprawled bodies of colonists trying to sleep. Thanks be there are no children in this colony yet, she thought. How they would take this, I don't know.

She noticed that the Marines guarding the inner entrance doors were looking uneasy and pressing their ears to the door. She ran quietly down the stairs and over to them. 'Trouble?'

'Listen,' said one of them. She pressed her ear to the panel. There was a definite whispering rushing sound from outside. The shadow was moving against the dome.

'Open them up, I want to listen at the outer door,' Bernice instructed, in the manner she hoped appropriate to a Special Emergency Council Advisor. 'Be ready to shut them quickly if it gets in — whether I'm back inside or not.' They hesitated for a moment, then unbarred the doors. She slipped across the short vestibule to the heavy outer doors. The sound was more distinct. It suggested a surging motion in her mind, to and fro, like shingle on a beach. Bernice came back through the inner doors quickly. 'Close them up,' she directed. She turned on her radio. 'Dome top, this is Professor Summerfield at the main door. What's the shadow doing right outside here?'

There was a pause. 'Hard to make out, Professor. You can't make out its contours. Uh, but I think it's sort of bulging up against the door.'

Bernice ran back up the stairs to the office. The Doctor and Paak turned to her as she burst in. 'I think we've got a problem,' she said quickly. 'The shadow's carrying something and I think it's going to try to use it like a battering ram.'

The missile launcher nestled peacefully in the little glade scraped out of a long earth bank. The still duplicate forms of its crew lay beside it. 'Santony to dome. First find, reference:' He gave the coordinates of the glade. 'If you send a crew in the aircar it's all yours.'

'Well done, but you'd better hurry,' came the reply. 'The opposition is trying something.'

Santony and Flyn exchanged an anxious glance, then cut in their jets and took off through the trees.

The dome trembled as the ram struck the outer doors. From the observation gallery ports they poured fire down onto the mass of the shadow. The Doctor's spray bound the top layer of the shadow, but it was three metres deep around the entrance. It sloughed off its immobilized substance like shed skin and fed fresh material in from its core in the forest. The swell of the dome hid from them the part of it that was closest to the entrance. 'If we try rolling grenades down the skin of the dome, we'll only crack it open ourselves,' Paak shouted above the sound of the battle. 'Move your spray gun down to the main hall, Doctor. We'll need it there if it breaks in.'

Bernice, Sorren and the engineer − Bernice kept forgetting to ask his name − helped the Doctor move his equipment. In the hall, the colonists were being evacuated to the upper levels of the dome, while Marines were setting up a heavy semiportable rifle opposite the inner doors. The engineer handled them two pieces of plastic cloth. Bernice realized everybody was tying similar pieces about their feet. 'They'll help a bit,' the engineer said simply.

Bernice saw the Doctor frown in thought. 'Shall I tell Ace to hurry along a bit?' she suggested.

He smiled grimly. 'You can be sure she won't be stopping to pick the flowers along the way.'

'Well if she doesn't get here soon, she might as well pick

some for a wreath.' She saw the Doctor's frown deepen. The thumps on the doors were getting louder.

He turned to Sorren. 'Did I see some backpack sprayers in the storeroom?'

'Why, yes. For spraying the test crop fields. But they've got no range.'

'I know. Get me one please,' the Doctor said. Sorren did as he asked.

'Doctor,' said Bernice anxiously, 'how close are you planning to get to it?'

'It's overextending itself, you see,' said the Doctor, half listening. 'There's only one of them laying siege; the rest are too busy burning or loading the *Atlas*. Maybe we can take advantage of that.'

Sorren returned with the backpack sprayer. The Doctor poured some of his concoction into its tank and pressurized it. He took off his pack and retrieved his umbrella. He fished a thick roll of wire from his pocket and started wrapping it round the shaft. They watched as he tucked the wire through his belt and let it hang down to his feet. Bernice realized he was wearing rubber boots. Wordlessly the engineer handed him wire strippers and he bared the trailing end. He strapped on the sprayer, opened his umbrella and held it at the ready. Even a few of the Marines stared at him, distracted from the crashing at the door.

He beamed back at them. 'You work the sprayer,' he instructed Bernice. 'Don't forget the gloves.' He turned to Sorren and the engineer. 'Use the earthing rods — keep it contained. Just give me a chance to get past it.'

'But where are you going?' said Bernice.

'To tackle its only vulnerable spot, of course.' He went over to Sergeant Ashton, who was commanding the heavy rifle. After a few words the Sergeant nodded, and handed the Doctor something from his belt.

Paak came down the stairs to stand with his troops. He stared at the Doctor, who spoke to him quickly. There was a crash and the outer doors went down. Blackness flowed up the transparent panels of the inner doors and their hinges groaned under increasing pressure. 'Get ready,' said Paak calmly.

* * *

They found the second vehicle in a gully a kilometre into the forest. It was a self-propelled blaster cannon. 'This is it,' said Santony. 'We can use this one close in.' They dropped down beside it in a cloud of blasted leaf litter. Flightpacks were stripped off and they bundled inside: Santony to the fire control console; Flyn into the driving seat. The motors hummed into life and the vehicle surged forward.

The inner doors burst open and the black wave poured into the hall. Blaster fire burned and cut through it. Electric bolts cracked back. Bernice hosed spray over the flowing mass and saw it swell up behind its fused and bound skin, which split and rolled beneath a fresh tide of shadowmatter. The wave poured further into the hall, spreading and flattening. Now it was a metre deep, half a metre deep. Tendrils grew up and over their heads, spitting electric bolts. They were forced back to the stairs. The air in the hall was scorching with energy and ringing with cracks and zips of power.

And then the Doctor darted forward, spraygun hissing before him, and he ran up and onto the top of the shadowform, his boots sinking into the pliant skin formed by his spray, almost making him bounce forward as through on an inflatable. Tendrils curved over his head; electricity cracked and earthed through his umbrella frame and down the trailing wire. And he ducked through the doorway and was out into the fresh light of morning.

The blaster cannon carrier hit the waters of the ford and threw up a wall of spray. It surged forward, the bow-wave breaking almost up to the driver's window. Flyn leaned forward, urging it on, willing it to go faster against the resistance of the river. The domes of Touchstone rose above the far bank.

The bolt almost knocked Bernice off her feet; her ears were ringing from the crack of air. Sorren was down, contorted, back arched, her face burned. The engineer lunged forward with his earthing rod, but a tendril curved around it, dividing into two horns with electricity arching between them. He fell, his chest smoking. Damn thing, you're learning, cursed Bernice. And

215

I didn't know his name. She kept blasting spray onto the thing and watching it split and pour forward again. She was pressed back against the wall under the stairs. Wrong side, you fool, she thought. The floor was a matt-black lake flowing heavily towards her, trying to swallow her.

The Doctor ran forward on light feet, skipping to one side then the other as tendrils arched over him. One divided at the tip and he thrust his umbrella between the horns and they crackled and collapsed, shorted out. He ran on, eyes searching the black river that snaked out of the trees, looking for — there! A swelling in the shadowform at the edge of the forest. It had overextended itself. He raced towards it.

The carrier surged clear of the water and ground up and over the bank. Tearing strips from the turf, it rolled forward, Sorren swinging its power turret around to cover the main dome.

The wave of blackness lapped at Bernice's feet. She braced herself for the last sensation she would feel; nothing. She opened her eyes. The shadow was retreating, flowing and rippling back out of the doorway, chased by a hail of fire from the upper galleries.

The carrier skidded round the last of the outer domes. Santony saw the river of darkness flowing through the entrance of the main dome. Then a wave of shadowmatter surged back out of the shattered doors: rolling back on itself, gathering and swelling and reaching up into the sky and curling, as though about to break. And the Doctor was standing on the shadow's tail where it flowed out of the trees, firing his blaster pistol at a basketball clump of shadowmatter, electricity crackling and earthing through his smoking umbrella. As the avenging wave rose over him, he cast his pistol aside, threw something into the hole he had burned in the clump, and dived to one side — and Santony burned the wave at maximum power, shearing off its crest which disintegrated into a cloud of soot and charred fragments that showered over the Doctor as he rolled onto the grass.

The clump exploded.

Sparks discharged along the length of the shadowform. For seconds it writhed and pulsed, then, slowly, settled and spread and was still.

Marines edged cautiously out of the dome. The Doctor picked himself up and started dusting the worst of the soot from him. Flyn halted the carrier beside him as Bernice appeared at the entrance. She arrived in time to hear the Doctor explain: 'That was its core, the relay to its controlling intelligence. It used all its body-matter to overwhelm the dome, leaving it exposed and unprotected.' He looked at the smoking remains of his umbrella. 'Well almost unprotected. Hello, Benny, you're all right then.'

'Doctor, it was as close as I *ever* want it to be.' Her face fell, the exhilaration of being alive fading. 'Sorren, the engineer – they didn't make it.' They were silent for a moment.

Then the Doctor said briskly: 'Well, we must proceed. There's still much to do.'

'What?' Bernice felt dazed.

'One down, eleven to go.' he turned back to Santony. 'I suggest the Lieutenant sends for that missile carrier you found immediately. We are going to need it.'

The remaining shadowforms reeled and shivered in sympathy with their central mind as the loss of their fellow resonated between them. For long moments they were motionless as their controller considered a response. The loading of the *Atlas* with as much shadowform material as it could carry had to continue, as did the gathering of the precious ore spilled from the tangled remains of the ferries. The threat to those processes must be eliminated.

Two decisions were made. The first caused three of the shadowforms to leave their tasks and flow towards Touchstone.

As the aircar lifted off and sped across the river, the first of the colonists started making their way across the ford.

Flyn backed the cannon up close to the dome entrance. The Doctor and Bernice appeared from inside, dragging a heavy cable. Santony opened a panel in the side of the vehicle, made the connection, then slapped the side. 'Okay, Flyn. Mains on.'

'The other weapons are being recharged as well,' said the

Doctor, 'but I doubt if the shadows will allow us much time.'

'We'll hold them here as long as we can,' Santony said firmly. 'That'll give the colonists time to get clear. They've got a chance now that it's light.'

'But why should the shadows pursue them further?' asked Bernice.

'It depends how vindictive they're feeling,' responded the Doctor. 'You really can't tell with a mind as different as this one.'

'But *what* is it? What's controlling the shadows?'

'Ah, well. I have an idea about that.'

'Here they come!' said Santony.

The last kilometre of the track was wreathed in smoke, slowing their progress. Suddenly, the first breeze of the morning snatched it away and they were out from between the flanks of trees and Touchstone was before them. Ace took one glance, then set her carrier racing forward. *Get ready*, she warned the Shenn gunners and Kim. *Fire at three hundred metres.*

From the main dome a heavy-duty blaster cannon was firing furiously at three monstrous black amorphous forms which were edging towards the settlement. An aircar flew over them, harassing them with rifle fire. There were people struggling across the river. As they closed on the combat zone, Ace saw a missile carrier speed along its far bank, firing a salvo at the shadows as it went, then turn and plunge into the waters in a cloud of spray. Come and join the party, she thought fiercely. Over the open radio link she shouted: 'The cavalry's coming! Everybody target the one on the left first!'

The carriers slewed to a halt between the domes and the forest. *Fire!* ordered Ace. The left-hand shadow disappeared in a multiple flare of energy blasts and exploding missiles. The blaster at the dome and the oncoming launcher added to the intensity of the bombardment, the noise merging into one continuous pounding roar. Even she could not recall seeing such a concentration of fire power. The shadow flared and disintegrated into dust. They shifted their aim and in moments the second one was gone. The third flowed back towards the trees, scattering fused and blazing fragments as it went. Then it collapsed and blew away.

The firing stopped.

'Nice timing!' Santony's cheery tone came over the radio.

'We try to oblige,' Ace replied. As she started to move the vehicle forward, she thought: *Kim?*

I'm here. That was something, wasn't it?

And frightening.

Yeah, a bit. Ace didn't need to ask how the Shenn were, she *knew*. They had simply done what had been necessary, but she could feel their displeasure at the destruction. Perhaps some of it was rubbing off.

They drew up beside the dome. She saw the Doctor and Bernice and a handful of Marines. Santony waved from the turret hatch of his blaster cannon. Bernice's voice came over her radio. 'What kept you?'

She tried to sound offhand. 'Don't you know? The cavalry always come *just* in time.' The Marine-crewed missile launcher rolled up from the river. She pulled at her door —

An intolerably brilliant bolt of light seared across her vision at a low angle and struck the Marine's launcher, punching a hole clean through it and sending it tumbling onto its side.

Ace, Kim, jump!

There was a blaze of light and a shatteringly loud blast of sound and pressure that caught her like a rag doll and flung her through the half-open door as the carrier exploded behind her.

Flyn lunged forward, knocking Bernice and the Doctor flat.

Santony reached for the blaster control, jerking his head round for a target — and his carrier disappeared in an eruption of flaming metal.

A bolt of fire struck the dome and it burst into fragments.

Through air rent by intolerable light and noise, Ace fell, hitting the ground agonizingly hard fifteen metres from the remains of her vehicle. She bounced and tumbled. Only her suit and toughened duplicate physique saved her. She rolled to a halt, stunned and uncomprehending.

It did not register on the detectors. We are sorry.

Ace looked up. A strangely shaped ship of pure black hung above them.

Chapter 28

'Don't move. Don't move any of you.' It was the Doctor's voice on her helmet radio, cutting through her confusion. I might as well stay still, Ace thought; you don't fight a warship with handguns.

The black ship hung above them, cannon zeroed in, its jets remarkably quiet for the bulk they were supporting. Perhaps they could convince it that they were dead. Perhaps it didn't care. 'Why doesn't it just finish us off?' That was Bernice; she was okay then, for the moment. Ace turned her head slightly. There was thick acrid smoke and blazing wreckage everywhere: all the carriers she could see were burning. There were the remains of a Shenn duplicate protruding from under the tangle.

'Ace? Can you hear me?'

'Yeah, I'm okay, Doc. I got thrown some way from you. Is Nat there?'

'Sorry, Ace. I think he's dead.'

Oh. Shit and hell and damn! Why the good people? He was nice and we thought that we'd just won. It's not fair. And I know that, but it doesn't help. *Kim? Kim?* There was nothing. Okay, she can't actually be dead, but . . . *Shenn nest, can you hear me?*

Yes, Ace.

Start growing new bodies for me and Kim at once, do you understand?

How will this help you now?

Because if this body dies now, then it means me and my friends will be dead too — and I must be ready to go after whoever's responsible. Start searching for more mobile weapons as well, while you've got the chance. You might need them yourselves.

We understand.

There was a distant building whine, then the scream of jets.

Over the trees and through the smoke, the *Atlas* lifted ponderously into the sky. They watched it climb and grow smaller and disappear. 'Was that what they were waiting for?' wondered Bernice.

'Possibly,' the Doctor replied slowly. 'Perhaps the black ship's controller just wanted us to know we had failed. Rather childish of it really, in a malicious way.'

'Were the rest of the shadows on board, do you think?'

'One to fly it, certainly. But I think the rest will stay.. They want to burn more trees.'

'I just hope,' Bernice's voice faltered slightly, 'that if they're going to kill us they'll do it quickly. I don't want them to send the shadows.'

'Then we'd run,' said Ace firmly, 'and they'd have to shoot or let us go. No shadow's eating *me*.' Frag it, this is hard, she thought. Do they realize I wouldn't die, that I'm onto a better dean that the Doctor's twelve lives at the moment? I swear I'll get them if they hurt you. I swear —

The black ship moved. It was sinking, coming closer. They're going to make sure, Ace thought. What will it feel like to be killed but not die?

There was a sudden scream and the hurricane blast of jets shredding the smoke from the burning carriers, and then the black ship was lifting, turning, trying to gain height. There was a brilliant explosion against its shields, then another. It shook. The black dart of an interceptor flashed across the sky, trailing a sonic-boom tail. More missiles burst against the black ship. Its own beams lashed out.

Something huge streaked across the sky. There was a sunburst of light as it passed over the black ship. The sound of artificial thunder beat upon them, then was overwhelmed as the mind-numbing sound of a monstrous tunnel of air falling in upon itself boomed out of the heavens. A wind tore through the trees, churning the smoke of the forest fires into writhing streamers in its wake. With a roar of jets the black ship sped after it.

Ace was on her feet, cheering. 'It's the *Broadsword*! Burn the bastards!' Figures appeared out of the swirling smoke: the Doctor, Bernice, a few Marines. Was that all that were left? There was no reunion, they were simply together again, watching the empty sky. The only sound was the confusing rumble of old and fading sonic boom tracks.

Still alert, they started checking the wreckage, but there were no more survivors. Those few seconds of fire from the black ship had been devastating. Lieutenant Paak, Sergeant Ashton . . . Ace felt sick. No last-minute heroics, she thought, just suddenly gone. She saw what was left of Santony's body. She turned away quickly. 'You know why he was uptight when we first met him? He was on compassionate leave from the garrison here; his mother had died.'

They found Kim's remains. 'She'll be all right,' Ace said. 'It's like this . . . ' She explained quickly. The Doctor nodded; Bernice looked at her curiously.

The Doctor looked at the sky again, but there were no ships or fighters, and no sound. 'I think we had better cross the river and join the colonists. The shadows may be moving again soon.'

Something seemed to burst in Ace's brain. Raw light and sound pulsed through her for a moment, then faded.

She was lying on the ground, the Doctor and Bernice bending over her, looking concerned. 'Wow. That was an experience.'

'What happened?' demanded the Doctor.

'It was over the hypergem links. The Shenn nest felt it too.' She sat up quickly, pushing their hands away. 'I'm okay now, it's gone.'

'For goodness' sake, Ace,' Bernice said in exasperation. 'Just for once let people fuss over you a bit!' For a moment they stared at each other.

'Thanks,' said Ace quietly.

'And now we had better be moving,' said the Doctor. 'We can do nothing more here.'

'Look — up there.' It was one of the handful of surviving Marines. He was pointing. Kilometres up in the sky, a fireball was slowly tumbling from space, leaving a spreading smoke tail in its wake.

'Which is it, the *Broadsword* or the black ship?' whispered Bernice.

The Doctor switched on his helmet radio. 'Hello, *Broadsword*. Doctor calling *Broadsword*, come in please.' There was an agonizing pause.

'Hello, Doctor, this is *Broadsword*.'

Twenty minutes later, the first of the big Marine landers were arriving at Touchstone.

Hello, Ace. Can you hear me?

Kim? How are you? Are you okay?

Well, I'm back in a vat again of course. You were right, it was the hard way to do it. But the Shenn say they'll have another body ready tomorrow, so I guess I can't complain. How is everything?

All the Marines' heavy weapons are down. The rest of the shadows have disappeared into the forest — they know we've got them licked now, I guess. The place is crowded: Colonel Charters is in charge, the colonists are returning from over the river. We'll be going back up to the Broadsword in a minute; the Captain wants a report on what's been going on here.

And the Doctor and Bernice, are they okay?

Yes, thanks to a duplicate trooper called Flyn. She knocked them flat when the first blast came, took the damage herself. I guess her real body's okay back in the mountain nest, so I can thank her properly in a few days. But we lost Santony I'm afraid — he was still in his carrier when it got hit.

Hell — I'm sorry. I liked him.

Yeah, so did I . . . Look, we'll be relayed through to the Command Room soon. The Council wants a report from its special advisors. Any messages for your grandfather or parents?

Tell them . . . I'll be just like my toy plane. They'll understand.

Here we are again, thought Bernice: the same group around the briefing room table. She exchanged hurried greetings with the others. As she took her seat, she noticed Santony's empty place. Not quite the same, she amended.

The screen showed Marshal Talevera and Prefect Delray. Both displayed identical expressions of puzzlement and frustration. 'Please tell us, Doctor,' said the Marshal firmly, 'if you now know, what this has all been about? As I understand it, the duplicate builders were not our real enemies. Something called Umbra was. Who or what, is Umbra, and where is it?

The others in the room all turned expectantly to the Doctor. 'Yes,' said Bernice, 'we'd like to know as well.'

The Doctor sighed. He sounded wistful. 'I can make a reasonable extrapolation. Many, many years ago, a fluke of nature created a form of life in a most isolated place.' He paused and half smiled. 'Once upon a time, there was an asteroid —'

'Oh come *on*', said Ace.

'No, really. It's a rather sad story, you see, about a lonely being that wanted to grow, but couldn't.'

'Nevertheless, Doctor,' countered the Marshal, 'please tell it in language more suitable for the records.'

'Very well. Many years ago in this system, a comet came unusually close to an asteroid at the gravitationally stable L4 point, sixty degrees ahead of Arden in its orbit and equidistant from Arden and its sun. The result of the encounter was to leave the asteroid rotationally locked to the sun, and to deposit on its surface a layer of the more unusual carbon formations that develop only in space, together with certain trace impurities. Since one hemisphere of the asteroid was always light and the other dark, there was a current flow through the semiconductive medium due to the thermocouple effect. And at some point, the analogue of a neural cell formed and reproduced.'

'That's most improbable.' interjected Strek. 'The chances are —'

'I know: infinitesimal — but not non-existent. This may have taken millions of years, but eventually it happened. It's a big universe, Professor. Anything that's not impossible, is merely waiting to happen. Anyway, the neural net spread over the asteroid, and very quickly found it could not spread or grow further. So it reached out; not physically, but through the electromagnetic wavelengths it had been bombarded with since it was formed, and which it had probably learned to focus and transmit using craters on its surface as natural dish antennae. It found Arden. There was more body material for it: carbon bound up most obviously in the trees. It found the Shenn group mind that it could influence with the analogue of thought-wave frequencies, and pushed it towards developing a technology that would be able ultimately to bring what it desired to it. And it found hypergems. Now *they* were a bonus. With them as part of its mind—body structure it could expand as it wished: no light-speed limitations on its thoughts with hypergems as relays. No danger of it fragmenting into multiple competing beings which, considering its nature, must have been a possibility. It just wanted to be one big growing baby.'

'Baby?' exclaimed Kausama.

'Well, adolescent perhaps. It's very immature in some ways, brilliant in others — the typical product of a sheltered upbring-ing. Its appreciation of reality is, shall we say, one-sided and rather selfish. So, that was its aim. And then you came along to colonize Arden, and it had to make changes.'

He paused reflectively. 'We'll never know exactly what was planned for Tairngire and Arden. It probably involved the duplicates among the military, in combition with these shadow-forms, engineering some form of takeover that would allow it to continue growing and spreading. Beyond a certain size, of course, these shadows would be almost impossible to stop. I suppose we might ask Umbra itself . . . '

'What!' exclaimed Delray.

'Naturally,' said the Doctor, looking about him in surprise. 'Umbra has been listening to your communications channels for years; its a born eavesdropper, you might say. Where do you think the name "Umbra" came from?'

Quillon broke the silence that followed. 'Doctor, if for no other reason, I must make contact with this Umbra being to lay charges against it for crimes it has instigated, both here and on Tairngire.'

'Going to read him his rights?' Bernice enquired mildly.

'Need a big pair of handcuffs,' added Ace.

Quillon maintained a straight face. 'The law is the law,' he stated with dignity.

'I think we would all be interested to hear this conversation,' the Marshal said. 'Please arrange it, Doctor.'

'All we need to do is to beam a hyperwave signal at the appropriate point in space. Umbra has hypergems now, so it's certain to be have a suitable receiver.'

Kausama relayed the order to communications. They waited expectantly for a few seconds, then the Doctor said: 'Umbra, can you hear me? We would like to speak to you. There's no point in hiding any longer because we know where you are. Your plan has failed. You can't win, so it's time to talk peaceably.' There was no response.

'One load of shadowmaterial and hypergems isn't enough. You haven't the power to move your mind-core yet, and the fleet will be here in a few days, so why not talk and prevent more suffering?'

For a long moment there was nothing, then: 'Umbra *is* strong. Umbra will win.' Bernice shivered. The Doctor had been right. There was an eerie petulant quality to the voice that she associated with skinned knees and shrill belligerence.

'But not strong enough or big enough,' responded the Doctor, just as though reasoning with a child. 'The Shenn won't run the duplicates for you anymore, and your shadows on Arden are being hunted down and destroyed by the Marines. You've *lost*.'

'What will you do with Umbra?' Suddenly the voice sounded wheedling and anxious.

The Doctor looked at the others, his expression grave. 'If it was up to me, I would not hurt Umbra, but I would not allow Umbra to grow further until it had learned responsibility, and was sorry for what it had done.'

'Stop Umbra growing?'

'For now, yes.'

'No! Umbra wants to grow now,' The thing bawled. 'Not to be alone anymore. To be big. To be everywhere, to touch things and make more of Umbra.'

'No,' said the Doctor firmly. 'You'll have to be patient. You must grow *within* before you can grow without.'

'We're taking away your toys,' added Ace.

There was a silence, then: 'Umbra knows something you don't know.' Suddenly it sounded sly and cunning.

The Marshal interrupted: 'What do you know?'

'If you don't let Umbra grow *now*, Umbra can hurt you.'

'We can't let you grow, Umbra,' said the Doctor.

'Then Umbra *will* hurt you.'

Kristen Barr tiptoed through the shadows of the passageway between the campus courtyards and checked the sensor again.

Yes, the reading was still there. Now's your chance to play detective, she thought.

Somebody had been tapping into the university's power supply — but cleverly, intermittently. The maintenance people couldn't trace them, so she thought she would. Students drawing power for some clandestine use shouldn't be too hard to find. After all, she'd survived meeting some *real* thieves — and duplicates as well. She checked her watch; it was nearly dawn. She didn't want to miss the latest news on Arden.

Kristen followed the strengthening reading. There must be a concealed power line that nobody knew about. She followed the signal across a corner of the campus park. Ahead of her, between the trees, was the glass wall of the museum exhibition hall. Now what did they want to power in there? Some of those massive antique electric engines? They were valuable; she hoped they hadn't damaged them.

Kristen stepped forward — and all the lights on the campus flickered and dimmed. She looked at the meter scale and could not believe the reading. She ran to the glass, shining her torch into the great chamber and over the blocky forms within. The beam fell on her old friend the nodding donkey, and she saw it grind to a halt.

The ground began to tremble and the glass wall shimmered where her torch beam passed through it. A panel jerked free and crashed to the ground, crumpling around its laminations. A deep bass rumbling pulsed through her frame, rising in pitch, growing louder and more shrill. Kristen ran for the trees as, inside the hall, the floor beneath the nodding donkey heaved, toppling the structure and blasting pipework, safety valves and floor tiles through the roof of the building. The sound was screaming into the ultrasonic. Kristen fell flat behind a tree and looked back.

Blackness surged into the exhibition hall, fountaining heavily out of the ground and flowing up the glass wall, bursting open the panels. But it was not oil.

'Umbra hads done it! Umbra has done it!' it chanted.

'What have you done, Umbra?' demanded the Doctor.

'Done what Umbra said. Going to hurt you because you won't

227

let Umbra grow.'

Kausama opened the line to the bridge. 'Go to alert level two immediately.'

'Not *you*, silly,' mocked Umbra. 'Them on Tairngire.' On the screen the Prefect turned aside and spoke urgently.

'What can you do on Tairngire, Umbra? Your duplicates are gone,' said the Doctor.

'Before they went, they planted some things for Umbra.'

A tongue of shadow two metres deep rolled across the grass to swallow her. Kristen sprinted desperately away, aware that all the lamps in the park were flickering. She clawed at her phone as she ran. 'Chief. Emergency, get help . . . ' A bud swelled up on the surface of the wave behind her.' Something out of the ground.' The tendril grew upward. 'From the oil pump.' It curved over. 'It's *alive*!' The electric bolt burned and crackled down. Her charred body crumpled to the ground and disappeared under the tide of shadow.

'What did they plant?'

'Shadowseeds, of course. Not quite like those on Arden; they grow slowly, but they grow *big*.'

'But shadows need hypergems, and you didn't have any then.'

'Had a few. Duplicates brought just a few early on. Not enough — had to be secret, needed more, but had a few to practise on.'

'Where were they planted?' The Doctor's voice was harsh.

'You'll find out. Then you'll leave Umbra to grow. or else . . . '

'Doctor.' the Prefect's voice was uncertain.' 'We're getting reports of a minor earth tremor and some electrical disturbance. It seems to be located in the university area.'

A terrible braying laugh rang through the room. 'Umbra said you'd find out. Now you learn how Umbra can hurt you.' The channel went dead.

The Command Room screen showed both the Marshal and the Prefect issuing orders. Bernice and Ace leaned towards the Doctor. 'Bluff?' queried Bernice. 'Are there really more shadow seeds?'

'I don't know,' replied the Doctor. 'The question is, can we take the chance?'

'But what is it feeding on in New Byzantium?' wondered Ace. 'And why didn't it trigger the seed earlier?'

'It didn't trigger it earlier because it wanted to strengthen its core first, I expect. As to what it's growing on . . . ' He turned to the shocked faces of Quillon, Strek and York. 'I know you're concerned for family or friends, but you can help them best by thinking clearly. What source of carbon is there associated with the university, besides vegetation, people and what it might be able to draw from the air?'

They conferred in muted tones for a few moments, then Strek started suddenly and said, 'Doctor, I'm afraid it may be feeding from an oil field.'

The Doctor looked grave. 'That is very unfortunate.'

The lights of the university flickered and pulsed. Confused, half-dressed people were spilling out onto the quads from the residential blocks. The ground was trembling. There was a distant sound like the rush of a wave. It was getting closer. Lightning seemed to play over the roof tops. Portlyn ran through the quads 'Get out!' he ordered. 'Evacuate the campus.' Then he shouted Kristen's name. She shouldn't have wished for excitement, he thought. All he ever wanted was a quiet life. A wave of darkness erupted from between two buildings and engulfed him. And then there was perfect peace and quiet.

The first aerial pictures were relayed to the *Broadsword*. The lights in the heart of the city were being overwhelmed by the spreading shadow.

'You must turn off the main power,' said the Doctor. 'It's feeding off that as well.'

'We daren't until daybreak,' came the Marshal's voice, rough-edged. 'The panic is horrific enough as it is. Some parts of the city are already cut off. We're airlifting people out, but we're already lost craft to these electric bolts by flying too low. The army are attacking the thing, but it is far more massive than those you reported on Arden — and still growing. We cannot use the heaviest weapons while people are still trapped.' The picture cut to show the Command Room again. The Marshal and Prefect appeared resolute, but shaken.

'The Council has decided,' said the Prefect, in a formal tone. 'Captain Kausama: you are to proceed at once to the asteroid occupied by the being known as Umbra and neutralize or destroy it at all costs. Confirmation of these orders is being transmitted over the Fleetcomm channel.' She paused. 'We have decided that we cannot capitulate to Umbra's demands. Such a being could not be trusted, and ultimately the result would.be the same.'

'You're quite right,' the Doctor confirmed sadly. 'There is no alternative now. Umbra has the selfishness and single-mindedness of a child, but with terrible power. And you have annoyed it.' Bernice felt the air grow thick around her for a moment.

Kausama spoke. 'We are already underway at maximum acceleration, Prefect. Including one hyperspace micro-jump, we will be in the L4 region in just over five hours.'

Chapter 29

'Ship status?'

'All personnel to combat stations; shields activated; all weapons charged and armed. The ship is ready, Captain.'

'Time to target zone?'

'Two minutes.'

'Command team, take your places. Prepare for computer interface.'

'Marshal,' said Lieutenant Khan in a taut voice, 'the army can't hold the corridor out of the city any longer. The Defence Building will be cut off.' The Command Room screens showed mobile blasters burning a wall of blackness that was rolling over what had been a travel-tube station. The shadow fused and vaporized but kept coming.

'Is the building itself still secure?' enquired the Marshal in measured tones.

'Yes, sir. For the moment.'

'And the roof landing pad?'

'Still clear, sir.'

'Then we needn't worry for the while,' he said reassuringly. 'While we can still do some good coordinating the operation, we stay here.'

'I wish these suits were more comfortable to sit down in,' said Bernice.

'Why not take yours off then,' suggested Ace.

'In the circumstances, I think not.'

'Well don't complain about them.'

'That wasn't a complaint; that was an observation.'

'Well I'll make an observation in a minute about people who can't keep quiet —'

'Do be quiet, both of you,' requested the Doctor.

They were both silent. Ace could feel the tension in the air like a palpable thing, built from anticipation and thoughts of the last scenes relayed from New Byzantium.

The special advisory group were seated around the briefing room table watching the relay from the bridge screens. They were all wearing lightweight pressure suits. Ace had laid her blaster conspicuously on the table in front of her. Nobody commented.

'Entering zone of gravitational stability now. Beginning scan for asteroid,' came the voice from the bridge.

'I wouldn't have thought an asteroid would be so hard to detect at this range,' said Professor Strek.

'You can be sure Umbra won't make it easy for us,' said the Doctor. 'It will try to conceal itself as it did the black ship. Remember, it has the contents of the *Atlas* to work with.'

'But that can only be a few hours ahead of us. It can't have done much in that time.'

'I think it has a powerful incentive,' said the Doctor. 'Survival: basic instinct. Just like any living thing, it wants to survive. Pity to destroy such a unique being, but it has given us no choice.'

'Yes,' agreed Strek. 'Such a pity. It would have been fascinating to study it.' He hesitated. 'Almost a . . . crime to kill it.'

'Killing anything is a crime,' stated Quillon flatly, to no one in particular. Ace looked up from contemplating her blaster and thinking of Santony to frown at him.

'Tell that to Umbra,' she suggested.

'Perhaps,' Strek said slowly, 'we don't need to kill it. Maybe we can restrain it somehow.' Ace blinked hard, thinking she must have missed something. But her flip remark about needing a big net froze on her lips.

'Now that's a very humane suggestion, Professor,' said the Doctor, staring into the air, his eyes not quite focused.

'Quite right,' said York. 'We must show we are civilized. I think we are letting military thinking cloud our options.'

'I am sick of war — and the military mind,' Bernice stated firmly. There were vague nods of agreement from round the table. Ace was quite still.

'There is such a thing as negotiation you know,' continued York. 'I was given special ambassadorial status for this mission in case there was a chance of a peaceful settlement. I represent', she said proudly, 'the government, and I think we should sit down around a table with Umbra and discuss this problem like civilized beings.' And to Ace's horror, the mad idea was greeted by nods and murmurs of approval from around the table.

'And,' said Chiminoe brightly, 'I'll bet Umbra knows a thing or two about hypespacial transmissions; bound to in the circumstances. Now I would really like to have a talk about that. Might learn something useful, maybe something that can be developed commercially.'

'That's an idea,' said York. 'Trade is the basis of good relations. Friendly commerce. There must be something Umbra wants from us.'

Clutching her blaster in one hand, Ace reached over slowly, grasped the Doctor's forearm and began to squeeze hard. She could feel the touch of Umbra now, trying to reach through the hypergem link to her real mind, trying to confuse her, to make her forget their purpose. Whatever mental force could influence a Shenn group mind over a distance of hundred and fifty million kilometres, was taking them over at a few thousand. Umbra was . . . not so bad really . . . Why shouldn't they talk instead of . . .

Then she felt the mind of the Shenn nest wrap itself around her and strengthen her resolve, and Kim's voice was saying *Fight it. Don't let it fool you!*

'Doctor!' she hissed. 'Fight it. Put up a mind block, please.'

'Hmmm, what?' He seemed half in a trance. 'Don't squeeze my arm, Ace, there's a good girl.' She gritted her teeth, swung him round in his chair, pulled back and slapped him hard enough for him to feel it through the light helmet.

The map screen showing the spread of the shadow suddenly blossomed with new sightings in a halo round the city. Prefect Delray looked at the fresh outbreaks in dismay.

'How did it get that far?' she demanded. 'It's jumped nearly two kilometres in places. Wait a minute.' She scrutinized the

233

map. 'They're all tube terminals — it's spreading along the travel-tubes!'

'Doctor. Doctor! I'm sorry, I didn't mean to hit you so hard. I forgot about being a duplicate, but you've got to snap out of it.'

None of the others seemed to notice her bending over the Doctor as he lay on the floor. York was speaking to the bridge. ' . . . and we feel, Captain, that this aggressive action against Umbra should not be pursued.'

The Captain's voice came back: 'I agree, Councillor. I have cancelled the alert and have ordered all weapons systems disarmed.'

'No!' Ace bellowed. 'That's what Umbra wants. Fight it, it's getting at your minds. Benny, think what you're doing!' For a moment Bernice half turned, a puzzled expression on her face, then her eyes glazed again.

' . . . and we are proceeding to Umbra's asteroid with our shields lowered as a gesture of good faith,' continued the Captain in frighteningly reasonable tones. Ace felt the fields tighten as the ship altered course. She turned back to the Doctor, shaking him violently. Puppets! This whole thing had been about puppets used by Umbra: duplicates, Shenn, the shadows — and now them.

'Please, Doc, wake up. Please . . . '

The shadow rolled through the narrow streets of the old town, flowing over Lantern Market Square. A gunship flew overhead, its energy cannon blazing. Electric tendrils reached up towards it, but the pilot held a safe height, and the cannon started to chew away at the shadow's edge. A spout extruded from the shadow's surface and there was a sharp bang. A fist-sized ball of shadowmatter arced into the air, trailing a wire-thin tendril behind it, and struck the gunship. Lightning crackled up the wire. The gunship's jets cut and it fell out of the sky.

Umbra was learning.

The Doctor's eyes suddenly snapped open and he sat up abruptly, causing Ace to jerk back. 'Doc, are you all right?'

His voice was strained; his face pale. 'Yes, I'm blocking it out — for the moment. We must get to the bridge.'

She helped him to his feet and they staggered to the door, leaving the others apparently oblivious, immersed in a surreal debate about trade with Umbra. 'A tax of one tree per person for the privilege,' York was proposing reasonably.

They crossed the central access core to the bridge. Suppose the door's locked and shielded? Ace thought. But it slid open easily. Of course, the alert's been cancelled. That's a mistake, Umbra.

Everyone on the bridge sat neatly at their places as though all was perfectly routine. Their sudden entrance went unremarked. The Doctor ran to the manual weapons control panel, pushing aside the operator who sagged confused in his chair. He rapidly scanned the displays. Ace was at the adjacent panel, stabbing at buttons. 'Doctor, the main power links to the force shields have been cut manually from engineering. And the main drive has been shut down.'

'And so have the weapons circuits.'

'How long will it take to reconnect them?' On the screens, a dark mass was growing, blotting out the stars.

'Too long, I'm afraid,' said the Doctor.

The Command Room shuddered, damping the babble of voices for a moment as its occupants exchanged anxious glances. Behind the Prefect, Peter van Buran spoke urgently over the building's intercom. There was a pause, then he leaned forward. 'The shadow has broken into a basement level, chief.'

The Prefect took a deep breath and opened the general address channel. 'Your attention please,' her amplified voice said throughout the complex. 'The shadow has entered the lower levels. Begin evacuation to the roofdeck immediately. Prepare transfer of command links to Heliopolis City.' There was a stir in the room; some support staff began to file out. She could see people leaving the gallery.

The Marshal was talking on another channel. '*Broadsword*, have you detected the asteroid yet? *Broadsword*?'

'Hello, *Broadsword*. Marshal Talevera calling *Broadsword*.' The voice sounded from the communications panel. The Doctor crossed to it, reaching past an unheeding Le Paz.

'Yes, Marshal, I can hear you.'

'Doctor? The shadow has broken into the building. We are preparing to evacuate. It's still spreading over the city. We can't contain it.'

Prefect Delray's voice cut in. 'There are still people trapped in parts of the city. If they are to be saved, you must destroy Umbra. Have you found its asteroid yet?'

'Yes,' replied the Doctor, 'we have found the asteriod. One way or the other, it'll all be over in a few minutes.' He closed the channel.

'Or to put it another way,' said Ace, trying to keep her voice level, 'the asteroid's found us.' The screens showed them coasting towards a dark lozenge-shaped mass of rock, crater-pitted and scarred by ancient impacts. Ace read the scale on one of the screens: fifteen kilometres by ten approximately, the long axis pointing to the sun. 'That's where Umbra hangs out. I suppose.'

'Yes. Ah, there's a welcoming committee, coming up for us,' the Doctor said. Ace could just make out the dark forms flitting across the sunlit limb of the asteroid. 'The stolen fighters, I would assume, coming to put a shadow controller on board.' She saw his eyes flickering from the view on the screens to the display readings and back again, as though calculating.

Ace looked about her at the vacant expressions of the crew. Even if they could rouse them, what could they do? She didn't want Umbra to think they had simply given up; it wasn't in her nature. Perhaps it knew of their helplessness and was gloating, just like a malicious child savouring its victory. 'Doctor,' she pleaded, 'isn't there *anything* we can do to stop it?'

The Command Room was nearly empty. The lights flickered, then failed. Dim red-tinted emergency lights cut in. They could hear the distant sounds of gunfire from the lower levels.

'Come on, chief, you've got to get out of here,' van Buran insisted. 'I've got your things.' He was grasping the official briefcase. Lieutenant Kahn held the Marshal's valise. An army escort waited at the door.

'Yes, we'd better go, Annis,' the Marshal said gently. Delray took one last look around, confirmed that the gallery was empty, then strode towards the door. The escort opened the doors and flanked them down the corridor. The sound of gunfire was louder.

'Sorry, Marshal, Prefect, but we'll have to use the stairs: We can't trust the lift-tubes,' the Captain of the escort said apologetically.

'That's all right, son,' the Marshal said gently. 'We've been sitting down for hours; we could do with the exercise.'

At the top of the flight of stairs leading down, they saw a squad of soldiers peering intently into the depths, semiportables and plasma bazookas at the ready. Their leader urgently waved them past and onto the up flight. 'Move it,' he said without deference. 'It's broken through another wall down there.' They started up briskly. Delray realized they had fifteen levels to ascend. Glad I remembered to wear my comfortable shoes this time, she thought.

As they reached the top of the third flight, there was a fierce crackling from below and a volley of energy weapon blasts in response. The escort Captain looked anxiously down the stair-well for a moment, then urged them on. Lightning flashed below. The stairs seemed to rise endlessly before Delray. By the gods, they were cutting it fine; she hadn't realized things were so bad. They staggered as the stairs shook. There was a roar and a blaze of light. Multiple explosions rang in her ears and a blast of smoke-filled air billowed up past them. The echo of a hoarse cry was cut off by a harsh crackle of energy.

From below came a rushing, hissing sound.

'Isn't there anything?' Ace repeated.

The Doctor's eyes were still flicking between displays. He seemed to choose his words carefully. 'Nothing to speak of.' She grasped at that ambiguous phrase. Nothing he could *risk saying*, he meant — in case Umbra could hear them through the minds of the crew. The screens showed the fighters coming nearer. 'Sometimes you have to be prepared to do things for the greater good, you understand?' She nodded. 'You might have to hurt innocent people to save others. Are you ready for that?'

She nodded. This was going to be bad.

'Now!' The Doctor leaped at the pilot's chair, heaving its occupant to the floor and sliding into his place. His hands flashed over the manoeuvring thruster controls. 'Keep them off me!' he shouted as the ship turned. Ace stood at the back of his chair, facing the crew — and every eye on the bridge suddenly turned to them.

'The Doctor and Ace are a danger to the ship,' Umbra's voice rang out over the ship's speakers. 'Kill them.'

The tongue of shadowmatter was rising up the stairs faster than they could climb. They were on the fifth level above ground. It's my fault, Delray thought bitterly, gasping for breath, forcing her legs to keep pumping at the steps. I wanted to set an example, to be the last one out and not run away to safety before the others. Now people are going to die trying to save me because I can't climb stairs as fast as they can. Should've kept fitter. Sixty's only middle-aged.

'Leave me . . . I'm slowing you . . . ' she grasped.

'Never,' panted the Marshal. Lieutenant Khan grasped one arm, van Buran the other and they pulled her along with them. The escort fell back. She heard the shrill of an energy weapon on continuous discharge. The stairs were blurring before her. There was a crash of lightning from below.

Lieutenant Ruban lunged forward at the Doctor. Ace knocked him aside with duplicate strength. But there were too many to take on hand-to-hand. 'Fight it!' she shouted at them, swinging her blaster in a warning arc. 'Don't listen to it!'

'No good, no good,' crackled Umbra. 'They think you're their enemy. Doctor, stop doing that. Get away from the controls. This is Umbra's ship now. Stop them.' He ordered. The crew moved forward. None were armed, Ace realized. But how soon until the security guards appeared? Behind her, the Doctor was working the manoeuvring controls, heading the ship for the sunward side of Umbra's asteroid.

'I don't want to hurt you!' she shouted into their faces. They were set in expressions of fixed determination, not quite seeing her. She swallowed. She was going to have to shoot these innocent people: people she knew, now worse puppets than the duplicates. Silently she cursed herself — why don't you carry a stunner? This was what the Doctor anticipated.

'You'll have to kill them,' Umbra chortled: a terrible sound. 'Or you'll have to stop, then you'll be Umbra's toys.'

Shit — the little bastard is enjoying this! she realized. He's playing it out. But he can't know the Doctor has something definite in mind. So I've got to give him time.

With icy precision, she shot a blaster bolt into Le Paz's leg. She swung round and shot Commander Foss's leg from under him. And they both continued forward, crawling along, faces set in pain but still coming. 'You bastard!' she raged at Umbra. 'Leave them alone.' Armed security men appeared at the bridge door, and her reflex took over and she blasted them, shooting to kill, almost sobbing with despair. Umbra's voice cackled over the speakers. He was playing with them!

To her sharpened senses and reflexes, time seemed to be running down into nightmare slow motion, her gun swinging to and fro, blasting down officers and crew, who kept dragging themselves forward. She kicked the nearest ones away, but they threatened to overwhelm her by sheer weight of numbers. Unless she killed them. Oh no . . .

Through the ring of advancing figures she saw Captain Kausama turn jerkily, as though fighting every step, and bend to pick up one of the fallen security guard's weapons. She saw Kausama's shaking hands adjust the setting and raise the gun, swinging it towards her. Ace levelled her own blaster. She couldn't see Kausama's legs; her arms were before her body; she would have to shoot to kill. She saw Kausama's agonized face, as though she was fighting Umbra and knew what she was doing.

You have to do it, Kim said in her mind.

Ace saw Kausama nod —

Ace's blaster crackled —

'Go on,' shouted Umbra. 'More, more. This is fun.'

Ace screamed in range and hate. She blasted shots over the heads of the crew through the open door and heard them explode in the corridor. An alarm started sounding. 'Benny!' she shouted. 'Help me.'

239

Two levels to go. Only the four of them were left. The seemingly unstoppable thing boiled up the stairs behind them. A tendril reached up and crackling blue-white radiance lit the stairway. Delray jerked with the secondary shock, and van Buran fell away, blackened and smoking, and vanished into the shadow.

Bernice stirred. There was noise: an alarm was ringing. Ace's voice . . . She felt Umbra's attention slip away a little. The others paused in their senseless debate, looking puzzled by their words, but still uncertain. She bit her tongue hard and deliberately, feeling the hot blood. Don't let it take over again; focus on the pain. She punched the edge of the table. Quillon jerked to his feet, gun in hand, and staggered for the door. Whose side is he on? she thought. She forced her legs to move and stumbled after him, seeming to swim through the almost tangible waves of mental force tugging at her mind. They were out in the corridor, across the central stairway core. Smoke was in the air: alarms were sounding. Crew swayed on the stairs, locked in confusion.

She stumbled into the bridge over the bodies of two security men, a stride behind Quillon. She saw the Doctor hunched over a control panel, Ace at his back facing a semicircle of crew who clawed at them like mad things, and Ace was kicking them back and blasting at their legs, her face a mask of despair and horror. Some were clearly dead, but the rest still kept coming, urged on by the shrieking voice of Umbra.

'No!' shouted Quillon, levelling his pistol. Ace's reflex snapped her round; Bernice lunged at Quillon's gun arm. She felt the blaster bolt strike him as his stun pistol buzzed and whined, sweeping the room. Then he fell, Bernice on top of him.

Ace had staggered back, shielding the Doctor from the worst of the beam. Most of crew were down, stunned. The Doctor half slumped over the board, his legs dead. Ace's face was pale with shock, fighting the stun effect on her duplicate body.

The Doctor pointed desperately across the control boards. 'Benny, pull that lever now!'

'No,' Umbra wailed in fear for the first time.

Bernice forced herself on against the thing tearing in panic at her mind, focusing on the one big manual lever among all the delicate touch-sensitive controls on the bridge. A lever to pull when all else had failed. She tore off the protective cover and heaved down.

There were shouts from above. They were on the last flight of stairs. Kahn turned and burned the thing behind them with her blaster. Electricity crashed and she fell back, charred and ruined. A shadow arm reached upward.

The *Broadsword*'s solar sail blossomed and unfurled, tugged open by tiny gas-jet rockets, sparkling in the sun. Bernice watched on the screens as millions of square metres of micro-thin foil unfolded, and a monstrous shadow grew across the face of Umbra's asteroid.

'No!' it shrieked from every speaker in the ship. 'Don't take away the light. Umbra will die without the light. Don't hurt Umbra . . . Umbra only wanted to grow . . . to be big . . . Not fair, not fair . . . Poor Umbra . . . mind . . . going to . . . sleep . . .'

The arm collapsed to dust and soot and billowed back down the stairs in a whispering power-soft wave, crackling gently as its powder drained away, leaving a midnight shroud over the bodies of Khan and van Buran as it flowed past them.

The Marshal and the Prefect lay sprawled in a corner of the last landing, panting and gasping for breath. Outside, the sound of firing slowly faded away as a shadow covered the last sunlit sliver of Umbra's asteroid.

Chapter 30

Hours later, Ace was curled up on her bunk in her cabin on the *Broadsword*, staring at the wall.

Kim was trying to talk to her, but she had shut her out.

Ace needed to think.

There was a knock on the door. She didn't answer. The knock came again. 'Go away,' she said. The door opened. Bernice and the Doctor came in. They sat on the side of the bed.

'I thought you'd like to know,' said the Doctor, 'that we've found the TARDIS. It was sitting in a crater on the dark side of the asteroid, next to the *Atlas*. I wonder what Umbra thought it was? Another toy, I suppose.'

'Just shut up about it, all right?'

'You can't blame yourself for what happened,' said Bernice gently. 'You had to shoot those people to save the rest of the ship and hundreds of people on Tairngire. You had no choice.'

'But I *did*.' Ace punched the cabin wall, leaving a dent. 'If only I'd been carrying a stunner, but no . . . ' She punched the wall again. 'Stupid bitch Ace always has to pack the most firepower, doesn't she?' There was no Umbra left for her to get even with, only her conscience.

'A stunner wouldn't have stopped the flyer in the park.'

'Well, a stunner and a blaster then. Or a duo.'

'You won't be able to move if you carry a weapon for everything.' The Doctor smiled ruefully. 'And do you think Umbra would have allowed that terrible game to be played out on the bridge for so long if you *had* been carrying a stunner? No, we only had time to do what was necessary *because* you had a blaster, and Umbra wanted to savour your dilemma. You never really had a choice. But it was *Umbra* who killed those people, as surely as if it had pulled the trigger itself.'

There was a long silence, then Ace said: 'I shot the Captain.

She was fighting it . . . She knew I had to — she nodded.'

'That was extraordinarily brave,' said Bernice simply. 'I think the Concordance choose their officers very well.'

'But what about Quillon? Was he going to shoot the crew or us? I'll never know. It was the worst thing I've ever done, I think — but it was reflex, you understand?' She was sitting up now, looking at them, anxious and fierce at the same time.

Yes, thought Bernice, we understand. Even you need reassuring occasionally, Ace, for all your toughness. Even you aren't an island. But you'll never admit it. Aloud, she said: 'We understand. Look, we're going down to the TARDIS in a minute, and the Doctor thinks we'll just slip away, hop a few weeks into the future and pick up the real you from the Shenn nest when you've mended. And then . . . '

'Yes?'

'I was thinking about another holiday,' said the Doctor.

Ace smiled ironically. 'I think I've had about as much holiday as I can take.

The Doctor frowned. 'Actually, I was thinking of a holiday on my own.'

'We're not that bad, are we?' Bernice said.

There was a long pause. Then, seemingly shaking off his momentary gloom, the Doctor said, 'It started well, don't forget that. And perhaps things would have been worse for Arden and Tairngire if we hadn't been here.'

Ace swung herself off the bunk. *Kim?* she thought.

I'm here, Ace.

Do you forgive what I did?

There is nothing to forgive, Ace. There's only understanding. Both the Captain and Inspector Quillon would say that. They knew it was for the best.

'Yeah,' Ace said aloud. 'Well, we have to believe that, don't we?' She sighed and looked at the Doctor and Bernice. 'Okay, then. We'll see the Shenn and get me back again. I want to say thank you to them properly, and see how Kim's getting on. Let's go.'

Donal Robson looked out over the great forest of Arden from the foothills of the Phebe Range.

A year had put a thin film of green back over the burned-out areas, that reached from Touchstone almost to Oberon. But the great trees would need help to reclaim their lost ground. Grassland was all right, but Arden was a forest world.

He patted the pack of tree seedlings beside him and glanced at Rusty, who was chewing a nut next to him. The bushtail brushed his bib-front clean and looked at him. 'Chirrip-choo?' it enquired.

'Yes, Rusty, down the quick way. And plant a few more trees.'

As the flightpack carried them down the hillside, Robson could see the tiny dots of figures in the clearing, already at work. Some of them were giant Shenn duplicates, he knew. They bothered some people, but oddly, considering what had happened to him, he quite liked them. Perhaps it was because they wanted the forest back too, and they were letting a small colony of humans stay on Arden.

The events of the previous year seemed like a bad dream now. Indeed, if it wasn't for the Shenn and the great burnt swathe of forest, it might have been. Don't dwell on the past, he told himself. Be like Rusty: take each day as it comes and enjoy it for what you can find that's good in it.

He thought of the seedlings he was carrying. He'd be an old man, perhaps dead, before most of them reached their maturity and the forest was whole again.

But he wouldn't let the idea worry him.

Already published:

TIMEWYRM: GENESYS
John Peel

The Doctor and Ace are drawn to Ancient Mesopotamia in search of an evil sentience that has tumbled from the stars — the dreaded Timewyrm of ancient Gallifreyan legend.

ISBN 0 426 20355 0

TIMEWYRM: EXODUS
Terrance Dicks

Pursuit of the Timewyrm brings the Doctor and Ace to the Festival of Britain. But the London they find is strangely subdued, and patrolling the streets are the uniformed thugs of the Britischer Freikorps.

ISBN 0 426 20357 7

TIMEWYRM: APOCALYPSE
Nigel Robinson

Kirith seems an ideal planet — a world of peace and plenty, ruled by the kindly hand of the Great Matriarch. But it's here that the end of the universe — of everything — will be precipitated. Only the Doctor can stop the tragedy.

ISBN 0 426 20359 3

TIMEWYRM: REVELATION
Paul Cornell

Ace has died of oxygen starvation on the moon, having thought the place to be Norfolk. 'I do believe that's unique,' says the afterlife's receptionist.

ISBN 0 426 20360 7

CAT'S CRADLE:
TIME'S CRUCIBLE
Marc Platt

The TARDIS is invaded by an alien presence and is then destroyed. The Doctor disappears. Ace, lost and alone, finds herself in a bizarre city where nothing is to be trusted — even time itself.

ISBN 0 426 20365 8

CAT'S CRADLE: WARHEAD
Andrew Cartmel

The place is Earth. The time is the near future — all too near. As environmental destruction reaches the point of no return, multinational corporations scheme to buy immortality in a poisoned world. If Earth is to survive, somebody has to stop them.

ISBN 0 426 20367 4

CAT'S CRADLE: WITCH MARK
Andrew Hunt

A small village in Wales is visited by creatures of myth. Nearby, a coach crashes on the M40, killing all its passengers. Police can find no record of their existence. The Doctor and Ace arrive, searching for a cure for the TARDIS, and uncover a gateway to another world.

ISBN 0 426 20368 2

NIGHTSHADE
Mark Gatiss

When the Doctor brings Ace to the village of Crook Marsham in 1968, he seems unwilling to recognize that something sinister is going on. But the villagers are being killed, one by one, and everyone's past is coming back to haunt them — including the Doctor's.

ISBN 0 426 20376 3

LOVE AND WAR
Paul Cornell

Heaven: a planet rich in history where the Doctor comes to meet a new friend, and betray an old one; a place where people come to die, but where the dead don't always rest in peace. On Heaven, the Doctor finally loses Ace, but finds archeologist Bernice Summerfield, a new companion whose destiny is inextricably linked with his.

ISBN 0 426 20385 2

TRANSIT
Ben Aaronovitch

It's the ultimate mass transit system, binding the planets of the solar system together. But something is living in the network, chewing its way to the very heart of the system and leaving a trail of death and mutation behind. Once again, the Doctor is all that stands between humanity and its own mistakes.

ISBN 0 426 20384 4

THE HIGHEST SCIENCE
Gareth Roberts

The Highest Science — technology so dangerous it destroyed its creators. Many people have searched for it, but now Sheldukher, the most wanted criminal in the galaxy, believes he has found it. The Doctor and Bernice must battle to stop him on a planet where chance and coincidence have become far too powerful.

ISBN 0 426 20377 1

THE PIT
Neil Penswick

One of the Seven Planets is a nameless giant, quarantined against all intruders. But when the TARDIS materializes, it becomes clear that the planet is far from empty — and the Doctor begins to realize that the planet hides a terrible secret from the Time Lords' past.

ISBN 0 426 20378 X

DECEIT
Peter Darvill-Evans

Ace — three years older, wiser and tougher — is back. She is part of a group of Irregular Auxilliaries on an expedition to the planet Arcadia. They think they are hunting Daleks, but the Doctor knows better. He knows that the paradise planet hides a being far more powerful than the Daleks — and much more dangerous.

ISBN 0 426 20362 3

LUCIFER RISING
Jim Mortimore & Andy Lane

Reunited, the Doctor, Ace and Bernice travel to Lucifer, the site of a scientific expedition that they know will shortly cease to exist. Discovering why involves them in sabotage, murder and the resurrection of eons-old alien powers. Are there Angels on Lucifer? And what does it all have to do with Ace?

ISBN 0 426 20338 7

WHITE DARKNESS
David McIntee

The TARDIS crew, hoping for a rest, come to Haiti in 1915. But they find that the island is far from peaceful: revolution is brewing in the city; the dead are walking from the cemeteries; and, far underground, the ancient rulers of the galaxy are stirring in their sleep.

ISBN 0 426 20395 X